CIRCLE OF BLOOD BOOK ONE.

LOVER'S REBIRTH

Other books by R. A. Steffan

The Horse Mistress: Book 1
The Horse Mistress: Book 2
The Horse Mistress: Book 3
The Horse Mistress: Book 4
The Complete Horse Mistress Collection

The Lion Mistress: Book 1
The Lion Mistress: Book 2
The Lion Mistress: Book 3
The Complete Lion Mistress Collection

Antidote: Love and War, Book 1

The Queen's Musketeers: Book 1
The Queen's Musketeers: Book 2
The Queen's Musketeers: Book 3
The D'Artagnan Collection: Books 1-3
The Queen's Musketeers: Book 4

Sherlock Holmes & The Case of the Magnate's Son

Diamond Bar Apha Ranch
Diamond Bar Alpha 2: Angel & Vic
(with Jaelynn Woolf)

CIRCLE OF BLOOD BOOK ONE:

LOVER'S REBIRTH

R. A. STEFFAN & JAELYNN WOOLF

Circle of Blood Book One: Lover's Rebirth

INTRODUCTION

This book contains graphic violence and explicit sexual content. It is intended for a mature audience. While it is part of a series with an over-arching plot, it can be read as a standalone with a "happy ever after" ending for the two main characters, and a satisfying resolution of the storyline. If you don't intend to continue the series, you may wish to avoid the epilogue.

TABLE OF CONTENTS

ONE

Human blood always tasted sweetest when the world was falling apart around you. That indisputable fact was one of the great ironies of vampirism, Tré reflected. It was a bone-deep truth that spoke to the bottomless well of darkness within his soul—if he could still lay claim to having such a human thing as a soul, at any rate.

Once, he had been Vladimir Illych Romanov III, a man of importance, respected by all. Now, he was merely Tré, a shadow hidden among shadows, lost in the night.

What was left of Tré's soul was little more than a tattered flag planted on a barren, muddy hill where the battle had already been lost, and the war had moved on to richer, more fertile fields. A remnant. An overlooked scrap too unimportant to bother tearing down and burning.

Yes, that was his soul in a nutshell. His soul, and the souls of his fellow vampires.

The unremarkable blond-haired, hazel-eyed young human currently slumped in Tré's strong grip shifted restlessly, a low moan slipping free from his throat. Tré could feel the vibration beneath his lips, through his sensitive fangs.

Reluctantly, he disengaged. Around him, the shadowed corridor at the back of the seedy New Orleans nightclub slipped back into focus, the sound of jazz replacing the low, steady *shush-shush, shush-shush* of a human heart pumping blood through veins and arteries.

A few drops of that sweet, sweet blood dribbled from the neat bite mark over the kid's jugular before the healing power of Tré's saliva sealed the two small, circular wounds. Tré swiped the trickle of red with his thumb and licked it clean.

Destroying the evidence.

His victim that night was a typical Midwest frat boy, drawn to the Big Easy by the siren call of plentiful alcohol and loose morals in the run-up to Mardi Gras. He'd made the drunken mistake of wandering off on his own after his friends decided to head back to their hotel, and now he'd become lunch for an apex predator.

Fortunately for him, however, the days of Tré's uncontrollable bloodlust and hunger were long past. This particular plain-faced prey animal would live to enjoy his hangover in the morning, with nothing more than an additional bit of weakness and dizziness to encourage him to make better life choices in the future.

As if the phrase *better life choices* had been some sort of mental summons, Xander chose that moment to stick his head around the corner.

He took in the scene and raised an eyebrow. "Oy, fearless leader—stop playing with your food, and let's get a move on. Sun'll be up soon, and even the rioters over in the Lower Ninth Ward are probably ready to call it a night at this point."

The broad vowels of Old London were out of place amongst the rich Creole drawl of the city's natives. Other than that, however, Xander fit right in with his tailored trousers, leather shoes polished to a high shine, and black silk shirt open at the neck — a shameless hedonist to the core.

Xander's pupils were blown wide and dark. Tré wondered if he'd managed to find a heroin addict to drink from tonight.

Again.

The blond frat boy grunted and scrubbed a shaky hand over his face. "Oh, wow," he said. The voice of middle America. The wholesome boy next door. "Sorry I checked out on you like that, bro." He reeled a bit, and Tré steadied him. "Not sure what happened there. Maybe I had… had a bit too much to drink?" He laughed awkwardly. "So… um, right. Sorry. What were we talking about, again?"

"It's not important," Tré told him. "You have your phone?"

The boy fumbled in his pocket and nodded, still dazed.

"Call a cab," Tré ordered, making eye contact and placing a bit of will behind the words.

The frat kid nodded. "Yeah, I'll… uh… I'll just call a cab now, I think. Anyway, it was good hangin' with you, man — "

Tré didn't bother to reply, already turning away to join Xander as they headed for the back door of the club.

"You seen Duchess?" Xander asked, as they exited into the humid winter chill of the Louisiana predawn.

The lazy energy of the city at night prickled against Tré's skin, sharper than usual and with a heavy air of anticipation that he didn't much like.

"Not since she disappeared into one of the back rooms earlier, with a couple of boy toys in tow," he said, unconcerned.

"In her element, then," Xander observed. The words were wry. "Guess she'll make her way back in her own time. Or not, as the case may be." He took a deep breath, as if scenting the air. "Something's off today. S'like a storm coming. But not an *actual* storm, you know? Can't say I'm too broken up about it. It's getting boring just waiting around for something new to happen. You can feel it too, right?"

"Yes," Tré said. "I can feel it, too."

Xander drew the night air into his lungs again, and rolled his neck from side to side, the vertebrae popping one after the other. "Damn. That was some *really* good smack, Tré. Even second-hand. We should totally go clubbing more often."

Around them, the city held its breath. Waiting.

-o-o-o-

These days, Delaney LeBlanc dreamed in riddles.

A swirl of hazy, nonsensical images. The touch of a hand, rough calluses dragging against the soft skin of her cheek as she smiled and pressed into the contact. Whispered words in a half forgotten language. Children's laughter. The purr of a cat and the excited yip of a dog. The chatter of voices speaking words that seemed both strange and strikingly familiar. If she listened just a bit more closely, she'd be able to understand them, she was sure —

Della woke with a start, dizzy from the series of disconnected scenes that had haunted her sleep. Rolling onto an elbow, she glanced at the glowing red numbers of the clock on her bedside table and groaned.

"*Argh*! It's *four-thirty in the morning*. What the hell, brain?" she rasped, the plaintive question disappearing into the silent room around her. The darkness did not reply.

Her long honey-colored hair, insane from restless sleep, was plastered against her face, a tangled mess on top of her head. Flipping it back, she sat up in bed and started to comb her fingers through it, attempting to soothe her raw nerves with the mindless, repetitive motion. As the tangles came free, she closed her eyes, carding her fingers slowly through the heavy length. Feeling her heartbeat gradually slow.

The dream had made no sense, but it had still felt *so real*. Della couldn't quite shake the feeling that she'd had the same dream before, many times, always culminating in waking up early with this disconcerting feeling of loss and need. It was almost as though she were seeing images from someone else's life. Someone she had long forgotten, like a childhood friend.

Of course, that was absurd. She had grown up in suburban New Jersey. None of her usual playmates had spoken a different language. And that part of the dream was *very* clear in her mind. What perplexed her most, however, was that she felt she should have no trouble understanding the voices of the happy children who chattered away in—what language could it be?

She had no idea. It didn't sound like French, or Spanish, or German, or any language she'd heard people speak in the real world.

Probably something I've made up, which is why I feel like I should be able to understand it, Della thought with a yawn. *Dreams are weird. It's just my subconscious blowing off steam. I hope.*

Della decided that her subconscious must be really messed up, given how bizarre her nighttime visions had grown of late. Sometimes, she felt like she was going honest-to-god insane, a feeling heightened by the stress and anxiety she had been under recently.

Not wanting to start her thoughts down that particular path this early in the morning, Della threw her legs over the side of her bed and stood up, toes digging into the deep shag of the carpet. With the ease of long practice, she flipped on the lamp beside her bed without looking and straightened, reaching for the ceiling, as high as her arms would go.

She stretched her short, five-foot frame as far as she could, feeling her joints pop and crack in protest. Wriggling her toes, Della concentrated on the sensations under her feet and throughout her body, dragging her attention away from the dream images and into the present. Where it belonged.

Focus, girl, she coached herself, trying to shake the disturbing remnants of her subconscious delusions. *Life goes a lot smoother when you pay attention to the real world, not an imaginary one.*

When she felt awake and more or less calm, she padded across the bedroom and slipped out into the main room of her dark apartment. The gloom this morning felt oppressive. Not at all like the cozy, sleepy stillness that had greeted her early morning habits in years past. This darkness felt malicious and full of intent.

She suppressed a shudder and fumbled for the light switch. With her living room bathed in the harsh yellow light of cheap, compact fluorescent light bulbs, Della blinked and glanced around, checking for an intruder. She felt like she was being watched from the shadows, yet she was completely alone in her apartment.

She sighed, suddenly weary.

Jesus. I'm getting paranoid. Maybe I need to go to the doctor for something to help me sleep better, because this is getting ridiculous. If I don't get at least a few uninterrupted of hours of rest tonight, I'm going to start hallucinating pink elephants instead of imaginary burglars.

Della stifled an ugly snort of laughter at the irony. She already felt like she was losing her mind without adding sleep deprivation on top of everything else.

"Coffee," she muttered aloud, heading into the kitchen to brew a pot. Maybe she would go into the office early today and get a few reports done. Might as well be a productive insomniac.

When she was growing up, Della had never once fantasized about being the receptionist for a small insurance company in New Orleans. Yet, despite all her good intentions, here she was, stuck in a dead end job and with no prospect of changing that fact or moving on to better things.

Life had been going okay until just a few years ago. For a given definition of *okay*, at any rate. Her family was kind of a train wreck, admittedly. Her older sister had been killed in a car crash when Della was ten, and the strain of the tragedy had eventually driven her parents apart. Her mom eventually remarried, to a guy Della could barely stand. Her dad had pulled away, to the point that her only contact with him was an occasional stilted email on her birthday or Christmas, when he didn't forget. With her grandparents dead and no real contact with her far-flung aunts and uncles, she was essentially alone.

That was all right, though. She loved her parents, of course, but it was a remote, intellectual sort of love. The kind that was better served by distance. When she'd headed off to college, rather than homesickness, she'd felt... *relief*. She'd graduated four years later with a degree in graphic design and started working for a greeting card company, putting together cover samples to be vetted by a panel of marketing analysts.

The job was great, the money was decent, and she lived comfortably in an apartment about two miles from work. On beautiful days, she had been able to walk there with a friend. Even though it seemed like everything was going perfectly, Della had struggled with feeling out of step with the world around her. It was a feeling of waiting for the other shoe to drop. Like the calm before a thunderstorm.

Maybe that was why she had a lot of trouble understanding—or sympathizing with—her peers' petty concerns about boyfriends, hair, drama, celebrities, and fashion. Oh, she would smile politely and tell them she loved their new outfits and would exclaim in horror when her friends complained that their most recent dates never responded to their text messages, but on the inside, Della had a deep longing for something more. Something *real*. Something that had meaning beyond the shallow, two-dimensional lives the others around her seemed to be leading.

Be careful what you wish for, right?

She'd had a couple of good years at the greeting card company before the market plummeted suddenly and they had been forced to downsize. Della's job was eliminated and she was laid off with a modest severance package.

The memory still brought the ridiculous burn of tears to her eyes. She swiped a hand across her face and shoveled spoonful after spoonful of coffee grounds into the white filter. She needed something strong this morning to combat her sleepless night.

"Coffee should put hair on your chest," her late grandmother used to say, while making a brew so bitter that Della's jaw hurt while she drank it.

The memory brought a wistful smile to her lips as she started the brewing cycle. Soon, the smell of fresh coffee wafted through her kitchen, waking her more effectively than anything else could have.

If there was one thing that defined Della, it was her ability to survive. She had taken some hard knocks in life, but she prided herself on her ability to come up swinging every time. After being let go from her job in Hoboken, Della decided that it was the perfect opportunity for her to pursue a secret dream she had long harbored in the back of her mind.

Della's father's family had originally come up from New Orleans in the early 1900s. She had never been able to visit the city as a child, but after learning about her family's history, she became fascinated by the rich culture and vibrant soul that seemed to explode from the seams of the city, as if it could not be contained.

Even though she had no connections there, she had packed up all of her possessions in one small moving truck and driven southwest until she reached Louisiana. Within a few days, she found a relatively inexpensive apartment a few blocks away from A.L. Davis Park, and applied for several jobs in the design field.

It quickly became apparent, however, that she needed to set her sights lower. She settled for a receptionist position with Lighthouse Insurance Company, telling herself it was only until she landed something better. That had been more than a year ago. And, although she was fond enough of her coworkers and her boss, the pay was barely sufficient to keep her afloat in the small one-bedroom apartment she rented.

The benefits are very competitive, I think you'll find. She could practically hear the weary hopefulness in the owner's voice as he'd conducted her second interview—hoping that she'd accept the position; hoping that he wouldn't have to go through the hiring process again a month from now.

And so, there she remained. Too loyal to leave the company for another dead-end job outside of her field. Too poor to look for a different place to live. Feeling like she was way past her expiration date. Her life was boring and quiet, yet not the quiet of peace. It was the quiet of vague, half-hearted desperation, struggling beneath a thick layer of inertia. Della knew she was just waiting for something big and inevitable to happen, even if she had no idea when it would occur or what form it would take.

How long can I keep doing this? It was the constant mantra in her life. *What happens when I can't any more?*

Of course, it wasn't as if she thought she was the only one. No, Della knew that it wasn't just her life that seemed to be teetering on the edge of some precipice. She could barely turn on the television without hearing horrific stories of rapes, kidnappings, stabbings, mass shootings, bombings, and natural disasters that claimed the lives of innocent people going about their day-to-day business. The growing wave of fear and violence was like an infection, spreading across the world, into every town and every city.

New Orleans was no different. In fact, it seemed like in the last few months, things here had gone from bad to worse. There was rioting and violence in the city almost every night now, occurring at rates that baffled FBI crime statisticians and forensic psychologists. No one could explain why everything seemed to be going wrong all at once.

"It's like living in a freaking war zone," one of her coworkers had said in frustration, after being mugged outside a restaurant the evening before. "All we need now is for another hurricane to hit us. That would just be icing on the cake."

Della could only nod sympathetically and murmur vague agreement. Things really were out of control, as if more and more people were losing their minds and turning into wild animals, preying on the weak.

Well, at least she wasn't alone in the *losing her mind* department.

These depressing early morning thoughts swirled around her brain, not helping with the fuzziness caused by lack of sleep. She sighed and rubbed gritty eyes. Since her damn coffee wasn't ready yet, she'd have to take more direct action to shake the fretful worries still clinging to her like shadows.

"I need a shower," she told her goldfish, Jewel, who was swimming sedately around her fishbowl. Della wasn't allowed to have pets other than fish in her apartment, so she talked to the little creature like it was a dog or a cat. It felt good knowing she had something to come home to, even if it *was* just a stupid fish.

Fifteen minutes later, she was slumped forehead-first against the cool plastic liner of the walk-in shower. Hot water pounded against her back, relaxing tense muscles that felt like they had been knotted for weeks. Afterward, as Della flicked water off her skin with a towel, she caught a whiff of coffee coming under the door of her small bathroom.

Wrapping up in a fuzzy robe, she walked out into the kitchen and poured a much needed cup. Despite the scalding temperature, she took several deep gulps, feeling her eyes water from the heat.

Thank God for coffee. Now I'm finally ready to face this day.

I hope.

-o-o-o-

At five minutes to seven, Della unlocked the office door and slid inside with a sigh of relief. She hated walking alone through her neighborhood in the early morning darkness to get to her tram stop, but thankfully most of the crazies seemed to have either gone home or passed out in the gutter by the time she ventured forth today.

The streetcar operator looked about as frazzled and red-eyed as she felt, but he'd at least spared her a strained smile when he glanced at her phone to check her thirty-one-day RTA pass as she boarded at Third Street, in the Garden District. The tram was nearly deserted. She huddled in a seat near the back, cardigan wrapped around her body to hold the late February chill at bay.

One transfer to the Canal Street line, followed by another ten-minute walk, brought her to the unprepossessing brick and concrete building that housed the insurance agency. There was a musty smell in the air as she flipped on all the lights. The carpet was old and as the humidity started to rise in the mornings, the smell would begin to rise as well.

Her desk was neat and comfortingly familiar, with the picture of her family—before a drunk driver had taken Jaymie away from them—set in a modest frame near the back edge. Her area was situated near the front door where she could greet any visitors, but could also assist the insurance agents with anything they needed, back in their offices. Besides her direct boss, Rich, there were three other women, two agents and an office manager, along with two other men who worked at Lighthouse.

It wouldn't be long before her coworkers would begin arriving, she knew. She was looking forward to the hustle and bustle of people around her. The noise would be welcome after feeling as though the silence around her was pressing on her, like someone trying to suffocate her with a pillow.

To dispel the image and the unnatural quiet, Della flipped on the small radio she kept on her desk. She always turned the station to the oldies, because they rarely played any current news reports. She was beyond tired of hearing about all the death and violence around her. She didn't need a reminder of it every hour of every day.

The sound of the music relaxed her. It helped to keep some of her jitters at bay. Even so, she was really happy when Ryan and Sean showed up an hour and fifteen minutes later.

"Good morning," Della said, knowing her smile must look forced and unconvincing.

They both murmured good morning, Ryan yawning widely behind his hand.

"You're here early," Sean observed.

"Yeah, couldn't sleep. Thought I might as well be productive."

"That's mighty enterprising of you," Ryan answered in a deep southern drawl. His kind brown eyes twinkled at her as he made his way towards his office.

Della turned back towards her computer screen and started sorting through emails. She flagged a few on her to-do list, and decided that she could get started on this month's expense reports.

The day passed without serious incident, although after the first couple of hours, the familiar tedium seemed to bore into Della in a way that nearly drove her crazy. By lunchtime, she wished she could go home, but then she remembered that she was likely to face another lonely and restless night of disturbing dreams.

I just can't win, no matter what I do, she thought miserably. She really was starting to feel like she was losing her mind. *Maybe I do need to go see a doctor or something. This can't be right — I don't think normal people feel this way all the time. I just need to sleep. That would make everything a hell of a lot easier.*

"Hey, Earth to Della. Can you hear me?" The voice was mere inches from her ear, and startled her into a flinch.

"Huh? Oh, sorry Alice." Della stared up at her co-worker's face like a deer in the headlights. Alice stared back, looking distinctly concerned.

"Della, are you okay, honey? You seem really out of it today," Alice asked, her brow furrowed.

Della wondered how long she'd sat there staring into space. The look of worry seemed out of place on Alice's thin face—her friend was usually upbeat to the point of being annoying.

"Yeah, sorry," she said quickly. "I, uh, just haven't been sleeping that well in the last few weeks."

Alice frowned in earnest. "Uh-oh, why's that?"

Della sighed. "I wish I knew, to be honest."

"Well, if you need anything, don't hesitate to call me, okay?"

"Yeah, okay."

Alice smiled at her and turned towards her office. Della watched her go, thankful for the presence of at least some friendly faces in her life. Even if they seldom socialized outside of work, it was about the only thing she had going for her these days.

By the time six o'clock rolled around and everyone had cleared out to head home, Della was completely exhausted. She could barely keep her eyes open as she turned off all the computers, locked the doors, and walked towards the first of the two trams that would take her back to the nearest stop to her apartment. It was an unseasonably cold evening in February, and Della shivered against the chilly gusts of wind blustering against her back.

As she was walking toward Canal Street through the deepening dusk, she followed a group of commuters, most of whom were clutching their bags and jackets to themselves, trying to stay out of the wind.

"I haven't felt this cold here in years," one woman commented, turning up her coat collar.

"Well, it's definitely not a record low," her companion answered, "but I'm ready for our typical balmy weather to come back. This is gonna be hell on the new palm trees Jim and I just had planted in the back yard."

Della felt like she was two minutes away from falling asleep on her feet, which probably explained why she reacted so slowly to what came next.

A group of people dressed in black with masks pulled down over their faces barged onto the street from a side alley. They were all clutching handguns, and one was holding what looked like an assault rifle, cradled against his chest like a baby.

Several gasps and cries broke out as the crowd stuttered to a stop, pressing together like a squeezed accordion. The gunman standing at the front raised his weapon in the air and screamed, firing two shots into the sky. His eyes were crazed, and unhinged laughter spilled out from the blank mouth opening of the dark balaclava.

Pandemonium broke out around Della, who was standing frozen with shock, her eyes glued to the gunmen. The crowd that she had been following scattered in all directions, screaming and pushing and shoving against each other as they

ran. The sharp retort of gunfire shattered the evening.

Above Della's head a window shattered, rain-
ing glass down on her. A large, burly man with a
bushy beard slammed into her in his attempt to get
away. She staggered as his huge frame plowed into
her and she began to fall. Miraculously, he paused
long enough to grab her arm and keep her from
hitting the ground. With his help, she was able to
steady herself on her feet. Before she could wrap
her stunned brain around the idea of thanking him,
however, he fled down the sidewalk towards the
corner.

Della took a few stumbling steps after him, still
dazed. Her breath was ragged in her lungs, which
burned with pain as she tried to pull cold air
through her mouth.

*This can't be happening, this can't be happening,
this can't be happening.*

Her brain was stuck on an endless loop, unable
to jerk free from the terror spilling onto the street
around her. Her vision was tunneling and she
couldn't focus on the figures rushing past her and
out into the street. Car horns blared, tires shrieking
as several vehicles crashed into each other, trying
to avoid the panicking people now flooding into
traffic.

Della knew she needed to get away, but it felt
like her legs were mired in quicksand. She couldn't
run and she felt an enormous pressure constricting
around her chest, as if she were being suffocated.

*Oh, God. I'm going to die right here on this side-
walk.*

The thought ripped through her mind like a lightning bolt. The adrenaline burst that accompanied the terrifying realization propelled her forward so quickly, she almost fell to her knees again. Still mindlessly following the man that had stopped her from falling, Della tried to make it to the corner.

An explosion of sound seemed to fill Della's awareness, and the man with the beard crumpled to the ground ahead of her. At first, she didn't connect the two things—not until she saw the bright red splotchy patch blossoming over his gray jacket.

Della was moving, but she felt like her arms and legs were made of lead. She stumbled towards him, completely horrified at what she was seeing. The man was face down, gagging and gasping for air on the sidewalk, his breaths coming in terrible, wet rattles. Della knelt down beside him, the spreading puddle of his blood soaking into her dress pants and she placed a hand on his back.

Before she could even begin to help him, she felt him shudder and go completely still.

Della's heart was pounding so hard and fast, she felt like it was going to leap out of her chest, yet the thumping in her ears was sluggish, and everything around her seemed to be moving in slow motion. The gunmen were making their way in her direction. More explosions of noise echoed against the facades of the tall buildings around her. More bodies were falling to the ground. Terrified shrieks seemed to reach her ears as if she were underwater, muffled and distant. Yet Della remained on her knees, unable to leave the still body under her shaking hand. Sudden, crippling grief poured out of her for the man who had helped her—however briefly—at the cost of his own life.

Fuck this, Della thought savagely, anger surging behind the sorrow. She'd heard on the news that experts now recommended fighting and throwing things at gunmen in a mass shooting situation, rather than trying to flee or hide.

The man's messenger bag was lying on the ground next to her, as well as a small, decorative metal trashcan that must have been knocked over when people stampeded through the outdoor seating area of the café nearby. With fumbling fingers, Della reached for the strap in one hand and the trashcan in the other. She stood in one swift movement, bracing herself for a fight to the death, adrenaline lending her muscles a sudden, unexpected strength.

One of the gunmen was just behind her; she could hear his excited breathing and then the press of cold metal against her back.

"Are you ready to die, little kitty?" he sneered in her ear.

Her answer was to plant her feet and swing the bag and trashcan around so fast that the gunman, who was clearly not expecting her to fight back, didn't have time to duck or get out of the way.

As she spun, Della felt her makeshift weapons make contact with the man's shoulder and side. He let out a loud *oof* as the air was forced out of his lungs. The impact caused him to take one heavy step to the side, but he didn't fall and he didn't drop his weapon. Della dropped the bag but clung to the trashcan, raising it in both hands like a bat.

The gunman swore at her and pointed the gun straight at Della's face.

Completely terrified, she threw the trashcan at him as hard as she could, which caused him to lower the gun so he could knock it aside before it hit him.

"You're going to regret that, bitch!" he growled, lunging for her. Della stumbled backwards, trying to get away, but he grabbed her shoulder and spun her around, wrapping his arm around her and pressing the cold barrel of the gun against her temple.

TWO

Della held her breath and gripped the meaty forearm that was wrapped around her chest with clawed hands, trying desperately to pull the man's arm away. Even if she had managed to rip herself free, though, she knew that the minute she made a move to get away, the gunman would blow her head off. She simply held on, fingernails digging into the heavy black material of his shirt, feeling the seconds tick by one at a time, like dripping molasses.

With the gunman behind her, she could see the chaos on the street again. At least ten bodies lay in pools of blood. The dark red puddles seemed to shimmer under the streetlights. It was as though a heat haze had descended on the block, making everything waver in her vision. Her eyes flickered around, going in and out of focus, searching for any sign of the police or a SWAT team. Praying for help.

There was no one. She was alone with the dead, and the deadly. The other gunmen were chasing stragglers down the block and shooting bullets into fallen bodies. They blasted out windows of shops, including the one she and her captor were standing in front of, which caused him to yell in anger at his comrade.

"What are you doing, you stupid fuck! Trying to get me killed? Point that damn thing somewhere else!"

Della gasped aloud, despite trying valiantly to remain silent. She could hear a dull whine developing in her mind, an all-pervasive buzzing noise that drowned out any thought of defending herself. Panic was flooding her, followed by shock, preventing her from formulating any sort of coherent thought.

"Now, time to deal with you, pretty kitty," the man said, jerking Della from behind so that her feet slipped out from underneath her. He dragged her backwards towards the building as she scrambled to find her footing.

"Let me go," she pleaded.

"Not until you've fucking paid for that little trick with the trash can, whore," he said, spinning her around to face him. His breath was hot and smelly on her face. She gagged and fought to get away from him, desperate for fresh air.

He slammed her down on the ground, and her head hit the pavement with a sharp crack. She sprawled there for a moment, stunned by the blow. Lights popped in front of her eyes and Della lay completely still, forgetting where she was or what was going on around her.

The sound of gunfire above her jerked her back to reality. The man standing over her had shot at a car that had driven by, blowing out the windshield and passenger-side window.

Della clapped her hands around her head and curled into a ball, her ears ringing from the repeated blasts so close to her.

Suddenly the man was back, kneeling over her and yanking her arms away from her body. She fought back furiously, swinging and clawing at every square inch of him she could reach. He used his body weight to pin her legs down and pressed the gun against her cheek.

"Lie still," he commanded.

Della struggled for a moment more, but went limp when he pressed the barrel harder against her face.

She looked up into the face of pure evil, seeing his cold, blank eyes gazing back at her. There was only dark mirth and chilly indifference to be found there. She knew with complete certainty that she was going to die any moment now.

Out of nowhere, a mist descended around the site of carnage, swirling as if caught in a high breeze, even though everything in the night had gone completely still. It wrapped itself around the man crouched over her, flowing across his face. He jerked his head to the side, completely bewildered, and tried to swipe at the fog. His fingers passed straight through it, but the mist blew on towards the middle of the street, drawing his gaze. By the way the other gunmen were staggering around and waving their arms, Della guessed that something similar had happened to them.

The mist seemed to solidify in a dense patch in the middle of the blocked street, coalescing to reveal five dark figures. A strange aura of power radiated from them. Several of the gunmen backed away, raising their weapons.

"What the fuck, Benson?" one yelled in confusion in the direction of Della's attacker.

The man called Benson grabbed Della by the hair and dragged her to her feet. She shrieked in pain, clamping her hands around his and scrambling desperately for purchase, trying to find her feet and support her weight.

"Don't just stand there! Kill them!" Benson roared, making Della flinch in fright.

All at once, the shadowy figures burst into motion. Their speed was inhuman, Della realized with a jolt. No one could run that fast, not even if they were being pushed by a huge dump of adrenaline. They were moving *unnaturally* fast, almost as if they were flying towards the cluster of gunmen.

Della watched in open-mouthed awe as two women in the group launched themselves at the man carrying the assault rifle. He stumbled back in shock and fired off several rounds, all of which missed the newcomers and buried themselves in a building across the street with an explosion of brick dust. One of the women used a powerful blow to turn the barrel of the rifle towards the ground and slammed her fist into the man's face. His nose erupted in a gush of blood. He fell back onto the ground and both women landed on top of him.

The man who appeared to be in charge of the group of newcomers surveyed the scene with startling light gray eyes that seemed to glow silver in the low light. He effortlessly swiped the legs out from underneath the gunman standing closest to him before his pale gaze fell on Della and her captor. Benson growled and raised his gun, pointing it at the man with a shaking hand.

"Help the woman," the silver-eyed newcomer said, apparently unconcerned by the threat. His tone was deep and rich. Crushed velvet over tempered steel.

Somewhere in the back of Della's overwrought brain, she realized that he had the most amazing voice she had ever heard. She would have probably gone weak at the knees if she weren't already shaking like a leaf in a high wind.

Della heard a rushing sound and blinked. When she opened her eyes, a large man was standing in front of her, looking at her attacker with the intense green eyes of a hunting tiger. He took a calculated step forward, fists clenched as if he were about to strike. Benson stepped backwards, pulling her with him, and Della could feel him trembling against her. He fired off another deafening round from his handgun, and her would-be rescuer jerked to the side as it hit him in the chest, under the clavicle.

To Della's utter surprise, the man did not crumple to the ground. Instead, the wound only seemed to make him angrier. He surged forward, grabbing Benson by the head with both hands. Benson dropped Della, who fell to the ground as her tormenter began to scream and struggle wildly, waving the gun around. She rolled quickly out from between the two and watched, horrified, as the newcomer lifted Benson from the ground by his head and threw him into the nearest wall, face first.

He crumpled to the ground—a discarded rag doll, lying in a heap on the dirty pavement, obviously unconscious. The man with the gunshot wound in his chest walked over and stomped his heel down on Benson's face, assuring that he would not be getting up again.

Ever.

The crunch of his skull smashing made Della's stomach churn. She felt bile rising in her mouth and coughed, trying not to vomit. She crawled backwards on her elbows, using her feet to propel her, trying to get away from the grisly tableau.

The movement seemed to catch her rescuer's attention. He walked forward slowly, his hands raised in a peace token, and dropped to one knee next to her.

"Hey, now. Easy, there. Are you all right?" His tone was soothing, and very, very British. Della could still feel the aura of raw power radiating from him, which terrified her just as much as the armed man who had taken her hostage. Yet, she could not help but be captivated by his eyes, which seemed almost to glow in the low light. They were mesmerizing, and she realized that she was staring at him like a fool, silent and slack-jawed.

She shook her head, trying to clear it, and raised a hand to her pounding temple.

"Y-yeah, I think so," she answered in a shaking voice.

He knelt next to her.

"It's okay. Take a moment. You've had quite a scare," he said, his voice calm and collected. Della's eyes strayed to the gaping hole under his collarbone, oozing blood that looked almost black in the low light.

"Ah. Yes. Sorry about the gore," he said, noticing her gaze. "It's really unfortunate, that. Smarts like hell, actually, now that I think about it." He winced, lifting a hand to prod at the wound and craning his neck to try to look at it. "Son of a bitch, that's gonna leave a mark. I do *not* get paid enough to deal with this shit while I'm sober…"

Della's mouth was still hanging open, but she couldn't speak. She looked around wildly, wanting nothing more than to just go home and pretend that none of this had ever happened. She felt a bone-deep weariness underneath her pounding heart, and she was still fighting down nausea that threatened to overcome her willpower.

She could see the other figures walking towards her through the darkening evening, all converging on them.

The gray-eyed leader walked over to her rescuer and looked down at the wound on his chest, a crease of worry forming on his forehead. His hair was dark, falling tousled above a serious brow, sharp cheekbones, and full, sensuous lips.

"Xander, you obviously neglected to duck again," he said in that deep velvet voice. "We've talked about this before, have we not?"

Della felt her heart skip a beat despite her terror.

The man called Xander had a hand clamped over the wound now, trying to stem the bleeding. "That we have. And I believe I made it perfectly clear that we need to keep a flask or two of the good stuff on us when dealing with this kind of crap. If I'm going to get shot through the lung by some redneck shithead with crooked teeth and halitosis, I'd prefer to be considerably more intoxicated than this, beforehand."

Ignoring the litany of complaints, the leader knelt and reached out a hand to steady Xander, who had started to sway.

"Well, fuck," Xander said matter-of-factly, and half-collapsed into his friend's supporting grip. Trying to keep both of them upright, the leader set his hand down hard on the ground for balance. His fingers grazed the skin on Della's wrist — the barest of brushes.

It was like touching a live wire. An electric jolt shot through Della's entire body. She felt as though she had been punched in the stomach. Air was forced through her mouth in a sound of shock that was echoed by the leader's surprised grunt. He jerked his hand away and leapt gracefully to his feet with his injured friend held securely in his grip, staring down at Della on the ground as if he had never seen anything like her.

Their eyes met, and she saw something like dismay flicker behind his silver-gray eyes. His lips parted, as if he wanted to say something to her, but no sound escaped his mouth. They stared at each other for several moments, the wounded man next to him flicking his eyes back and forth between the two. His eyebrows furrowed in confusion.

"Tré?" he asked.

The gray-eyed man did not respond, just continued to stare into Della's face. She thought she saw *recognition* flash behind his eyes.

But that was impossible. How could he recognize her? They had never met before. She would have remembered if they had, she was sure.

"*Tré*," The wounded man said, more insistent this time. "Police approaching. Time to leave. Unless you'd like to try answering their questions while I bleed out in the back of a human ambulance?"

This seemed to startle the leader out of his reverie, and he broke eye contact with Della.

"Oksana," he commanded in a hoarse tone. "Wipe her memory."

"Wait. Wipe my *what*?" Della demanded, jerking into a sitting position. She tried valiantly to scramble away from the female figure descending upon her. "No. *No!* Stay away from me."

"It's all right, sweetheart," the woman said in a soothing voice. "Hey, look at me. Relax. That's it."

Della felt all the tightness in her muscles start to drain away. She shook her head, trying to clear it, but a dreamy veil seemed to fall in front of her eyes, making everything foggy.

"No... wait," she said in a weak voice, feeling everything around her grow dim. Grayness seemed to swirl around the edges of her vision and she tried to shake her head again, feeling it flop back and forth in slow motion.

The glare of the streetlights and the chill of the rough pavement beneath her slipped away, sending her into warm, soft darkness.

-o-o-o-

"Ma'am? Ma'am, are you all right?"

Della's eyes jerked open, rolling drunkenly in their sockets, unable to focus on anything. "*Wait…*"

"Ma'am? Are you injured?"

Della's vision gradually cleared. She realized that she was being pulled into a sitting position by a police officer who looked deeply shaken. "Ma'am?"

"I—I don't know," Della answered in a hoarse voice. "What just happened?"

"You were involved in a shooting. Please, we need to get you to the paramedics. Can you stand?" he asked.

"I think so," Della said, and the police officer helped pull her to her feet. She swayed as all the blood in her head rushed toward her feet.

"Easy, now," the police officer said, wrapping an arm around her shoulders. "Take it easy."

Moving slowly, he led her around the corner to where a barricade was set up. Behind the line of police—all pointing weaponry in their direction— Della could see the flashing lights of ambulances.

"Ma'am, did you see what happened to the gunmen?"

Della stumbled, leaning against the cop heavily. "I don't know. I don't remember anything."

She wracked her brain, trying to remember the shooting, but only feeling terror threaten to paralyze her on the spot. No mental images formed in her mind. She couldn't even remember how she got onto the street. The whole day seemed hazy and distant. She looked around, trying to orient herself, the flashing lights and wail of sirens dominating her immediate surroundings.

Where am I? How did I get here?

"It's okay," the officer said, his tone soothing as he patted her arm.

"Why can't I remember?" Della breathed, feeling as if something inside her was falling away. Darkness swirled around in her mind, making her stomach churn uncomfortably. "Why—*Jesus*. Why can't I *remember* anything?"

-o-o-o-

"Of course they had to have assault rifles. *Assault rifles*, seriously? God, I hate this country. Have I mentioned that lately? And here I am, sober as a fucking *nun* after a damn bullet punched a hole through my chest. This shit is evil, I tell you. Pure evil. And they call *us* the demons…" Xander complained, the strength behind his words fading as he slowly bled out.

Tré ignored him, exercising all of his self-control merely to keep his friend propped upright between him and Eris. If he allowed himself to think about what had just happened, he'd lose his shit completely. And they couldn't afford that right now.

Of all the insane, astounding, unexpected things to happen, he never would have foreseen this. It was *impossible*. How could *she* be here? Now? All of these centuries later?

"I've just decided," Xander slurred. "I hate bullets. Do you hate bullets, Tré? Because I do. *Hate* 'em."

"I hadn't realized it was possible for a vampire to become delirious after an injury," Eris said conversationally. "I thought that was just a human thing."

Tré allowed himself a bitter snort. "Trust Xander to break the mold."

"I'm one of a kind, you know," Xander protested. His feet dragged as sudden exhaustion seemed to overwhelm him.

"You'd better stay with us, in that case," Tré said dryly. "Since you'd be impossible to replace." He turned his attention back to their footing as they stumbled across the rickety bridge leading up to the abandoned plantation house they'd been using as a base of operations.

They had discovered the place, deep in the Louisiana bayou, several months ago. Since then, they'd hidden themselves here, fixing it up enough to be marginally habitable, and venturing into New Orleans only as necessary.

Tré had sent the others ahead to prepare, knowing that time would be of the essence once he and Eris arrived with Xander.

The air was thick with humidity, mist rising around them as Tré and Eris stomped through mud and sludge, making their way up the hill to dry land.

"You know what?" Xander said suddenly, his voice somewhat clearer. "Walking sucks. Why do humans do this all the time? I wouldn't bother."

Eris and Tré's eyes met over the top of their friend's drooping head. "You're the one who morphed back into solid form half a mile shy of our destination," Eris pointed out, a look of consternation crossing his handsome Mediterranean features.

It was true that they would normally have traveled as mist, or in the form of owls. But Xander's owl would have manifested the same horrific injury he now sported in vampire form. And by the time Oksana had wiped the human woman's memory, Xander had lost enough blood and life force that he couldn't maintain his transformation into mist all the way back to the plantation house. Tré supposed they were lucky he'd made it as far as he did.

But... *the woman*.

Tré's mind wandered back to her. He felt a complex tangle of emotion surge through him as he recalled exactly how her skin felt as it brushed against his. It was a touch so old — yet so familiar — that he had momentarily been paralyzed by the unexpected warmth of life flowing through his cold limbs.

His thoughts carried him all the way to the door of the old house. Oksana opened it for them, looking deeply concerned as the trio slipped quickly through the entrance.

"Tré," she called after them. "We've put some clean linens down in Xander's room."

"Thank you," he responded. "With luck, he's lost enough blood by this point that he won't end up bleeding all over them."

"You're a terrible friend," Xander muttered. "You know that, right? Because I feel it's important for me to drive this point home."

Eris snorted in dark amusement as they trudged up the stairs to the second floor, listening with some trepidation to the creak of ancient wood under their feet. Thankfully, the old boards supported their combined weight without cracking, and they passed awkwardly around the bend in the steps, reaching the landing without mishap. The second door on the right, Xander's room, stood ajar and they shuffled him across the threshold in an awkward three-way dance.

After lowering the wounded vampire's limp frame onto the bed, Eris nodded silently to Tré and slipped out of the room, shutting the door behind him with a quiet click.

Tré propped Xander's feet up on a stack of pillows and removed his boots.

"I don't care to make a habit of this," he told the other vampire, who seemed more aware of his surroundings now that he was fully reclined. "Particularly not when you are, as you have repeatedly pointed out, completely sober."

Xander's flat gaze was unimpressed. "I assure you, this was not how I intended to spend my evening."

After freeing the buttons, Tré pulled Xander's sticky, blood-soaked shirt back, and examined the wound under his collarbone.

"That will take some time to heal," he murmured, using his fingers to press the skin back down around the gaping hole. If they were lucky, it would heal correctly and not leave a substantial mark on Xander's marble skin. "Still, I suppose it could be worse. You have lost much of your life force, though. I can feel it weakening."

"Don't fuss. I'll recover," Xander said. He sounded confident, yet Tré noticed that his eyes had drifted shut. He looked as comfortable as he could be, under the circumstances, so Tré pulled up a chair next to him.

"Here. You need to feed," Tré said, offering his wrist.

Despite his earlier protestations, Xander barely hesitated. Like a child, he opened his mouth gratefully, revealing sharp fangs that sank into Tré's skin.

Tré felt his flesh pierced, but he did not flinch as Xander suckled weakly at the blood dripping into his mouth. Knowing that he was in for a long night, Tré adjusted his position in the chair to a more comfortable one, and rested his elbow on the bed next to Xander. After several quiet moments, color seeped back into his friend's pale skin, and Tré could feel the steady throb of Xander's power growing stronger. The blood he had shared was already beginning to do its job.

"How do you feel now?" he asked when Xander paused in his feeding.

"Like shit… but better than I did earlier," Xander admitted. He sounded tired, but more aware and centered than during his ramblings on the journey back to the house.

"Good. Rest for a while. Then you will need to feed again. Every few hours throughout the night, I'd expect."

Xander nodded and blinked several times before meeting Tré's eyes directly and holding them.

"What happened to you back there, Tré?" he asked quietly.

Tré frowned. "What do you mean?"

Xander refused to be put off. "With the woman we saved? I felt something strange happen when you touched her, and you looked like you'd seen a ghost, afterward."

"It was nothing, just stirred up some old memories. Nothing for you to be worried about right now."

"But—"

He shook his head. "Xander. You need to rest and focus on healing. Here, please feed some more. I'm strong enough, and it will help knit the wound back together more quickly."

Xander looked as if he wanted to argue, but instead he sighed and latched on to Tré's proffered wrist again.

While his friend drank more forcefully, Tré allowed his mind to drift again towards the woman. He could not seem to banish her from his thoughts, as much as he tried to.

He had touched her skin and for a moment, his power had nearly exploded out of the bounds of his body. He'd felt the absolute, overwhelming certainty that he knew her. This no casual acquaintance from days past, however. No, he had recognized her as his long lost Irina. The only woman he had ever loved.

But that was truly impossible. She had died, centuries ago, a horrific death, wrought by his own blood-soaked hands. The same hands that were supposed to protect her and shield her from all suffering.

Memories flooded Tré's mind, very much against his will. He had been haunted by these memories every single day of his endless, immortal life, stuck in a brooding cycle of guilt and self-loathing that would never cease. Not for all eternity.

Tré had been turned from a mortal man into a vampire at the hands of the most evil power the world had ever known—the demonic spirit, Bael. Among other horrific abilities, Bael had the power to tear a soul into two pieces and cast the Light side into the depths of hell, leaving only the Dark behind.

According to the doddering old village priest, Tré had been marked by evil from the time he was a small child. Yet Bael did not succeed in capturing him until he was a young man, barely twenty-three years of age when it finally happened.

The demon had come upon him in the dead of night, surrounding him like a suffocating cloud that burned his skin and eyes and tore the air from his lungs. Tré could remember how he thrashed and struggled, trying to fight off the force of darkness that felt like it was permeating his entire being. He had been dragged down into a hole—a grave designed for the living—and at the bottom of the pit, the torture had truly begun. He'd fought with everything in him—with the crazed frenzy of a cornered animal, all his strength pouring out to no effect.

He could not escape the demon's clutches. The agony of having his soul torn into two pieces, the Light and the Dark, was a torment he would never forget, despite the hundreds of years that had passed since that time. But something had happened. Something had gone wrong.

Instead of submitting to the rape and defilement of all the good in him, Tré had managed to claw his way out of the pit that Bael had cast him into. He still remembered Bael's unearthly shriek of fury upon seeing that his victim had escaped. But Tré had cared nothing for the demon's dismay.

A burning thirst seemed to ignite in his gut, spreading up into his throat and his mouth until he felt he must surely die from the craving. He could feel his body shuddering, changing, and strength he had never known flooded through his limbs.

It was at that moment that his life changed forever. With his soul torn in two, he had left the mortal world and stepped into the night as a vampire. He was crazed, desperate, and panicked by the lust for blood that made his head spin and his canines lengthen into fangs.

He had crawled along the ground, pulling himself forward by his fingernails, an inch at a time, dirt and ashes filling his mouth. At that moment, he had looked up through the haze of pain and rage and seen a graceful figure making its way towards him. Tré blinked rapidly, averting his eyes. It seemed as though a dazzling light was pouring from her, shining against his burning skin. Shining into his very soul.

It was his beloved, Irina. They had been betrothed for nearly a year, and Tré loved her with a passion that seemed terrifying at times. They were soulmates, destined for each other and no one else.

He snarled, drawing his arms and legs up underneath him, ready to spring towards the source of life, light, and blood that he could smell radiating from her. He needed her to quench his bone-deep thirst. Nothing else would do. Nothing else could stop his agony.

Irina had seen him, covered in dirt and mud, a broken specter of the man that she loved. She had rushed forward, drawing her hood back and revealing her distraught face, tragically beautiful in the moonlight.

"Vlad!" she cried, falling to her knees in front of him. He sprang at her, feeling a burst of strength he had never experienced before, propelling him forward through the air.

He crashed into her delicate frame, pinning her to the ground beneath him. She screamed, terrified by his twisted features, his burning eyes. He bared his fangs with a feral growl and —

Tré shook his head violently, trying to free himself from the memories that had assaulted him, seemingly out of nowhere. He could not afford to think about that terrible night. He needed to focus. He needed to maintain discipline.

There was work to be done, and many things to be considered. Bael was behind everything dark, all the evil in the world. Tré had sensed his presence during the shooting today, even if the demon had not shown himself directly during the attack.

He and his fellow vampires had vowed to spend eternity fighting against Bael, to seek revenge for all of the mortal lives that had been lost, including their own. They were the products of Bael's failure, as each of them had somehow managed to escape his clutches before being turned into lifeless, animated puppets, capable of only evil. Their miraculous escapes, however, had come at a cost that could never be repaid.

The last flicker of Light inside them had only been shielded by the willing sacrifice of a true love, which formed a fragile bond between the two broken halves of their souls. In Tré's case, the sacrifice had come from Irina, who had cowered on the ground, rolling over and covering Tré's body with her own protectively as Bael had descended upon them.

The memory of that terrible moment threatened to shatter Tré's divided soul into a million shards and scatter them into the wind. He trembled as he sat next to Xander, whose eyes were open, studying him closely and with no small amount of concern.

Tré broke eye contact and forced his mind back to the ever-growing problem before them. It did no good to revisit old memories of Irina's sacrifice. Such indulgence was a weakness.

It was clear to all of them that Bael's power was growing, and the tides of the long war between Light and Darkness were turning in the demon's favor. This perplexed Tré. Why now? What had changed? How many more lives would be lost or destroyed before Bael could be forever defeated?

Could he be defeated?

Eris—the scholar among them—had done a vast amount of studying over the centuries. He'd discovered that a handful of ancient texts predicted the downfall of Bael at the hands of thirteen failed undead, a council of immortals who would join together and cast the demon into his own hell, forever condemned to the same mutilations he had inflicted on the world.

He and Tré had scoured the globe, discovering four more vampires in turn, but never finding any more than that despite their ongoing search. It appeared that only six of them had survived the turning with their sanity intact... though that assessment might be a bit optimistic in Snag's case. The oldest of the vampires, a sad skeleton of a creature that had been turned long before Tré, long before Eris, was hardly what you would consider *sane*.

At any rate, Eris had told them the ancient texts pointed towards that very love, which had saved them from Bael in the first place, being the uniting force that would ultimately be the demon's demise. This, in Tré's opinion, was errant nonsense. Laughable, even. There was no love left in him, only cold bitterness. With the possible exceptions of Eris and Oksana, they were all a bunch of ancient, bitter ghouls who probably should have been staked centuries ago.

So why—*why*—had the touch of that woman awoken such feelings of peace and belonging within him? It made no sense. Perhaps, he thought, she was some distant relative of his long lost love? But that would be impossible. Irina had died before she had borne any children. How could there be any connection?

Xander's voice broke into his morbid musings. "Tré, no offense, but your blood tastes like some punk emo kid angsting over his latest existential crisis. Are you absolutely sure you don't want to share your thoughts with the class?"

Tré frowned at him. To his private relief, Xander looked almost completely normal again, after the healing blood he had provided. "Not really. It's merely a ghost from the past."

Xander gave him a look that was almost pitying, but to Tré's eternal relief, he didn't press the issue.

"Right. Whatever you say. Thanks for the top-up, anyway. Though, you know—if you really loved me, you'd've downed a bottle or three of Glenmorangie beforehand to help take the edge off." He stretched carefully. "Now, go brood somewhere else for awhile and let me sleep. I'll let you know if I need you."

Without a word, Tré pushed the chair back against the wall and left the room, his thoughts still swirling around the honey-haired, hazel-eyed woman who seemed to somehow possess Irina's long dead spirit.

THREE

"Okay, try to stay calm." The blonde police officer—whose nametag identified her as Sgt. Diane Sheffield—spoke in a soft voice, rubbing Della's shoulder. Della wished she would stop.

She was sitting on the tailgate of an ambulance, wrapped in a reflective, crinkly blanket, unable to do more than huddle there and shake. Her fingers trembled violently as she tried to wrap the blanket more tightly around herself.

"I—I can't remember much," Della said for the dozenth time, feeling her teeth rattle together from the force of her tremors.

"That's okay. Just try to tell me what you do know. What happened after the gunman knocked you down and you hit your head?"

She strained her memory, attempting to focus on the hazy images. "I lay there for a minute, but I was too scared to really move because he was still pointing the gun at me."

"What did the gun look like?"

Della furrowed her eyebrows, trying so hard to remember. "Black handle, but it was made of silver metal."

"Was it an automatic or revolver?"

Della blinked in confusion at the police officer. "What?"

"Sorry," Diane said. "Did it have a circular chamber that spun when he fired? Like out of one of those old west movies? Or did he have to cock it like this?"

With her hands, she made a sliding motion back and forth.

Della shut her eyes, trying to remember. It was all so dim and jumbled together. The paramedics had assured her that it was normal for the mind to short circuit like that during a traumatic situation, but it didn't make the experience of memory loss any less terrifying.

"It's like your brain tries to take in too much information and your fear makes things spill back out. You may never get these memories back, and that's perfectly normal," one of the EMTs had told her, while shining a bright light in her eyes.

Della believed him, but there was still something about the whole thing that felt... *wrong*. She felt like there was something on the edge of her mind, obscured by the haze. She was *sure* it was important. Drastically important. Life changing, even. Yet, she could not draw it forward into her conscious mind, no matter how hard she tried.

It wasn't all that surprising, she supposed. Her heart was still thudding out of control and she could feel her pulse pounding in her eyes and face. She knew that she was fighting shock at this point, which was why the paramedics had insisted that she speak with police while wrapped up. They were trying to keep her body temperature from falling.

"Miss LeBlanc?" The police officer said.

Della realized that she had been silent for several long moments, lost in thought. She had completely forgotten that the officer was waiting for an answer.

"What? Oh, the gun. Sorry. Um, I don't think anything on the gun spun, but I can't be sure," she said, staring at her knees.

"That's okay, we just want to make sure that we haven't missed any weapons that may have been dropped in the street."

"What do you mean?"

"The gunmen were still holding their weapons when—" The officer's voice trailed away and she shook her head. "Well. Never mind about that part. We just want to make sure we haven't missed anything."

Della nodded, wiping cold sweat from her face with the edge of the blanket. She could feel the adrenaline that had been coursing through her body for what felt like hours draining away. She was left feeling weak, shaky, and nauseated. As her stomach gurgled uncomfortably, she leaned against the side of the ambulance and looked up into the officer's face.

"Can I go home now? Please?"

Sgt. Sheffield gazed sadly at Della, who knew she must look completely weak and defeated.

"Of course," said the officer. "We'll have someone take you home in a few minutes. And, Della?"

"Hmm?" Della answered, not looking at the woman.

"Please make sure that you follow up with someone — a therapist, or a doctor, or a pastor, or *someone* about this. We may also need to call you in for more information, but not for the next couple of days, probably. Are you willing to help us?"

"Of course," Della answered, clearing her throat. She slid unsteadily to her feet, feeling Sgt. Sheffield grip her arm above her elbow to support her.

Della let herself be guided towards a police car and another officer, who drove her home.

Along the way, Della stared mutely out of the window, unable to see much through the heavy blanket of darkness. It was as if the streetlights weren't penetrating through the gloom as well as they usually did, or maybe her eyes weren't working properly.

She couldn't even muster up enough energy to rub at them to try to bring everything into focus.

"Are you going to be all right, there?" The officer asked. She jerked in surprise and looked over at him. She had barely paid attention to who was sliding into the car next to her, so she was surprised to see an attractive young cop with sandy blonde hair glancing back and forth between her and the street ahead. On a normal day, she might have thought he was kind of cute. Today, she would be happy never to see him again.

"Yeah," Della answered in a dull tone. "Thanks."

When she finally made it home, the officer walked her to her apartment, tipped his hat to her, and left as she slipped inside. With her back against the door, she locked the handle, deadbolt, and the chain above her head before standing stock still, hugging herself.

Everything felt unreal. Della looked down at her hands, amazed to see fingers attached. She rubbed them together, but couldn't feel the slide of skin against skin. She was completely numb, only aware of a vague tingling that was passing over her entire body.

Knowing that she desperately needed sleep, Della tossed her handbag onto the ground right next to the door, not even bothering to grab her cell phone out of it first. She supposed she was lucky that one of the officers had retrieved it from where she must have dropped it, and returned it to her. She stepped out of her shoes and stumbled into the bathroom.

After washing her face and brushing her teeth with rote movements, Della fell into bed, feeling ever so slightly more human after the splash of warm water on her face.

Sleep seemed to be waiting for her, dragging her down into her squishy mattress the second her head hit the pillow.

I should at least turn the light off, Della thought vaguely. Her eyes cracked open and she blinked at the offending lamp on the bedside table. Even though it was only a few inches away, she couldn't summon the energy to reach up and turn it off. The weariness in her arms and legs was so absolute, she felt like she weighed five hundred pounds.

At last, sleep overcame her, pulling her down into dark, fitful dreams.

-o-o-o-

She was standing on the edge of a small, quaint town, like one of those fake villages they dragged you to in grade school so you could see how people lived hundreds of years ago. Only here, there were no little hints of the modern world hidden around — no extension cords bundled along the base of a wall; no plastic water bottles stuffed hastily behind an olde-tymey market stall. By the indistinct light pouring out through the windows of the little cottages around her, Della could see that fires were lit inside. The sweet, rich smell of wood smoke lingered in the air around her.

A sense of urgency overcame her. She whirled and took off running, out of the village and into the trees, somehow knowing exactly where she needed to go. As she ran, she realized that she was wearing a simple dress of brown, woven cloth. The heavy skirts swished around her feet, which were bare.

She was traveling along a dirt trail, feeling her feet sinking into the wet earth. Mud squished between her toes.

Suddenly, through the darkness, she became aware of a creeping presence coming closer, ever closer. A chill ran up her spine and she recoiled, a suffocating sense of evil surrounding her. Looking ahead, she saw a dark figure writhing on the ground. Something was terribly familiar about it — the strong line of the man's back and shoulders, maybe. Or perhaps the timbre of the tortured cries floating towards her through the mist.

A swirling dark cloud exploded out of a pit and surrounded the figure, who shrieked in agony as it enveloped him.

Della felt a stab of shock as the man turned over, his limbs flopping like a broken doll's. Merciful God. She recognized his face — but where had she seen it before? The sense of familiarity she'd felt solidified into blank horror.

"Vlad!" she heard her dream-self scream. Tears were streaming down her face. She was terrified, but her heart propelled her forward through the fear. She stumbled over a tree root before righting herself and staggering the last few steps toward the man she... loved? She threw herself down onto her hands and knees at his side, mud splattering everywhere.

Her mind merged with that of her dream-self like double vision coming into diamond-sharp focus. Her betrothed panted on the ground, twisting and clawing at himself like a wounded animal. When he opened his eyes, Della saw a fire burning behind them that she had never seen before. They had always been a calm gray, like the sea on a cloudy morning. Now, they shone silver, glowing from within. She choked back another scream at the unnatural sight. His face and neck were covered in terrible scorch marks, and he barely seemed to recognize her.

But, no — something flickered in his eyes when he looked up into her face. Before she could draw breath, he moved faster than anyone she had ever seen. A heavy weight plowed into her and she was thrown backwards, sinking into the mud. A strong body, familiar but changed, crouched over her, caging her with arms and legs.

She could feel the black cloud of evil surrounding her, burning her skin, sucking the air from her lungs and leaving her gasping. She struggled under the suffo-

cating, intangible weight of it, to no avail. Her heart pounded as if trying to escape the prison of her chest.

The blackness had done this, somehow. This strange, evil force had attacked her beloved, and changed him into a tortured beast.

"No! Stop! Leave him alone!" she croaked, each word a searing pain in her throat.

A dark, malicious voice echoed with laughter inside her mind. It came, she felt sure, from the black cloud swirling around them as Vlad pressed her down to the ground. Her lover's hand came up and gripped her arm. Words swirled across her flickering awareness, confusing and dark. They did not come from her beloved.

"What will you give me in return?"

The voice was cold, yet sounded darkly amused by its own offer. Della felt the hair on her arms and neck stand on end as she realized that she was hearing a voice from the depths of hell itself. The pressure holding her down vanished as Vlad crumpled with a primal scream, landing next to her and convulsing in pain.

"I will give my life for his," she cried, throwing her body over her fiancé's as if she could somehow protect him physically from the forces of Satan.

Vlad struggled and groaned beneath her. To Della's shock, he pressed his mouth against her throat as if in a kiss. An instant later, Della felt a sharp stabbing pain. She shrieked and tried to tear herself away, but strong hands grabbed her like claws, holding her in place.

"Your love cannot save him," the voice purred in her ear. "He has already been turned. Your lover has forgotten you. You are nothing but meat to him now, and he will destroy you in your insolence."

"My life for his, then," Della ground out, feeling razor-sharp fangs sink deeper into her flesh.

More laughter, the sound making her skin crawl as if insects were scurrying over her body. The fangs pulled out and she was flipped over – tossed on her back again. The dark figure that had once been her true love loomed over her, salivating with bloodlust. Feeling the inevitability of what was about to happen, Della bared her bleeding neck to him, trying to keep his eyes locked on hers.

"Take what you need, my love," she whispered, forcing the words past the ruin of her throat. "I... give it... freely..."

With a flash, the beast that had once been Vlad sank his teeth into her neck as she let out a choked cry.

He did not answer, but continued to draw from her neck, a feral snarl escaping from his chest. The pain grew distant, but she felt terribly cold. The darkness of the moonlit forest seemed to be deepening to pitch black. Her hand slipped from Vlad's shoulder, flopping down into the mud as her awareness narrowed to a hazy tunnel.

-o-o-o-

Della struggled wildly, her legs tangling in the sheets and blankets. As she jerked awake, gasping for air, a black whisper rustled at the edge of her hearing.

"Oh yes, child. I do remember you."

Della blinked into awareness and found that she was on the floor, lying in a heap next to her bed. She must have tried to leap to her feet and ended up pulling all of her bedclothes with her onto the floor. She was panting as if she had run a marathon, covered in sweat. As she woke more fully, shaking the last vestiges of the dream from her head, she felt that terrible looming presence retreat and fade.

Clutching a hand over her heart, which was thudding loudly in her chest, Della tried to slow her breathing to a normal rate before she hyperventilated.

"I am *losing my goddamned mind*," she said to the empty room.

She stumbled to her feet, clutching the bed frame until her shaking knees stopped threatening to send her right back down to the floor. When she was steady enough, she grabbed her robe and slipped it around her shoulders, feeling the warmth soothing her tense muscles as she padded quietly through her apartment and out into the courtyard behind her building, still barefoot. She left her sliding glass door open to allow the fresh air to filter into the living room, and sat down on the lichen-encrusted bench.

The unusual cold snap had abated while she slept, leaving the night cool against her overheated skin, but not freezing. The dew had fallen and she stared into the sky, trying to see the stars past the bright city lights. Somewhere off in the distance, she could hear sirens wailing. She shivered at the noise, wondering what horrors were occurring beyond the confines of her little sanctuary.

A moment later, the faint rustle of wings caught her attention.

There was a live oak tree standing in the center of the courtyard. It had grown tall and broad over the decades, casting the apartments around her into shadow despite the bright moonlight that painted her bench pale gray. On one of the lower branches, she spotted a large owl perched silently, its round, silvery eyes gazing down on her. The huge bird ruffled its wings again before folding them neatly against its body.

She felt herself relax and exhaled the breath she hadn't been aware she was holding. The owl blinked slowly at her and then swiveled his head around, as if checking for other visitors. An unexpected sense of serenity settled over Della, making her eyelids droop as exhaustion caught up with her. A soft breeze caressed her face. She sat still and silent, listening to the sounds of the restless city around her.

Della tried not to think about the horrible events from the previous day, knowing that doing so would destroy the momentary calm that she seemed to have found, sitting here in the moonlight. In a way, she was grateful that she had few memories of what had happened. Even though it made the events seem disturbingly distant and unreal, she knew that she was less likely to be traumatized by memories that she did not truly possess anymore.

These thoughts passed through her mind, but she remained relaxed in the courtyard, untroubled by fear or memory. Right now, she felt like she could sleep peacefully for a week. Not wanting to waste the moment, she stood.

"Thanks for the nighttime company, owl," she said, and stumbled back to her bed. She was already half asleep when her head hit the pillow.

This time, Della didn't have any frightening nighttime visions. Instead, she drifted into a deep slumber, imagining a gentle touch running over her skin—the hand of a lover. She felt protected and safe, wrapped in a cocoon of sheets, peace and security warming her.

As the early morning hours slipped by, the imagined caress grew more intimate, rousing her blood without piercing the aura of drowsy contentment that draped over her dreams like the softest of blankets. When she awoke, she was covered in a light sheen of sweat, liquid heat pooling between her legs.

-o-o-o-

"Are you going to be all right now, Xander?" Tré asked, eyeing his fellow vampire with misgiving.

His injured friend had stumbled down from his room after a short nap, and was currently lounging on a dusty sofa that looked original to the early 1900s, a slow grin spreading over his handsome face. He was grasping a bottle of what Xander presumed was spiked blood, and he pointed his finger drunkenly at Tré with the same hand that gripped his drink.

"You," he slurred, "worry too much. You need to learn to let this shit *go*, Tré."

Tré scowled, skeptical. "We can't all drown our woes in drink. Also, do I even want to know where you got that bottle? Or how?"

"Almost certainly not," Xander mumbled, taking another drink and wiping away the trickle of deep red that escaped the corner of his mouth to drip down his chin. "Still, you should try it sometime as an alternative to your incessant brooding."

"Don't worry, Tré," a dry female voice said from behind him. "I'll keep an eye on him."

Tré turned, meeting Duchess' eyes with a raised eyebrow. Her blue gaze was as cold and depthless as the water at the bottom of a well. Her blond hair was draped elegantly over her left shoulder, falling in wavy curls far too perfectly formed to be random. Tré nodded his thanks and let his eyes slide back to Xander.

"Don't let him have another bottle," he said. Tré knew that Duchess was more than a match for Xander, especially when he was this drunk. She would manage to keep him under control by fair means or foul.

"You're the boss," she replied with a shrug, tossing her hair over her other shoulder and walking past Tré into the room.

"Behave," Tré commanded, looking at Xander, who lifted his eyebrows in response and made an innocent *who, me?* gesture with his free hand.

"I resent your implication," Xander said, forming the words with careful precision. "You should be more concerned with our resident man-eater's behavior than with little old me."

"I was speaking to both of you, actually," Tré clarified, and left the room without a backward glance.

Tonight, he had other concerns.

The woman. He had to see her. He had to know the truth. Tré's thoughts had been running along a single narrow path ever since returning from the battle where Xander had been wounded. He needed to find out the truth about the mysterious girl who—to all appearances—possessed the same gentle, loving soul as his long-lost Irina.

Stepping out of the front door, Tré took a deep breath, bringing all of his power into a central focus beneath his heart and lungs. Letting it flow once more through his limbs on a slow breath, he transformed into the shape of a huge gray owl. He spread his powerful wings wide and took flight, reveling in the way the ground fell away as he was borne aloft on silent feathers.

He could see much better in the darkness as an owl, and flicked his gaze back and forth as he flew low over the trees surrounding the old plantation house. Rodents scurried for cover as he flew overhead, but he ignored them. He was not on the hunt tonight. He headed toward the glowing lights of the city, a beacon in the moonlit night despite the lateness of the hour.

Less than half an hour later, Tré glided down to perch on the roof of a building, surveying the bustling crime scene below. Police, fire crews, and medical examiners walked back and forth between the dead bodies, talking to each other in low voices and comparing notes. Tré saw no sign of the woman. Knowing it hadn't been that long since the attack, Tré assumed that she would still be nearby—tied up in red tape, waiting for medical attention, speaking with police. He turned his head past ninety degrees to his left and saw that a mass of people were huddled around the corner and down the street.

He took flight again and settled on the eaves of another building, just in time to see the woman being led to a police car. A female officer with blond hair helped guide her into the seat and shut the door behind her, while another male officer stepped into the driver's seat.

Tré felt an unbidden stab of jealousy and possessiveness. He ruthlessly tamped it down.

Irrational. Ridiculous. This is not the time or the place, he scolded himself.

He followed the police cruiser all the way back to the woman's apartment building and watched as the officer escorted her inside. He flew low over the building, searching for a window that he could see through, only to find that shades or blinds blocked every one of them.

In frustration, he landed on a low branch of the tree in the small courtyard.

Even if I can't see her, he thought, *I just need to be near her. Just for a while, until all this starts to make sense.*

Perhaps if he stayed close by, he would be able to sense her life force. To discover if it was just a coincidence, a distant relation, maybe, or if it was truly his beloved Irina, reborn. Yet, how could such a thing be? How could Irina—brave, tragic Irina—*possibly* be here, of all places? It made no sense.

Tré grew lost in thought, turning the night's events over and over in his mind. He could not shake the impression that Bael was nearby, and centuries-old revulsion coursed through him. It was as corrosive as acid, this gut-deep hatred. It ate at the small reserve of Light that was still trapped inside him, for all that it was no longer unified with his soul.

And that was both the terrible power and the terrible failure of Bael. The demon had intended to rip the Light from Tré's soul and cast it into the pit of hell, but Irina had saved him. Her selfless, loving sacrifice had bound the Light inside him, turning him into a vampire rather than an undead puppet of his evil creator, filled with nothing but destruction and evil. A mere vessel for Bael's twisted desires.

According to Eris, ancient prophecy foretold that Bael could only be defeated in the coming War between Light and Darkness by a council composed of thirteen of his failures. Tré interpreted that to mean thirteen vampires, like himself. Thirteen people who had been saved by the sacrifices of true love, and transformed into powerful creatures who walked the empty spaces between the Light and the Dark.

But there weren't thirteen vampires roaming the earth. There were six.

Maybe Bael's cruelty and malice wasn't finished? Perhaps he simply hadn't created the other seven yet?

You'd think he'd learn from six mistakes, and stop trying, Tré thought bitterly.

His musings were interrupted by the sound of a sliding glass door being pulled back just below him. To his complete surprise, the woman from the mass shooting stumbled outside, wrapped in a robe and looking distraught. She dropped onto a bench near her door, leaving it open wide to the chilly night air, and scrubbed her face with her hands.

She was obviously troubled, despite Oksana's removal of her memories.

Tré wondered if she had been able to sleep at all, or if the events of the previous evening — those that she still remembered — were haunting her. Keeping her awake. Tré shook himself, ruffling feathers. He needed to keep his heart out of this matter. He was here purely for observation, to figure out what was going on. Not to satisfy the pangs of aching loneliness and desire he felt when looking at her.

He rustled his wings again, trying to shake free of the trance he had fallen into when she stepped outside.

The movement seemed to draw her attention and for a moment they stared at each other. Again, Tré felt a strong sense of recognition in his heart. It was as though someone had ignited a fire in his tattered soul, burning through him as he stared at the woman. He had never met her before that day, yet somehow, he knew her as well as he knew himself. He was drawn to her with an intensity that nearly knocked him right out of the tree.

Feeling an overwhelming need to protect her, Tré swiveled his head around, searching for any sign of danger that might disrupt the fragile sanctuary she seemed to have found in the courtyard. He could feel Bael hovering over the city, but the demon did not seem to be focused on this place. Tré's wary tension eased somewhat, and he looked back toward the woman.

He could hear her breathing, which was slow and tranquil now. At that, he felt a strange sensation somewhere between a deep ache, and the promise of peace that he had never known in the endless years since his turning. All this, wrapped up within one tiny woman huddled on a cold bench. He could hardly bear the sensation, which seemed to resonate between the two halves of his broken soul like a struck tuning fork.

Suddenly, the woman stood.

"Thanks for the nighttime company, owl," she said in a low, lyrical voice. A moment later, she yawned and turned back toward the sliding door. Tré could tell by her heartbeat that sleep was stealing up on her. He watched as she shuffled inside on unsteady feet and slid the door shut behind her. He could clearly hear the satisfying sound of a clicking lock, and then a thud as she rolled a heavy length of wood into the track of the door.

She will be safe tonight, he thought with satisfaction.

Still, it was difficult to leave. With the beat of mighty wings, Tré finally took flight and headed towards home, feeling as though he were leaving part of his heart behind.

FOUR

Tré's return to the abandoned plantation house did not go unnoticed, but the other vampires wisely decided not to ask him for details of where he'd been. Instead, he sensed them silently retreating further into the house. Staying out of his way.

With the dawn approaching, they would soon go their separate ways to sleep and recuperate from the events of the night. Indeed, when Tré walked into the dusty, moldering parlor, it was to find Xander looking pale, worn, and far too sober as he headed for the stairs.

"So, you didn't drink yourself into oblivion after all?" Tré asked without emotion.

"Your guard dog wouldn't let me," Xander said, with a yawn and a stretch. "I feel like shit, though—thanks for asking. I'm going to bed."

"Call me if you need to feed again," Tré reminded him as he watched Xander laboriously climb the stairs, his shoulders drooping with exhaustion. A careless wave of one hand was the only answer he received.

With a shake of his head, Tré continued through the house to the kitchen. The space was rarely used, except when Oksana decided to go on one of her human junk food binges. For some reason, that eccentric trait had never faded during the decades that he'd known her. With every passing year, it seemed that she would discover some new culinary abomination with which to drown her sorrows.

Personally, Tré didn't understand how she could swallow the stuff without choking. None of the other vampires retained any vestige of liking for human food, subsisting instead on a strict diet of blood.

Well. Make that *blood, alcohol, and psychoactive drugs*, in Xander's case.

Yet, Oksana could often be found stashing away bags of greasy chips and sickly sweet confections in crinkling plastic wrappers, the mere smell of which turned Tré's stomach. Her current obsession was something called *no-bake cookies*, which she insisted were the best thing that she had ever eaten.

Still, who was he to judge? As coping mechanisms went, it wasn't the worst he'd seen over the years. Case in point... *Xander*.

Tré pushed his way through the creaking kitchen door and found several of the others seated around a large table in the center of the echoing room. Snag, Tré noticed, was not present. Not that he had expected the ancient vampire to be here. The oldest of their group, Snag spent the vast majority of his time sitting in the back bedroom in total silence, his cold, mournful eyes staring unblinking at anyone who dared enter his sterile domain. Tré hadn't heard him utter a sound in a little over a century, and often wondered if he'd lost the ability to speak.

For all intents and purposes, the old vampire was barely alive, even by their standards. He was rail-thin, and his skin hung off him like wax paper — parched and colorless. He was covered, head to toe, in scars that looked like they came from burns and claw marks, but Tré had never asked for details of what had happened to him after his turning, millennia ago. He was reasonably certain he didn't want to know.

Mostly, Snag would sit alone, sometimes staring out of the window, sometimes staring at nothing. He refused to feed on humans. As far as Tré could tell, only Eris' careful tending kept him from slipping into the petrified, coma-like state that seemed to be as close as vampires could come to the release of death in the normal course of things.

Eris alone seemed able to break through to Snag. To a degree, anyway. All the others harbored the belief that the ancient vampire was deranged, and would eventually lose his mind completely. Not Eris, however. From time to time, Eris could convince Snag to feed from him. He had been known to sit and talk to the old vampire for hours, even if he never received an answer.

He claimed the two of them played chess sometimes. Though, to Tré's knowledge, there had been no independent confirmation of such a thing. And he, at least, found it very hard to picture.

"Hello again, Tré. You certainly look like shit this morning," Duchess observed, her eyes raking up and down Tré's body. She, of course, had already touched up her makeup and hair sometime following the battle. Her bright red lipstick almost seemed to glow from her perfect, cupid's bow lips.

Eris gave her a quelling look. "It's been a rough night, Duchess," he said, no real ire behind the words. "You need to lay off."

"No," Tré said with a sigh as he sat on an empty bar stool. "It's fine. Though I imagine Xander is still going to win the *looking like shit* award for today."

The others nodded with varying degrees of sympathy.

"Thanks for keeping him from getting completely plastered, Duchess, by the way," Tré added.

"I have no more desire to listen to him snoring like a freight train and talking to himself all day than you do," Duchess said.

Oksana drew a quick breath, as if she were about to speak, only to pause and chew her lip with a thoughtful expression. Finally, she said, "You know, it just seems odd to me that so many of these terrible things have been happening here in New Orleans over the past few months."

"Well, New Orleans *is* a city that stays up late and parties hard," Eris pointed out. "It always has been."

"Yes," she agreed, "I know that. But it still seems like everything is getting worse here. Like it's becoming some sort of... I don't know. *Locus.*"

"Things are bad everywhere, but you do have a point about the area feeling like a sort of focal point," Tré said. He leaned wearily against the edge of the table. "Eris, have you run across anything like this in any of the ancient texts about Bael?"

"What? Specifically about a surge of violence in one place, you mean?" Eris asked.

"Yes, exactly."

"Not really, no."

Tré swallowed his disappointment. He'd never placed too much stock in what was predicted in dusty old prophecies. Even so, he would have appreciated a little insight from any source at all, if the lore masters could have been bothered to come up with something that would actually *help* them.

"It feels to me as if things here are getting more organized," Oksana said quietly. "Take the gunmen last night. That wasn't an act of a random violence, like a riot, or someone snapping and killing his family, or a drive-by shooting. It took planning, preparation, and careful execution of a coordinated attack. I don't think the perps were gang members, either. And while I don't doubt that the authorities will play the Islamic terrorist card, I didn't get that vibe from them at all."

The other members of the group nodded agreement. Duchess ran her fingers through her long hair, ruffling it and tossing it casually over her shoulder.

"I think you're right that it's all related somehow to the growing pattern of violence we've seen in the city in the past few weeks, *ma chère*," she said eventually. "There seems to be no question that the attacks are growing in scale and organization."

"Agreed," Tré said.

Oksana yawned behind her hand and cast a longing eye towards a plate of cookies she'd left on the counter. Everyone was still and thoughtful except Eris. Eris looked troubled.

"Does… anyone else get the feeling that darkness is being *drawn* here, to New Orleans? Like we're standing at the center of a vortex?" he asked.

"Yes," Tré answered, the words striking a chord within him. "That's it, precisely. In fact, I was thinking about that on the way back. But… why *here*? Why now?"

"New Orleans does have one thing that the rest of the world lacks," Eris said, appearing decidedly disconcerted now. "It has the six of us."

"Why would that matter?" Oksana argued, frowning at Eris. "It's not like *we're* behind the attacks."

"No," Eris said with a shrug, "but it does seem like an odd coincidence that the only six vampires in the world would be residing in the city that's currently going to hell in a handbasket."

"But we're really only here in the first place because we *followed* the trail of destruction and violence," Duchess reminded Eris.

He nodded, but did not seem entirely convinced. Tré knew that Eris would spend hours — if not days — mulling over the theory. No doubt he would immerse himself the vast file of notes he kept on an old laptop, copied from the ancient texts that fascinated him so. Looking for some explanation, some *meaning* for what they had observed.

"There's something *different* about this place," Eris said in a quiet voice. "And it's new. I didn't feel it the last time I was here, a few years ago. It's also worth noting that, if the theory of darkness being somehow drawn to New Orleans is correct, it might explain why *we* were drawn here, as well. Vampires are, after all, dark creatures."

The words seemed to spark a connection in Tré's mind, and he frowned.

His mind wandered back over the last several weeks since they had arrived, following the reports of violence and unrest in hopes that it would somehow lead them to Bael. It was true that the incidents were getting deadlier and more public as time went on. It used to be that they could often manage small flare-ups with only one or two of them. Now, as the previous night had shown, it sometimes required all of them combining their strengths to stop the loss of life.

Yet, at the same time, they were utterly help-less to eradicate or eliminate the underlying source — the evil that seemed to possess some of the humans who acted as catalysts for the violence. On an almost nightly basis, there were riots across the city. The individuals involved did not appear to have any political or social aims. They simply seemed to enjoy getting into large groups, burning cars and buildings as they moved along the streets, sometimes even managing to force the police back with hails of rocks and Molotov cocktails.

Law enforcement presence didn't faze the riot-ers, who seemed almost impervious to normal crowd control and pain compliance techniques. The New Orleans Police Department was at a loss re-garding how to proceed, and simply attempted to manage the situation to prevent the spread of the rioting to residential parts of the city. Already, there had been calls for National Guard troops to be brought in to help support local departments. But, of course, New Orleans was not the only fire needing to be put out in the U.S. these days — it was merely the one burning the hottest, right now.

To Tré, it seemed bizarre that mass panic had not yet taken root among the populace. And yet, he knew that humans were notorious for their ability to rationalize things. No doubt, someone reading the newspaper over breakfast would tut at the headlines, marvel at the state of the world today, then shake it off with a muttered hope that none of it would come close enough to affect their little slice of the world.

It seemed likely, however, that a tipping point would come — a point after which everything would descend into total chaos. That, Tré knew, would be when the real nightmare began for humanity.

Eris was right. It didn't make sense, without some sort of catalyst. Why New Orleans? Why now? What was different about this city, compared to all the other cities in the world? Obviously, the Big Easy had always hidden a dark side, rife with tension between the *haves* and the *have-nots*. Every large city did, though in New Orleans, the divide between the rich and the poor had been exacerbated over the decades by natural disasters and economic hardship.

But that could not explain everything they were seeing. There was something else.

Tré's thoughts turned inexorably back to the woman who both was and was not Irina. A terrible suspicion entered his mind. Eris had pointed out that New Orleans was different because *they* were there. Yet, the six of them had moved from place to place for years, now. Decades. *Centuries.*

But *they* were not the only ones in the city. A ghost from the past was here with them, as well.

Tré took a deep, troubled breath and tried to clear his thoughts. He was jumping to conclusions. It was ridiculous to believe that a single human woman had anything to do with the violence that was spiraling out of control in New Orleans. It was just a strange coincidence, which happened to have popped up at a time when Tré was distracted by old memories and not on his best game.

Oksana yawned so widely that it looked like her jaw might break, and insisted that they all go to bed and prepare for another night of whatever insanity might come. He nodded agreement and wished the others a good day's rest, in a tone that was admittedly somewhat distant.

A few minutes later, Tré slipped gratefully in between the sheets of the grand four-poster bed in the room he'd claimed as his own. He'd left his door slightly ajar so he could listen for Xander, who was right across the hall, and hear him if he needed help during the day.

With a last, troubled sigh, Tré turned over and allowed his eyes to close, drifting into an uneasy sleep as the sun rose over the eastern horizon beyond the protection provided by the heavy crimson drapes.

-o-o-o-

Della stumbled into the office in a rush. She was nearly twenty minutes late for work—unheard of, for her. Her coworkers stared at her in consternation as she half-collapsed into the chair behind her desk, muttering hasty apologies as she did so.

Sean walked over to her, his blue eyes wide with concern. She could hardly blame him for being worried, Della had never been so much as one minute late to work since she'd been hired. She hadn't even realized any of her coworkers had a copy of the key so they could open the building without her.

"Della, you all right, there?" Sean asked in a low voice, leaning over her desk to get a closer look at her.

His concern threatened to stir up the deep well of shock and horror that was trapped behind her ribcage. But she couldn't... she could *not* afford to lose it at work. This job was the last marginally sane thing in her life. She *couldn't* screw it up.

To avoid having to speak, she nodded, the movement jerky. Sean raised his eyebrows at her and she looked back, trying to plaster a normal expression on her face. What did a normal expression even look like? She wasn't at all sure she'd pulled it off, but after a moment, he gave a quiet sigh and walked back towards his office.

Della let out the breath she'd been holding, not feeling as though she could come up with the strength and energy it would take to tell everyone that she'd been right in the middle of the mass shooting the previous evening.

She tried valiantly to power her way through the pile of reports clogging her inbox, but her mind kept straying back, replaying horrible loops of memories from the previous night. By mid-morning, Della was covered in clammy sweat and felt like she was on the verge of tears.

She hurried into the bathroom, locked the door, and tried to absorb the moisture from her eyes with dry, scratchy paper toweling from the dispenser. In the end, she achieved nothing more than making the whites of her eyes look even more blood shot.

When she returned to her desk, Alice wandered over, carrying an iPad in her right hand.

"Can you believe this?" she demanded, practically thrusting the little tablet under Della nose.

"Hmm?" Della replied, barely glancing up. The last thing she needed right now was for Alice to notice her tears.

"The shooting last night! Haven't you heard?" Alice said, her voice rising with emotion. "It happened not far from here and a whole bunch of people *died*."

Della didn't know what to say. Other than the police at the scene who helped her, she had told no one about what happened the previous day. She didn't feel like she could even *begin* to explain it to the righteously angry woman currently leaning against the edge of Della's desk.

"I just can't believe all the terrible things that are happening right now," Alice continued. "It really seems like things are getting worse, you know? I wonder if it's terrorists... I just can't understand why the politicians won't *act*—what the hell do they think we voted them in for?"

She continued ranting along these lines, the droning complaints failing to hold Della's fractured attention for more than a minute or two. The office went hazy around her, and she felt her heart pounding. In her mind's eye, she was again staring at the barrel of a gun as it swung upward and pointed directly into her face.

"…released the name of one of the men who was killed. Did you see that? Della?"

Della only caught the end of Alice's statement. She had become so lost in memory that Alice's words were drowned out by the rushing sound of panic in her ears.

"I'm sorry, what?" she asked, clearing her throat and trying to shake herself free of the flashback before she had a full-on meltdown right here at her desk.

Alice looked at her curiously and repeated, "I said, the police released some information about one the men who was killed. Did you see the news?"

"No."

"It's just so senseless and tragic! They say he was a single dad with twin girls. I guess they're orphans now. Apparently his wife died a few years ago from cancer. Who would *do* that to someone with children?"

Alice held up the iPad again. The screen showed a picture of a smiling, bearded man with two identical toddlers held in his arms. To Della's horror, she recognized him as the guy who had stopped her falling during the mass panic as the gunmen poured onto the street. She had knelt by his side, her hand pressed against his back, as he breathed his last.

Two girls? He had children*? Oh, God…*

Della felt like she was falling. She sat back against her chair and tipped her chin forward, trying to breathe through the dizziness and nausea that was threatening to overwhelm her. If it hadn't been for her, standing there frozen with shock, he might have made it around the corner. If it hadn't been for her, he might still be alive.

Something terrible was clawing up from deep inside her stomach and she tasted bile in her mouth. Her eyes began to water and she started to pant, distraught by the news that Alice had unknowingly shared. Della felt as if her whole stupid, meaningless life was crashing down around her.

It was her fault he was dead. *Her fault.*

"Della?" Alice was saying, and Della knew it wasn't the first time she'd repeated it. "Della, honey? What is it? Are you all right?"

Della clamped her eyes shut. She couldn't speak — not while she was concentrating on swallowing around the bile that was trying to rise in her throat.

"*Della.* Hey, now. You're scaring me," Alice said, coming around the desk and putting a manicured hand on Della's shoulder. She gave it a gentle shake, as if trying to rouse Della from sleep. "Seriously. Are you okay?"

Della let her eyes open slowly and glanced into Alice's pinched, worried face.

"No," Della murmured, the word coming out hoarse. She had successfully forced her stomach to subside—for the moment at least—but she felt like her tenuous control over her emotions and rebelling gut would not last for very long. "I'm just... not feeling very well."

"Yeah. No kidding, honey. You look terrible," Alice said, and frowned. "Maybe you should go home?"

Della sat silently for a moment. The idea of taking the day off was appealing, but on the other hand, the idea of being alone with her thoughts was not. Still, the last thing she needed was for her coworkers to see her like this.

"I think you're right," Della decided, rising to her feet and gathering her stuff.

-o-o-o-

Several hours later, Della was installed in a quiet corner of the public library. She had not gone home after leaving work. Instead, she'd decided to try losing herself between the pages of a book, something she'd often done as a child when she was upset. As she'd walked towards the public library at the corner of Tulane and Loyola, Della tried to distract herself by picking apart pieces of her nightmare. She had the strangest feeling that she'd dreamed the dream many times before. It was so familiar to her. Even the brush of coarse fabric against her skin had seemed like something she knew intimately.

But how could that be? She had no particular knowledge about medieval Europe or the type of clothing people wore at that time. Hell, it was even a mystery to her how she could tell for certain that the setting of the dream *was* medieval Europe. There was no way she could know that from the handful of scattered images she could remember, and yet she was as sure of it as she was of anything in her life.

With a stack of books in front of her, Della systematically flipped through pages, reading here and there and examining pictures of old tapestries and woodcuts. She never got a sense of familiarity from any of the books, though. Certainly not like she had from her dream.

Della rubbed tired, aching eyes as she pulled a book closer. She could smell the faintly musty scent of old paper as she carefully turned the pages of the well-used history tome.

Without warning, a shout shattered the quiet peace of the library. Della gasped and looked up, ducking down behind her stack of books in instinctive fear. She peered cautiously at the gap between two large pillars near the front of the library. A man, dressed in the tattered clothing of a homeless person, was screaming obscenities at the staff, all of whom were standing like statues behind the desk. His hand waved through the air as he gestured. As it passed through a ray of sunlight, something glinted silver. He had a knife clutched in his fist.

Fresh fear jolted through her. Was there no escape from the madness that seemed to be closing in around her? She scrambled back and hid behind a row of shelves, peeking through the spaces at the scene unfolding in front of her.

As she watched, feeling her pulse thundering in her ears, two security guards lunged forward and muscled the man to the floor. He continued to scream, his voice muffled as his face was pressed into the ugly, gray-brown carpet. Della could see the library staff huddling close together, looking shocked and frightened. She couldn't blame them — this was a *library*. Stuff like this wasn't supposed to happen in *libraries*.

Della returned to her table when it became clear that the situation was under control. She sat slowly, feeling her body going numb again and her eyes drifting out of focus. A fog seemed to be pressing down on her, weighing her down. Darkness passed in front of her eyes, and she blinked rapidly, trying to clear it.

There were no coherent thoughts in her mind, only a sense of dread and isolation. She felt suddenly alone, completely cut off from the world around her as the darkness and the damp chill swirled through her. Vertigo overcame her, and she realized that she was holding her breath and had been for some time.

Something is coming.

Della's thoughts ground back to life and, with a struggle, she was able to jerk herself back to reality. There was a presence here with her, like a breath of evil and decay on the back of her neck. Della whipped her head around. There was no one near her. And yet, she could not shake the sensation that malicious eyes were watching her.

She could feel icy prickling on her shoulders and head, as if an invisible spotlight had found her and was shining down on her with light so cold it burned. Della tried to focus mentally and banish the irrational, unsettling feeling. Glancing around, she found that the library was almost empty. The light coming in through the windows was a dim, golden glow.

"Shit!" Della exclaimed in shock. She had sat in the library all afternoon, and now it was evening. Had she... fallen asleep or something? Was the sense of evil just some crazy dream? Or had she really spaced out for that entire time, staring at nothing?

What was *happening* to her? She had to get out of there before dark. She suddenly wanted, more than anything, to be locked up safely in her apartment, with her stupid goldfish and her television and her pile of overdue bills.

She jumped up and gathered her possessions, shoving them in the small bag that she had slung over her shoulder.

"Oh yeah, this is just great," Della muttered as she hurried out onto the street. Already, the streetlights were coming on.

The tram stop was right outside, and she waited nervously for the next one to come along. When it did, she boarded gratefully and sat in her customary place near the back. It was about half full, but the other passengers seemed edgy, glancing at her and looking away quickly.

Della gripped the hard wooden back of the seat in front of her, feeling the edge dig into her palm. She counted ten stops, trying to push a vague sense of unease to the back of her mind. She got off at Martin Luther King and Lasalle, relieved when a handful of other people did as well. The small group headed downriver, in the general direction of A.L. Davis Park.

No one seemed in a mood to talk, only in a mood to get where they were going. Della ducked her chin and followed a woman wearing a long raincoat down the street. The uneven sidewalks, missing random bricks and heaving up wherever tree roots grew underneath them, were usually part of the city's strange, down-at-heel charm. Right now, though, they were yet another irritation, slowing her progress, threatening a stumble or a twisted ankle if her attention wandered.

Maybe I'll get lucky, Della thought with a hint of bitterness, *and just make it home without any problems tonight.*

The woman in front of her turned into a convenience store on the corner of the street. Della kept walking. Soon, the sound of other footsteps died away as her fellow commuters turned onto side roads, one by one. Feeling unaccountably nervous now as she hurried down the familiar streets, Della gripped her bag against her side with cold hands.

The dark, hovering presence that had seemed to dog her steps since the library persisted. She felt as if her footsteps were slowing — like she was wading through water or sand towards her shabby little apartment in the unfashionable part of town. Gritting her teeth, she pressed onward, desperate to reach the perceived safety of her building's front door.

Through the deepening darkness around her, Della could hear a low, evil laugh ring out. It sounded very far away, as if it were being projected through a long, echoing cave. Again, the sense of malevolent eyes on her back raised the fine hair on her neck.

Della spun, ready to face whomever was following her head on. To her surprise, however, the street behind her was completely deserted. The laughter continued as she whipped her head back and forth, trying to determine which direction the sound was coming from. Nothing was visible in the failing light. Indeed, nothing on the street was moving *at all*. The gentle breeze that had lifted her hair as she walked out of the library had completely died, leaving things still.

Dead.

A choking feeling threatened to rise up from Della's chest as she turned back towards her home, now only a few blocks away. Breaking into a fast, jerky walk, Della tried to hold her chin up and look confident, even as she fought not to succumb to the treacherous, uneven sidewalk and the sensation of wading through invisible, icy water that dragged at her feet. In reality, she was shaking so badly that she felt lightheaded.

I just need to get home. Home, where it's safe. Then, I can eat something, go to sleep, and try to relax so I can forget this whole, horrendous week.

The buildings along this stretch of road were mostly two stories tall, set close together with dark alleys in between, stinking of garbage and cat piss. Old businesses, many of them empty and boarded up for years now. *Looming*, in the dark. The silence around her seemed to press against her skin. Suddenly, she heard the noise she had been straining—and dreading—to hear. The soft scuff of footsteps behind her met her ears. Della gripped the strap of her handbag more tightly and pushed forward, even though she felt that terrible weight again, trying to hold her back.

With her peripheral vision, Della saw two large figures coming up to flank her on either side. Before she even had a chance to consider her options, she heard two more swing in behind her. Almost despite herself, she turned her head enough to look at them.

They were walking alongside her, staring with leering mouths and flat, cold eyes. Della reached into her bag and yanked out the canister of pepper spray nestled there. She ran forward and whirled around, so that she was facing her pursuers.

She held the pepper spray straight out in front of her, but she could see her hand trembling with fear. Gripping the cylinder tighter, Della sucked in a huge breath and yelled at the top of her lungs. "Stay back! *Get away from me!*"

The four men laughed as if she had said something terribly funny. The sound made her skin crawl, but it was not the same laugh that had pierced the night only a few moments previously. This sound was higher-pitched, more human, although the same flat, lifeless anger was audible behind it. Della shuddered, and started to hurry backwards, never taking her eyes off the men in front of her.

They exchanged glances, and one at the back crossed his arms with a shake of his head and a cold grin.

A foul odor hit Della in the face, reminding her of the rotting corpse of a dead raccoon she had come across while walking one day, as a teenager. She gagged and held her breath.

Who *were* these people? God, they smelled *awful*. Were they more crazy homeless people, like the guy at the library earlier?

For a moment, Della's attention was distracted the terrible stench forming an aura around the men. They were surrounding her again, and she reminded herself forcefully that she needed to stop worrying about body odor and focus on not getting killed.

"I'm warning you," she said in a loud voice. Anger was coming to her defense now, but underneath she could hear the hint of fear and vulnerability in her tone. The telltale signs of the cornered prey animal. It was seriously beginning to look like Della was cursed to die at the hands of one fucking nut-job or another, given the events of the last twenty-four hours.

"You're mine now, girlie," the man on her right hissed, as he grabbed her arm and wrenched her towards him.

Della's finger closed over the pepper spray canister and a cloud of *oleoresin capsicum* erupted between them, making her eyes burn and a cough try to choke its way free of her chest.

Her attacker blinked once, as if confused by her action. His eyes grew bright red, but he shook it off and continued forward as if she had merely sprayed water in his face.

Terror gripped Della, and she took two stumbling steps backwards over the uneven bricks beneath her feet, yanking against his grip on her arm.

She had deployed her only defense, and it had been completely useless. She was at the mercy of four men twice her size, and God only knew what they were going to do to her now.

FIVE

Della maintained her grip on the can of pepper spray, hoping that maybe the contents would have more effect on the other men who were now closing in around her.

The attacker on her right had only tightened his grip on her arm after she sprayed him in the face, and Della felt a sharp ache from the bruises she'd gotten the previous night — painful leftovers from her *last* life-or-death experience.

She tried again to pull away, feeling — if it was possible — even *more* afraid of these men than she had been of the shooters who had slaughtered innocent bystanders right in front of her. It was their eyes, she thought. They were just... *wrong.* Completely flat and empty, with no life behind them. The vice-like grip around her bicep was cold and clammy, like a steak left to thaw too long on the counter.

Everything in her screamed that they could not possibly be human. And this time, she wasn't just some random passerby caught up in something larger. Their attention was focused squarely on *her.*

Her attacker dragged her into an alleyway, the others following along behind. All four men only leered at her as she screamed. She felt her vocal chords straining and was sure that she was tearing her throat as she shrieked for help. In her heart, though, she knew she was completely alone. No one was coming to her rescue. Her cries of terror and rage at the unfairness of it all echoed off the walls of the stinking alley, sounding strangely flat.

Silence was her only answer. There was nothing around her but rubbish. No one nearby to hear her cries.

"Pretty little piece of meat. You're about to regret the day you were born," one of the men rasped at her.

Della opened her mouth to scream again, but only a whimper emerged. She could only imagine what was about to happen. She had no cash or expensive jewelry that they could possibly want to steal. That left *her*. They wanted *her*. What could four men with no souls do to one defenseless woman, with no witnesses around to stop them or hold them back?

In desperation, she lifted the pepper spray again, but a large hand effortlessly batted it from her grasp. She heard it clatter against the pavement. Her captor shoved her to the ground. She stumbled on the way down, striking her head against the brick wall behind her. Bright lights went off in front of her eyes like flashbulbs as she lay on her side in a dazed, crumpled heap.

Rough hands turned her over onto her back, and she blinked up at the four men, trying to clear the haze in her head. As if in slow motion, she saw one raise his open palm to strike her across the face.

It was odd. She could feel the distant, stinging pain and taste blood from her split lip, but it was as if her mind could not take in any more information.

Like she had already gone through too much, and her awareness was simply shutting down. She hadn't truly registered being hit. Maybe she was concussed or something—slipping in and out of consciousness.

Her arms and legs were completely limp, and she felt herself being dragged to the middle of the alley, bits of broken glass and gravel cutting into her back where her shirt had pulled up. One of the men was pawing at her exposed stomach, trying to pull down her waistband. Della felt herself retch weakly at the clammy, raw meat feel of his skin against hers.

From out of nowhere, a dark shape slammed into the man who was pinning her down. The impact knocked him away from her, further into the shadowed alley. Della's head was pounding, but she tried to crane around to see what had happened. The sickening sound of bones cracking met her ears, followed by the fleshy *thump* of a limp body falling to the ground.

The three other men were scrambling to their feet around her, balling up their fists as if preparing for a fight. The dark figure rushed at them, taking the feet out from one of Della's assailants with an almost casual sweep. He pounced on the fallen man, tearing at him like an animal. Blood sprayed across the alley.

Della could smell the coppery tang of it, and tried in vain to claw herself into an upright position. She wanted to flee like a frightened rabbit, but her legs were made of rubber and she couldn't even feel her hands or feet after the blow to her head. She tripped and felt the rough brick scrape skin from her forearms as she scrabbled for purchase.

Finally giving up, she curled against the base of the alley wall and clamped her hands over her ears, trying to block out the screams of agony coming from men who were being killed right in front of her. She squeezed her eyes shut, but no amount of sensory deprivation could block out the impression of bodies being torn apart, their discarded limbs hurled across the alley to lie in pools of dark, congealing blood.

Please, I just want to go home. Please, let me go home. Della rocked forward and back, curling into a ball and hiding her face. She could not even crawl away on her hands and knees, so great was her distress.

Barely parting her eyelids, Della peered out from behind her arms like a child peeking at a scary TV show. Her defender stood in a pale chink of illumination from one of the streetlights on the far side of the main road. He was rail thin and gaunt, with a shaved head. There was something exotic about his features, like an ancient stone statue, worn down to harsh angles by the passage of time. Despite his nearly skeletal aspect, something about his high cheek bones and straight nose seemed to recall a face of royalty. His eyes glowed with a fierce inner light as he lunged at the last of the men who had attacked Della.

She felt a thrill of combined terror and satisfaction as she watched her attacker drop all pretence and attempt to run. He turned and sprinted towards the street. Just as he was about to reach the corner, the man with the shaved head reached out with a movement that seemed almost lazy and caught the collar of his shirt. They both tumbled to the ground in a tangle.

With a snarl, her attacker rolled onto his back and attempted to punch the skeletal man in the face. He managed to land two blows that snapped his shaved head first to one side, and then the other, but the heavy impacts didn't appear to faze the newcomer in the least. In fact, he looked a bit bored as he stood and placed his foot in the center of the other man's chest.

The man on the ground bellowed in rage, the sound cut off abruptly when her defender pressed down hard with his foot. A sickening *crack* and several splintering noises threatened to make Della lose the minimal contents of her stomach as he smashed the man's chest, breaking every rib and crushing the organs inside.

With one last twitch, he lay completely still, obviously dead.

Relief poured through Della for a bare instant before it was swallowed again by terror. The gaunt man was turning toward her now, examining Della on the ground in a cold, distant sort of way. The same way a butterfly collector might survey a particularly interesting moth, right before pinning it to a board and sticking it inside a glass case.

She opened her mouth, intending to yell at him to stay back. But apparently she'd used all the air available to her, back when the attack had started. She couldn't even produce a squeak. She mouthed at him in silent terror for a moment before edging herself backwards along the wall, trying to get away from him as he advanced towards her, step by step.

There was no flicker of empathy, friendliness, or concern in his eyes, which were chilly and distant. Not *flat*, like those of the four men that were now scattered in pieces all over the alley, though. Rather, this man looked almost as haunted as Della felt. As if he had lived a million years of misery, and simply wished that everything would end.

As he passed through the illumination filtering in from the street again, Della could see that his skin was scarred and marked by what appeared to be claws. She stared, open-mouthed, as he came closer, wondering what could have happened to him to cause such injuries, when he was obviously so powerful and strong.

"*Please*," Della forced out, the word a hoarse, barely audible whisper. Fear of the man now walking steadily towards her pinned her in place. Perhaps it was her imagination, but it seemed that his movements were almost predatory in nature. He stalked silently forward, never taking his cold, glowing eyes off of her.

Darkness was gathering at the edges of her mind as the events of the past few minutes caught up with her. Fighting to stay conscious, Della pushed herself into more of a sitting position, but doing so only caused her head to spin and spots to erupt in front of her eyes. She felt sick and giddy.

She put her hand up, trying to motion for him to stop, but it seemed to waver in front of her, as if growing alternately close and far away.

Huh, that's odd, she thought numbly.

When the man was within arm's reach of her, the last of Della's strength seemed to evaporate. Blackness washed in around her like floodwater, and she slumped to the ground in a dead faint.

-o-o-o-

Tré's eyes flew open. It was as if someone had shouted in his ear, jerking him out of a fitful sleep. He sat bolt upright in his bed, the sheets and blankets bunching up around his waist.

He didn't know what had caused his abrupt return to consciousness, so he listened intently to the sounds inside the house. He could hear the even breathing of sleep coming from several of the others' rooms as his housemates slumbered peacefully on, untroubled by whatever had awoken him. Tré could also detect the soft sounds of Duchess one floor below in the sitting room, idly turning the pages of a book. He could tell that she wasn't really reading it that closely, since she often flipped back and forth, as if skimming for some bit of information.

He cocked his head while scanning the house more closely, searching for Snag. The last member of their clan appeared to be... *absent.*

Certain that he had simply missed the muted sounds of life from the half-dead vampire, Tré reached out with his mind to touch the life forces present. He could tell that Xander was starting to wake, roused by the brush against his mind. Oksana and Eris slept peacefully, lost in dreams of the past. Duchess raised an eyebrow when she felt Tré poking around. He could feel her flare of mild indignation at the fact that he was probing her thoughts. He searched through the rest of the house and found it empty.

"*Damn*. Where is he?" he muttered, rolling to his feet and fumbling for clothing.

Tré had been concerned for some time now that the oldest, most damaged of their group would eventually lose his reason and disappear into the night without warning. He had done everything he could to keep Snag safe and calm, a goal helped along significantly by Eris' inexplicable bond with the ancient creature.

From the time they moved into the abandoned plantation house, Tré was quite certain that Snag had never left. He never hunted, sustained only by the generous offer of blood that Eris provided him whenever he could be tempted into feeding. His absence struck Tré as very ominous, indeed.

He had always harbored a half-formed idea that Snag might snap someday, and Tré would end up having to protect the other vampires from him—or worse, some random, innocent human bystanders. Such protection would, quite possibly, come at the cost of his own life, since Tré wasn't at all sure he could best the powerful, ancient vampire in a fight.

He hoped that today was not going to be the day he found out—if nothing else, Eris would be devastated. Tré hurried downstairs and into the sitting room, where Duchess was still reading. Her back was to him, but he knew she was aware of his presence.

Sure enough, she spoke as soon as he came around the corner. "Looking for something in particular, oh fearless leader?" she asked in a dark tone.

Tré didn't mince words. "Where's Snag?"

Duchess went still in the act of turning a page. He could tell that she was listening hard, just as he had done moments before.

"He's not here," she murmured, turning a worried expression towards Tré. "How strange."

"That's what I thought," Tré replied.

Her earlier irritation vanished instantly in the face of the unexpected revelation. "You should go wake Eris."

Tré mulled that over for a bare instant before nodding agreement. He jogged back up the stairs and knocked on Eris' door.

A moment later, Eris pulled the door open, looking a little groggy and a lot confused. He was bare-chested, a pair of soft pajama bottoms slung low on his hips. "Tré?" he asked. "What is it?"

"Snag is missing."

"*What?*" Eris asked. Tré saw his gaze turn inward, searching.

"He's not here, or nearby," Tré said. "It looks like he's wandered off."

Eris raked his hand through his hair. "Okay. Right. Just let me put some clothes on."

Tré leaned against the doorframe while Eris disappeared back into the bedroom, a sense of foreboding settling in his stomach as he waited for the other vampire to get ready. He could hear Eris splashing water on his face from the ewer on the dresser, and changing clothes. When he emerged, he looked both alert and determined.

"Come on. Let's go find him," Eris said.

From nowhere, a terrified scream tore through Tré's mind, making him stagger as if from a powerful blow to the head. Eris reached out and steadied him on his feet, gripping his shoulders with strong hands.

"Talk to me. What just happened?" he demanded. "I felt something, but I think it was just the backwash from you."

Tré's heart was pounding out of control, as if he had just received an electric shock.

"Irina."

Tré knew that cry of anguished pain and fear anywhere. It was the same cry that had reverberated through his mind in a dark forest in fifteenth-century Moldavia, the night he had been turned by Bael. Usually, when his thoughts strayed down that dark road, he felt a surge of hatred toward Bael so powerful that he was barely able to control himself. This time, however, he felt nothing other than cold dread that something terrible was happening to his beloved *right now.*

It was the woman from the shooting the previous day. The woman he had followed and stood guard over during the night. It had to be.

She was in trouble, and this time, Tré was damn well going to save her, or die trying.

"'Irina'?" Eris echoed, looking completely bewildered.

"The woman," he breathed. "The one we saved from the shooters. Her life is in danger."

Without another word, Tré drew all of his power into a tight knot in his chest and changed himself into mist, hurtling out of the open window near Eris' bed and flying towards New Orleans.

The woman's cries reverberated in his mind, a beacon as bright as a lighthouse, drawing him to her side. Behind him, he could sense Eris following. He reached out with his mind to touch the other vampire's consciousness.

Where are we going, Tré? Eris thought. *You're following something, but I can only sense it reflected through you.*

It's Irina. The woman. I can hear her screams.

Tré could practically taste Eris' confusion.

But... how?

I've heard those same screams for hundreds of years. I know them better than I know myself. Only now, the veil of death no longer hangs over them.

Eris pulled back from the connection, lapsing into mental silence. Tré could hardly blame him for being taken aback. It was unprecedented that any one of them would have such a strong telepathic connection to a human.

Tré and the others were mentally connected because they had fed from one another many times over the years. If one of them became sick or hurt, the lifeblood of their fellows would strengthen them and speed the healing process. It bound the six of them together in fellowship. An unbreakable circle of blood. They were united as one in the face of Bael, and that unity extended to their thoughts as well as their bodies.

This fact was what made Snag's absence all the more startling. He would have to be very far away — or else purposely shielding — in order for Tré, whose mental capacity was incredibly strong and far reaching, not to be able to sense him. And what reason would he have to shield his thoughts?

A gripping fear and nausea that was not his own dragged Tré's attention back to the here-and-now. He could tell that the woman was injured, and it only made him press forward more quickly, hurtling toward the source of the terror. He followed her presence like a searchlight in the pitch darkness, guiding him to her, compelling him to her side.

A few moments later, Tré felt that beacon flicker and go out. The sensation very nearly sent him crashing back to earth in solid form. Eris swirled next to him, their forms mixing, as if Eris was lifting Tré up and keeping him moving forward.

Tré might have lost his mental grip on the woman, but it did not matter. They were close enough now that he could smell her.

He and Eris materialized at the mouth of an alley, stumbling to a halt as they took in the bloodbath around them. A powerful smell of dead flesh met his nose and he reeled, realizing that there were body parts all around him. Was Irina — ?

"Bael's minions," Eris said succinctly, looking at the corpses scattered in pieces on the ground. "But how —?"

His words trailed off as their eyes fell on the woman, huddled against the alley wall. A lone, skeletal figure loomed over her, reaching down to lift her limp form. Her head lolled, like a broken doll's.

Tré's breath caught. *Snag.*

The ancient vampire lowered his hand towards the woman's mouth, wiping a trail of blood away with apparent curiosity. He licked his thumb, tasting it, and pulled her closer to him.

Unthinking rage flooded Tré's body in an instant, and he stepped forward with a growl.

SIX

"Put. Her. *Down*." Tré demanded in a deadly voice. Snag froze, his mouth halfway to the woman's neck, and glanced back at the two new-comers with an arrested look on his face. He did not release the woman, and Tré's tenuous control snapped.

He sprang forward towards Snag, ready to tear him to pieces for daring to lay a hand on Irina. On his *mate*. The knowledge that Snag was a powerful vampire who could almost certainly best him in a fight fell away, unimportant. The understanding that, for their safety, the six of them needed to band together was as distant as the moon above them.

Tré forgot *everything* in the blind rage that poured through his body, eliminating all other thought and feeling. He snarled as he launched himself forward but was brought back sharply to reality when a strong grip jerked him around by the shoulder, halting his momentum.

The sharp pain as his back hit the alley wall cleared his head, at least partially, and he glared at Eris' face, inches from his own. His companion had grabbed him and slammed him against the wall, pinning him in place. Tré sometimes forgot that, despite his generally mild, bookish demeanor, Eris, too, was a vampire of great age and power. Older, in fact, than Tré. Older than *all* of them, with the exception of Snag.

But if he thought that would be enough to keep Tré from getting to Irina, he was sorely mistaken.

"Get off me!" he hissed at Eris, still furious. Tré shoved against his hold, still angry and determined to get to Snag.

"Tré, get a grip on yourself and *look around!*" Eris demanded. He gestured at the alley with a jerk of his chin, leading Tré's gaze toward the piles of body parts. "*Use your nose*, for fuck's sake!"

Tré finally shook Eris off and pushed away from the wall, brushing dirt from his jacket. With his angry gaze still locked on Snag, who had not moved, he took a deep breath through his nose and tried to separate the overpowering tangle of scents into something useful.

He could smell the woman. She was alive, but unconscious, and her sweet scent seemed to roll over him. Yet a putrid reek was rising as well, coming from the bodies lying all around them.

It was the scent of the undead.

Shock at this revelation pinned Tré to the spot, replaced by the cold realization of what Eris had already sensed, and tried to communicate to him earlier.

It was Bael.

Bael was behind this attack on his mate. Not Snag.

He took several deep breaths, forcing himself to return to a state of calm, and nodded brusquely at Eris, who had kept a hand on Tré's shoulder in case he made another attempt to attack Snag.

Throughout the entire thing, Snag had not moved or spoken. He remained crouched on the ground, supporting the woman's upper body in a loose grip.

Eris, seeing that Tré was in control again, squeezed his shoulder once and dropped his hand back to his side.

Tré moved forward and squatted in front of the pair on the ground. He avoided Snag's eyes, and stared down into the face of the woman he had both loved and destroyed. Her head had rolled to one side, resting against Snag's wiry bicep.

Tré could hear her heart beating. It seemed to be much faster and threadier than he thought it should have been. Dark shadows were smeared under her eyes. She looked ghostly pale under the glare of the distant streetlight.

He stretched out a hand as if to brush her soft hair out of her face. Just before he made contact, he jerked it back, misgivings flooding his mind.

What if she wasn't really Irina? What if he had been deluding himself? Perhaps he should have been worrying less about Snag's sanity, and more about his own. Nervousness bubbled up in his stomach—unusual, for him. He prided himself in being self-assured and confident; neither bold to the point of foolishness, nor timid to the point of paralysis. However, an unfamiliar chill was settling over him as this new fear awoke in his heart.

Tré was terrified that if he touched her, he would not feel that same bright spark of recognition. This woman had turned his entire world upside down and shaken the very foundation underneath him. He was captivated by her. But if it turned out she was not Irina, Tré was quite sure that the sense of grief and betrayal to the memory of his lost soul mate would tear the last, threadbare fibers of his soul apart.

Paradoxically, he was nearly as afraid that he would feel the same sensation he did the last time he touched her skin. He had mourned the loss of his beloved Irina. Had known that it was his fault she was irretrievably dead and gone. The burden of guilt lay heavily on him, only partially assuaged by his furious desire for revenge and his eternal battle against Bael.

That loss... that guilt... had defined him for centuries now. If Irina was *here*, lying in front of him, what would he do?

Tré felt Eris' mind brush against his softly, as if his friend had rested a gentle hand on his shoulder.

He looked back at Eris, who was standing a couple of steps behind him.

"Just trying to figure out what's going on with you, my friend," Eris said, watching him closely. "You've been staring at her for several minutes without moving or speaking, you realize."

Tré let his breath out slowly, and turned back to the woman in Snag's arms. "Just... thinking."

"I'm a huge proponent of thinking," Eris said, scratching the back of his head and looking around. "Unfortunately, we're standing in an alley full of undead body parts, so time is not really our ally at the moment. Did she see you?"

The question was clearly meant for Snag. Tré glanced up at him, still feeling self-conscious over his misjudgment of the ancient creature's motives. The older vampire merely stared back at both of them, his mouth a thin line. After a few moments, he gave a single, curt nod, barely perceptible through the gloom.

Eris swore quietly under his breath in Greek, his bright eyes searching the alley and the street beyond. "Well, I don't think we have much of a choice, in that case."

"What do you mean?" Tré asked, his sluggish mind struggling to keep up with the night's events.

Eris frowned at him. "I doubt a memory wipe will work on her while she's unconscious. I know *I* wouldn't be able to delve into her mind and find the correct memories to pull without risking significant damage to her cognitive abilities. She might wind up being a vegetable, and judging by your earlier reaction, I'm assuming you wouldn't approve."

Tré felt a flicker of annoyance at Eris' insouciant attitude, but did not comment on it. Instead, he nodded and rose to his feet. "We'll take her back to the house, then."

Eris gave him an appraising glance and raised his eyebrows. Tré knew exactly what he was thinking.

Of the six of them, Snag was the only one powerful enough to transform a human into mist with him, and travel great distances with speed. The knowledge stabbed at him as he watched Snag rise, pulling the woman more securely into his arms.

Tré approached the pair, giving Snag a burning look as he stepped up, face to face. For the briefest of moments, Tré thought that Snag was about to speak. His dry lips parted and he drew breath, but then at the last moment he seemed to change his mind. He sighed and brushed Tré's mind with his own, the contact so light that it was barely perceptible. There were no clear thoughts or words, just a sense of assurance and peace.

Tré relaxed his aggressive stance with effort. He knew he needed to trust Snag to get this woman back to the plantation house safely so he could care for her. His raging protectiveness was only getting in the way. Eris clapped a hand on his back, startling him out of his reverie.

"Come on," he said in a low voice, "let's just get out of here before the humans find this mess and start panicking."

Snag shut his eyes and straightened his spine. Tré watched as a mist swirled around him and the unconscious woman in his arms. A cool breeze wafted through the thick miasma of death and fear that had settled over the dark alley, and the mist blew away.

Tré pulled all of his life force inward. His body dissolved, and he sped after Snag and the woman, with Eris close behind. As he flew towards the abandoned house, he sank into the deepest parts of his consciousness, trying to contain the crazed emotions that were cracking his control and resolve.

Get yourself together, he thought, knowing that the next few hours would be nothing short of exhausting. *You can't afford to go to pieces now.*

As they flew, the last faint glow that had been illuminating the western horizon faded as total dark fell around them. The trees rustled as they passed and Tré poured everything into speeding towards the old plantation — his sole focus on the mysterious woman Snag was carrying.

He and Eris landed side-by-side at the front door, where Snag was already waiting for them. Tré immediately turned towards the older vampire. He was grateful for the power that had given the injured woman safe passage out of New Orleans, but now he felt an overwhelming need to have her in his embrace.

Snag relinquished his hold on her tiny, limp frame, transferring her into Tré's arms as Eris pushed the door open. To Tré's relief, he was able to hold her against his chest without their skin touching directly.

Coward.

Without a word or a glance, Snag walked into the manor house and headed towards his cold, barren room at the back. Tré paused, one foot on the top step of the of the porch stairs as he watched the other vampire go.

"Thank you," he murmured. He knew that Snag had heard him, and, indeed, the ancient vampire paused for a bare instant before passing out of sight.

After Eris shut the door behind them, Tré walked quickly up the stairs, cradling the unconscious body in his arms. As he stepped sideways through the doorway into his bedroom, he could hear her heart beating. To his relief, it sounded stronger than it had in the alley. Tré wondered if that meant she had passed from shock and unconsciousness into regular sleep. He placed her gently on his bed, hoping that was the case. Once she was settled, he strode quickly to the door and shut it, desperate for some quiet and privacy.

After listening intently for a moment, he could discern all five vampires in the house, present and accounted for. With a quiet sigh, he returned to the bed, and the enigma lying in it.

Tré stared down at the beautiful woman nestled against his pillows, barely resisting the urge to brush a wisp of honey-colored hair out of her face. It felt like his heart was swelling beyond the confines of his ribcage, threatening to burst free of his body.

What was *happening* to him?

Her beauty was like a song, calling to his soul, whispering to a place in his heart he had thought long dead. A great cloud of energy seemed to flow through his body, bringing warmth to his cold flesh and making his nerves tingle.

With trembling fingers, he reached out and touched the woman's arm.

Just as suddenly as last time, Tré felt a rush of shock—of *knowing*—pulse through his body. It was a bit more muted this time, and he wondered if that was because she was unconscious. Yet, there was no doubt in his mind that this was his soulmate. His beloved Irina.

He didn't know how she had come to be here, or how her soul could be in the possession of the sleeping woman in front of him. It was a complete mystery to him, but at the moment he felt no urgency to uncover the truth. He was blissfully happy just to be in her presence again, even if he dreaded the moment when she would wake up.

Unable to stop himself, Tré licked his fingers and reached out, wiping the dried blood away from her split lip with a gentle movement. He could smell its coppery scent on his hand. It intoxicated him, making his head spin.

How was he supposed to explain this to her? Where could he even begin?

In his mind, Tré rehearsed how the conversation might go. *"Hello, my name is Vladimir Illych Romanov III, but you can call me Tré. I'm a vampire, and you appear to be the reincarnation of my soulmate who has been dead for centuries, ever since I killed her and drained her dry in a frenzy of bloodlust after a demon turned me into an undead monster. Weird, huh? Let's be friends."*

Hysterical amusement tried to rise in his chest, and he pushed it down. She'd be screaming for the men with white coats and butterfly nets before he got the last word out. With a growing sense of doom, he pulled a chair closer to the bed and settled in, waiting for her to awaken.

-o-o-o-

A tangle of voices and the memory of rushing wind in her ears ushered Della back to awareness. She didn't immediately open her eyes, still feeling terribly confused and disoriented.

It felt like she was lying flat on her back, propped against a pile of soft, fluffy pillows and covered with a warm blanket. Rubbing her fingers back and forth with tiny movements, Della could feel soft sheets under her hands. They were much nicer than anything she had ever owned. Suddenly, she wanted nothing more than to nestle deeper under the covers and drop off into peaceful unconsciousness again.

She allowed herself to drift, wondering idly where she was and how she had gotten here. It seemed like there was something she had forgotten, something very important that was buzzing for attention at the edges of her mind. Yet somehow, she couldn't bring herself to be troubled by it. The memories were out of her reach, so instead, she let herself bask in the peaceful feeling that was wrapping her in a warm cocoon, whispering to her of sleep.

Knowing she would regret an extended slumber later, Della reluctantly tried to rouse herself.

With a sigh, she opened her eyes. It felt like it took longer than it should have before she was able to bring everything into focus. She blinked rapidly. When she was finally able to distinguish details, she saw that she was lying in a magnificent four-poster bed, with a gauzy canopy and beautiful deep red hangings pulled back around the posts. With what seemed like a great effort, she pushed herself into a sitting position. Her gaze fell on a man, sitting quietly by her bedside.

He was... holy *shit*. He was the most gorgeous thing she had ever seen. How was it even possible that this work of art was human? Good lord above. His cheekbones alone could probably cut glass, and his *eyes* —

She had to fight to keep her jaw from dropping open as she gawped at him like some kind of mental case. He leaned forward in his chair, regarding her in turn. Relief colored his beautifully sculpted features, but so did worry. She swallowed hard and blinked again, not wanting to look like a ridiculous schoolgirl in addition to her messy hair and crumpled clothes.

She couldn't help it, though — she continued to stare, wide-eyed, at the man.

He met her gaze with pale, intense eyes. The pupils were such a light, piercing gray that they appeared almost silver. Della felt her skin heat up as those eyes raked over her, looking at her like a starving man staring at a feast for the first time in years. She felt an inexplicable sense of familiarity with that hot gaze. A sense of *rightness*, as if she had met him years before, but had somehow forgotten.

Could she have known him when she was a child? He was about the same age she was, at a guess. Or... maybe a bit older than that? Perhaps in his late twenties. There was something timeless about those silver eyes —

The moment stretched, but neither one of them spoke. Burning curiosity pulled Della's attention away from his face, moving lower to take in the muscular frame hidden under finely tailored clothing that suited him, but also gave him something of a dark, mysterious air. She could sense a sort of… *chill*… emanating from him. A coldness, despite his hot gaze. It was a bit eerie, but she immediately shook it off, dismissing it as part of her growing paranoia after the past couple of days.

She sucked in a breath. *The past couple of days.*

Memory dawned, sweeping away any further frivolous thoughts she might have had about the inhumanly handsome man sitting next to her. *Jesus.* The alley. The men. They'd been about to—

Half-remembered images of unimaginable violence rose, murky and unclear. Something had happened, but then she'd lost consciousness, and now it was all one big muddle. She lifted a hand to the back of her head and winced when her fingers brushed a lump the size of an egg that throbbed and ached when she touched it.

The reality of her situation finally penetrated the haze surrounding her wits, and her heart began to race.

"Where am I?" she whispered. She clenched the comforter and blanket with white knuckles, feeling a flicker of growing fear as she searched the bedroom for any indication of where she was or how she got there. Would she never be free of the madness that seemed to be surrounding her life these days?

"You're in an abandoned plantation house, not far from the city limits. You're safe now. We rescued you from your attackers." The man's voice was velvet over steel—deep and dark, with a hint of an accent she didn't recognize. Della felt her heart slow down and her panic ebb, though she could not have said why.

"What happened to my attackers?" she asked cautiously.

The man's eyes lingered on her face for a moment before he spoke. "You don't remember?"

Once again, she concentrated on the memories, trying to sort through the muddle.

Clammy hands grabbing her. The horrible reek from the bodies pressed close around her. Leering smiles and flat, lifeless eyes. Pepper spray. The alley. Then... a shadowy figure. And blood. Blood everywhere.

She gasped and scrabbled back against the headboard, one hand coming up to clutch at her chest. She looked at the man sitting next to her in horror.

"How-? *Who*—?"

He frowned, as if choosing his words carefully. "I heard you screaming. An... acquaintance of mine arrived first, and defended you until I got there, accompanied by another friend of mine. You were injured, so we brought you here to this house so you could recover in safety. We didn't feel it wise to take you to a hospital. You might still have been in danger there."

Della struggled to grasp what he was saying. "Your *acquaintance* defended me?" She stared at him in disbelief. "From what I remember, it was more like he *massacred* four huge men without taking more than a couple of hits himself. *How*? What he did was not humanly possible!"

Before he could answer, there was a soft knock at the door. A moment later, it opened partway and a brown-haired, green-eyed man stuck his head into the room.

"Tré?" asked the newcomer.

So, her incredibly attractive rescuer and/or kidnapper was apparently called *Tré*. Before she could turn that new piece of the puzzle over in her mind, he turned to the newcomer and snarled, "*Get out.*" His full lips curled in anger, revealing pointed fangs.

The man who had just entered looked affronted, and parted his lips to snarl back. With another wave of shock, Della realized that his teeth, too, were long and sharply pointed.

It was too much. Della's mouth worked silently for a moment before she was able to drag in a ragged breath.

"*No!*" The word was a hoarse scream. Panicked, she scrambled backward toward the opposite side the bed, trying to get as far away as possible from the... *creatures* in front of her.

The sudden commotion seemed to startle both men. They turned and looked at her in concern, their growling match apparently forgotten.

"Stay the hell away from me, both of you!" Della shouted, holding out a hand to ward them off. She licked her dry lips, and found the copper taste of blood on them from where she had been struck in the face.

"Sorry," the green-eyed man said with a marked British accent, slinking back out of the room, his hands raised in gesture of peace. "Look, I'm sorry about that, Tré. I'll go."

Tré made a frustrated sound and turned back towards Della, who flung a pillow at him in her terror.

"Oh, *hell*, no!" she yelled, anger coming to her defense now. "I am *done* with this shit! You get back; don't come near me!"

"Irina... *please*," he said, lifting a hand toward her.

Della scrambled further away, very nearly catapulting herself right off the edge of the bed. She kicked at the heavy covers, trying to free her legs. She knew, deep down, that there was no escape from the madness that seemed intent on destroying her, but at this point, she was ready to die trying.

Before she could completely untangle her legs, though, she felt a heavy weight pressing down on her mind. The world seemed to be descending into a thick, gray cloud. Dizziness engulfed her. She clapped a hand to her head, trying in vain to fight the sensation. Her eyelids grew heavy.

"Not again," she slurred, exhaustion dragging at her.

Cool hands gripped her, drawing her back towards the center of the bed, settling her carefully against the stack of pillows. Her eyes fell closed, and she sank into darkness. The last thing she felt—or *thought* she felt, was a fleeting touch of trembling fingers, brushing her hair away from her face and tucking it behind her ear.

"Oh, *Irina*," whispered a deep velvet voice. *"What have I done?"*

SEVEN

When Della next gained awareness, it was not with the same slow transition back into wakefulness. Instead, she jerked awake with a cry.

Panting and sweating, she looked around with wild eyes.

"Do try your best to remain calm, if you wouldn't mind," said a bored female voice from next to the bed. "I find human hysteria dreadfully tedious."

Della's gaze flew to her immediate right, where she found a beautiful woman sitting in the chair next to the bed. Gaping at her, Della took in the woman's striking, porcelain-doll features.

Pale blond hair fell in graceful waves over the woman's elegant shoulders. Her bright blue eyes were accented by high, rounded cheekbones, finely arched eyebrows, and the blood red of her lipstick. Her expression was schooled into a haughty, disdainful look.

It took a moment for her words to register.

"Stay *calm*? *Seriously*?" Della asked, incredulous. She could have just as soon have detached her right leg and eaten it.

The woman shifted her position from where she had her feet propped up on the edge of the bed. She was wearing tight jeans, a black silk blouse, and high heels that matched the color of her lipstick. In a moment of completely inappropriate and shallow frivolity, Della realized that the shoes alone probably cost more than her last paycheck. A bubble of hysterical laughter tried to force its way up her throat, and she choked it back down.

Seeming supremely unconcerned with Della's emotional outburst, the other woman merely examined her perfect fingernails while Della attempted to regain control of her breathing.

"You're completely safe here, you know," she said, still sounding as though she found the whole situation hopelessly tiresome. "You can call me Duchess, by the way. I've been tasked with babysitting you while you slept."

When Della only stared at her, Duchess raised a sculpted eyebrow. "I'll take your generous expression of thanks as a given, then, shall I?"

Resuming her examination of her nails, the woman settled back in her chair.

Della's memories weren't working right. There were several things that she knew must be very important, but she was having trouble untangling the strands into a narrative that made sense.

"The men. The ones in the alley," she began, remembering that part well enough. "What happened to the men that attacked me?"

"One of my housemates found you, and managed to fight them off before they could do anything serious to you. Though you do seem to have hit your head. You've been in and out of consciousness for some time now. It's about three o' clock in the morning, in case you're wondering."

Della looked at the large picture window across the room. The heavy curtains were drawn back, and pale moonlight illuminated the skeletal branches of a tree outside.

"I'm surprised you remember it at all, to be honest," Duchess said, drawing Della's attention back towards her.

Della glanced into the perfect features that, despite their owner's dismissive tone, appeared focused and observant—as if she was feeling Della out for her responses.

Oh, I am so *not playing games with you right now, woman*, Della thought, as more memories surfaced—shocking, but far too clear and intense to have been a dream.

"And the two vampires that were in here earlier?" she asked pointedly. "Are you going to try to tell me I dreamt that?"

The two women stared at each other for several moments. Della was sure that Duchess was sizing her up. Measuring her.

"That depends. Are you going to faint again if I answer honestly?" Duchess asked.

Della felt her temper flare and she sat up in bed. "I've just been attacked and nearly killed twice in two days. Now, as near as I can tell, I've been kidnapped by a group of unemployed Calvin Klein models with extreme dental abnormalities. So, I'm not about to sit here and listen to—"

Without warning, Duchess grinned, showing her own pointed teeth, and set her feet down on the floor with a sharp clack of stiletto heels. She stood in a single, fluid motion and strode towards the door, ignoring Della's startled flinch.

"Tré," Duchess called, as she opened the door. "You might as well stop hovering and get in here. She knows."

The one called Tré stood in the doorway, looking strangely apprehensive as Duchess brushed past him and turned down the hall.

Della's gaze followed her departure before looking back to the man — *vampire?* — in the doorway. Their eyes met and held for a long, drawn out moment. Della felt her mouth growing dry as he shifted his weight, stepping fully into the bedroom and shutting the door behind him.

A million questions swirled around her mind, and she tried to form words with lips made numb by the complicated tangle of fear and fascination swirling around inside her.

"Who are you?" she finally whispered.

"My name is Vladimir Illych Romanov III. Though it is far simpler for you to call me Tré, as everybody else does these days," he said.

Despite the situation, a shiver of wholly inappropriate warmth slithered up Della's spine at the sound of his low voice. She tried valiantly to ignore it.

"What is this place?" she asked, not daring to tear her eyes away from Tré, who was leaning against the wall next to the door, with his hands shoved deep into the pockets of his dark, tailored trousers.

"This is my home. For now, at least. It's an abandoned plantation house, located a few miles south of New Orleans. My... housemates and I are restoring it and living here at the same time."

"And you're a vampire?"

Tré hesitated before replying. He looked unnerved, and licked his lips once.

"Yes," he said eventually.

Della felt a swooping sense of realization, as the obvious answer occurred to her.

"Oh, God. It's finally happened, hasn't it?" she asked, resigned.

Tré frowned. "Excuse me?"

She dragged a hand over her face, scrubbing at the cobwebs. Her answer was matter-of-fact. "I've lost my mind. Gone completely crazy. Certifiably batshit."

To her surprise, Tré smiled, his features relaxing for a moment before he sobered again. He crossed the few steps separating them and sank into the chair that Duchess had just vacated, his movements smooth as a hunting cat's.

"No," he said. "You most definitely haven't lost your mind. No more than the rest of us, at any rate."

Her eyebrows drew together in consternation. "Sure about that, are you?"

"Quite."

"But this is impossible!" Della insisted, her hands falling to lie limply in her lap. "Vampires don't exist! And those men... those *things* that attacked me? They stunk like rotting meat. I pepper sprayed one of them directly in the face, and he just laughed at me. They weren't... *human*." The mere memory raised a shudder of horror.

"No, they weren't human," Tré answered with a shrug. "Not anymore. There's a lot of that going around these days, unfortunately."

"Oh, terrific," Della answered, fighting the urge to roll her eyes. "You realize how all this sounds, surely."

Tré smiled again—a strangely sad expression—and gazed at Della's face as if drinking her in. It unnerved her, as she could find no basis for the look of affection and desire she saw in him. The sum total of their acquaintance consisted of him sitting by her bedside and—what? Perving on her while she slept? Then flashing his fangs at her, at which point she'd basically screamed in his face and fainted like the heroine in a bad Victorian romance novel.

He's not the only one who's been perving, now, is he, said the little voice that often seemed to whisper uncomfortable truths in her ear. Still, as the basis for a relationship went, calling it *flimsy* was an understatement.

"Yes. I realize how it all sounds," he said, replying to her earlier statement. "You must admit, though, as cover stories go, it's not the sort of thing you'd make up, now, is it?"

Almost despite herself, she smiled back at him for an instant before another question rose in her mind, turning her expression thoughtful as she struggled to recall details. "What did you call me earlier? Iris, or something like that?"

Tré's handsome face clouded. "Irina."

"Yes, that was it," Della said, remembering now. "Why did you call me that? My name is Della."

Silence stretched, until she thought perhaps he wouldn't answer at all.

"It's... very complicated," Tré said eventually. His face had grown drawn and distant, as if he was remembering something painful.

"I'm willing to listen," Della said.

"It's quite a long story, I'm afraid, and not a very nice one," Tré replied. "I have a question for you, first."

"Erm... okay?"

Tré leaned forward, stretching out a hand towards hers. He moved slowly, keeping his face calm and smooth, as if to assure her that he meant no harm. Della felt a flicker of fear, quickly subsumed by curiosity. She could not explain it to herself, but she wanted his touch. *Needed* it, as much as he seemed to.

Yes, it was true that he was the most beautiful man she'd ever laid eyes on, but that wasn't it. Not completely. There was something else, hovering in the air between them like the electric charge in the air before a thunderstorm.

In the infinitesimal slice of time before their hands touched, Della felt a thrill of foreboding, as if she was on the verge of remembering something huge and important.

Before she could make sense of the feeling, however, Tré slipped his fingers through hers. As soon as their skin touched, Della felt as if a wire had come alive from her hand straight down into

her soul. She gasped and jumped, but did not release Tré's hand. Instead, she gripped tighter.

"You feel it, then?" Tré asked, staring at her intently.

For a moment, his eyes lit with a fierce sort of
joy — an intensity that took her breath away.

"Yes, I--," she started to say, only to cut herself
off. She shook her head, as if to clear it. "What *is*
that?"

Tré hesitated, as if he did not want to speak his
thought aloud. "I'm not entirely sure. I think it's a
sign that the two of us are... *connected*... in some
way."

From the reluctance in his voice, Della thought
that he wasn't being entirely truthful. Or perhaps
he was withholding something from her. But she
did not press the matter as Tré spoke again.

"I need you to understand, Della, that there are
dark forces gathering around you." He swallowed.
"I don't know why, and I don't know yet how to
stop them. But I am making a vow to you right
now that I will protect you from them, this time."

This time?

Before Della could even open her mouth to
give voice to the many questions that were wheel-
ing and circling in her mind like a flock of birds,
Tré stretched forward and brushed her split lip
with his thumb. All of her thoughts and worries
froze and crashed to the ground at her body's unexpected reaction to the touch.

"You're hurt," he breathed. "Let me help."

Her mouth opened and closed several times
before she whispered, "How?"

He smiled again—with the same sad expression that did not touch the pain in his eyes. Rather than answer in words, he cradled her jaw with his fingertips and used the light touch to guide her toward him, stretching forward to meet her halfway.

She could have pulled back. Flinched away. She probably *should* have pulled back. Maybe she would have, if this were any kind of a sane situation. But, instead, she breathed in, the tiny gasp cut off when smooth, dry lips slid over hers. A sharp throb of pain made her flinch as the movement jostled the injury where her attacker had hit her, but it was all mixed up with a shock of pleasure spreading warmth along her overstretched nerves.

She couldn't help it—she moaned into the kiss, her heart racing with something other than fear for the first time in what felt like *ages*. Without even realizing she was doing it, her free hand came up to grasp the back of Tré's neck, holding him in place. She felt him smile against her mouth for a moment before he obligingly deepened the kiss.

He licked along the seam of her lips and pulled her injured lower lip between his teeth, lapping at the dried blood there. She shivered—*vampire*—and the pain flared for a brief moment before fading away to nothing. Goosebumps erupted on her arms as the nagging ache of swollen, split flesh gave way to the unadulterated pleasure of being kissed, and she practically melted beneath his sure touch.

There was no telling what she would have done—what she would have let *him* do—had they continued. Della was no innocent virgin, but she had never before been kissed like this. She could feel her blood rushing through her body like a drug. She wondered if he could feel it, too.

The thought was enough to bring her back to herself, at least a bit. As if sensing it, Tré pulled away a fraction, resting their foreheads together. He stretched up, brushing a kiss to her temple, and another to the top of her head. The fingers cradling her jaw slid back, urging her to bow her head as his slick, wet lips pressed against the bruise and cut where her head had hit the wall in the alley. Again, the dull pain of the injury faded. Her eyes slipped closed, only to fly open when she felt him retreat.

Tré pulled back, gazing uncertainly into her eyes.

"What did you do?" Della asked, barely recognizing her own voice.

"More than I probably should have," Tré answered, and rose to leave without another word.

Della sat still on the bed, staring after him, still lost in the sensations coursing through her body — too intent on bringing the spinning room back to stillness to feel particularly annoyed by Tré's abrupt departure.

She ran her tongue along her lips, feeling for the coppery split where she'd been injured. She could still taste the faint tang of dried blood, but the swelling was completely gone. The wound was healed, as if it had never been.

Confused and flustered, Della looked around as the quiet click of footsteps returned through the door. She was somewhat disappointed to see that it was Duchess, having hoped in vain that Tré would return to answer her questions.

And, y'know, maybe to kiss her again. That would be good, too.

"Where did Tré go?" Della asked, pushing the blankets completely off.

Duchess shrugged, unconcerned. "Not my day to keep track of our fearless coven leader's whereabouts, I'm afraid."

Della narrowed her eyes at the woman's flippancy. "Coven?"

Duchess stared at her. "That's what we are-- a coven of vampires."

She took a moment to digest that. "Oh. And... Tré is your leader?"

Duchess smirked. "It's a dirty job, but somebody has to do it. And no one else wants to."

"Right," Della said hesitantly. To her embarrassment, her stomach chose that moment to rumble audibly. "Okay. Look, I hate to ask, but... I'm actually starving right now. Do you have any food here? I honestly can't remember the last time I ate or drank anything, and, unlike some people, I'm a mere mortal."

"Ugh. Sounds dreadful. But never mind. Oksana can probably help you out," Duchess said carelessly. "Come on, we'll go find her."

Della rose cautiously from the bed, pleased when her knees didn't wobble. She was stiff, sore, and lightheaded, but at least she could walk. A thought occurred to her.

"Is Oksana a vampire, too?" Della asked as they headed out of the bedroom.

Duchess nodded. "Yes. We're all bloodsuckers, here. Present company excepted."

Della was busy concentrating on finding her footing down each of the creaking steps in the once-grand staircase. Despite her earlier relief at being able to walk unaided, hunger and dehydration were making her legs shake, unsteady beneath her. She felt strangely giddy.

"Don't worry, though," Duchess said, humor lending an unexpected lightness to her tone. "Oksana has a surprisingly eclectic palate for a vampire. We won't force you to adhere to our diet."

"Thank goodness for small mercies," Della managed, feeling like a clumsy moose as she plodded after Duchess, whose graceful steps practically seemed to float across the entry way and down a short hallway. The blonde vampire opened the door to a dimly lit kitchen that appeared largely unused.

Della was finally starting to take in the details of the house, as her initial shock faded. The bedroom had been a strange combination of creepy and luxurious, with expensive, high quality furniture and bedding, but cobwebs clinging to the ceilings and chunks of plaster missing from the walls. The staircase and entryway must have been like something from out of *Gone with the Wind* when they were new, but decades of neglect had left them shabby and in need of refurbishing.

The kitchen was ancient, and didn't look as though it had been updated since it was first built. It was lit, she realized, by candles. Thinking back, she realized that she'd seen no sign of electricity. The lighting had all been candles and oil lamps, along with a fire burning in the fireplace in the bedroom, which had beaten back the February chill.

At the table in the middle of the kitchen, a beautiful young woman, presumably Oksana, sat at the table in a pair of loose shorts and a tank-top. Her mocha-colored skin was smooth and clear. Flawless. The only imperfection on her body was an ugly scar just below her knee, disappearing into the sleeve of a high-tech metal prosthetic where her foot should have been.

As the two women walked through the door, she turned dark brown eyes on them and smiled, flashing dazzlingly white teeth. Della caught a brief glimpse of pointed fangs.

Duchess walked around Oksana, sliding her hand across the other vampire's shoulders in a surprisingly companionable gesture as she went.

"Hello, *ma petite*," she said. "Watch the human for me, would you? And feed her some of that garbage you call food, if you wouldn't mind. I need to go out for an hour or two and grab a bite, myself."

Oksana smiled up at her. "Of course, *ma chérie*. Be safe."

Duchess passed out of the back door as Oksana turned to Della. She frowned upon seeing the way Della was gripping the back of a chair for balance as her dizziness grew worse, and rose from her seat. Her gait was slightly uneven as she set her left foot down with a dull thud on the floor, but otherwise she seemed completely unencumbered by her distinctive injury. Della tried hard not to stare.

"Welcome," she said. "In case Duchess didn't tell you, my name is Oksana."

"Hi," Della said, feeling awkward. "I'm Della."

"Well, Della—it's nice to see you. Again," Oksana said cheerfully.

"A-again?" Della stammered, confused. There *was* something vaguely familiar about the lovely woman standing in front of her, but she couldn't place her. Possibly her low blood sugar and recent head injury weren't helping, but surely she would remember—?

"Yes," Oksana said kindly. "We've met before. Are you hungry? No offense, but you look weak as a kitten right now."

Distracted from her confusion, Della nodded, feeling her stomach clench hard. She hadn't really been up to eating anything the previous day, and she was paying for it now, in spades.

"Food would be... really good right now, thanks," she said.

"Well, lucky for you I'm a junk food addict," Oksana said matter-of-factly. "All the other ghouls around here ever want is human blood. All blood, all the time. I'd go mad."

Della swallowed a wash of queasiness as Oksana bustled around the kitchen. She'd gathered that was what vampires consumed, if all the horror movies were to be believed. Yet, she wasn't really prepared to wrap her mind around the reality of it right now.

Grab a bite, Duchess had said as she left. Della shivered.

After a few moments, Oksana returned from the large closet pantry, her arms full of packages and bags of food. Dumping them unceremoniously on the table, Oksana gestured Della over and said, "Please, eat something. You look dead on your feet."

Della sat down and picked up several bags, examining them. She was startled to see that the food was very ordinary, although the strange assortment suggested that Oksana wasn't used to dining with others. There were bags of Cheetos, Cracker Jacks, and a handful of boxed cookies. As she was perusing the options, Oksana reappeared at her side, handing her a full glass of something red.

"Uhh…" she said, eyeing the crimson liquid with misgivings.

Oksana laughed, a clear, bell-like sound. "Sorry, I wasn't thinking. It's Madeira, from the cellar. A '79, which I'm told was a good year."

"Oh," Della said, surprised. "Thanks."

"Don't mention it. I'd get you a glass of water, but all we have is a hand pump outside right now. I've no idea if the water is safe for humans to drink, so we'd better not risk it. Eris thinks he can teach himself how to run plumbing in here at some point, but… well. We'll see."

"How many of you are there?" Della asked curiously, popping open a bag of Cheetos.

"Six. You've met Duchess and Tré, I take it. The other three are Xander, Eris, and Snag."

"You all have very…unusual names."

Oksana smiled. "It's because we are old; much older than you children walking the Earth right now." She hesitated. "Well… except for Snag. In his case, it's because he won't tell us his real name. Snag's short for *snaggle tooth*. Which will make sense when you get a good look at him."

Despite the smile, Della thought that Oksana sounded sad, and heard her tapping the prosthetic foot rhythmically against the leg of the table.

"But all of you don't like human food?" Della asked, holding up a kernel of popcorn she had just pulled from the Cracker Jack box.

Oksana snickered and pulled the open box towards her, taking out a handful. She leaned back in her chair and tossed some pieces into the air, catching them easily in her mouth. "Nope. Not hardly. That's just me."

"But you *can* eat?"

"Of course!" Oksana said, around another mouthful. "Vampires are much more like humans than the stories would lead you to believe."

"How so?"

"Well, we eat—or we drink, at least. We sleep, just like you do—albeit during the day, rather than at night. We feel, and think, and have the full spectrum of emotions—that sort of thing."

"Do you have reflections?"

Oksana laughed aloud. "Yeah, I'm not really sure where that particular piece of folklore came from, but we joke about it a lot. If we didn't have reflections, do you think that Duchess could put on *that* much makeup every day?"

Della smiled, unable to resist Oksana's infectious good humor. She thought about that for a few moments, trying to dredge up everything she had ever heard about vampires. "There are differences though, right? Aside from the obvious fangs-and-biting-people thing."

A troubled look passed across Oksana's face. "Well—yes, there are many. We can't go out in sunlight. We have what I guess you'd call *special powers*. We do not age or grow, nor can we die a natural death. There are only a few ways we can be killed."

"A stake through the heart, or something like that?"

Oksana raised an eyebrow. "Not planning on doing a spot of vampire hunting, are you?"

Della's eyes went wide as she realized how that must have sounded, and she gave a horrified shake of her head. "No! I didn't mean—"

Oksana only burst into giggles again, though, and clutched Della's arm. Della hid her face in her hand, an answering laugh of relief choking its way free. "Sorry."

"Oh, Della, the look on your face was priceless!" Oksana said. She appeared to be trying to rein herself in and took several deep breaths, wiping tears of mirth from the corners of her eyes.

It was hard not to feel comfortable in Oksana's presence. Something that had been troubling Della spilled out of her mouth without her volition.

"Oksana," Della began, "Tré said that there are dark forces surrounding me, or something like that. Do you know what he meant by that?"

Oksana sobered, looking at her with clear sympathy. "We aren't completely sure," she answered after a moment of silence. "But it does seem like Bael is targeting you, somehow—sending his dark forces after you."

She had never heard the name before, so why did it send a shiver of dread through her?

"Bael?" she asked, not sure she wanted the answer.

A dark look passed across Oksana's face. "Bael is the demon that tore our souls in two, and condemned us to this half-life of vampirism. The six of us have sworn vengeance against him. We have vowed to fight him—for eternity, if necessary—and oppose him at every turn."

Della considered that, as she sat at a candlelit table with a vampire, munching on boxed cookies and sipping hundred-dollar wine.

"This is all so overwhelming. I'm still not completely convinced that I haven't just had a psychotic break or something."

Oksana gave her a sympathetic look and nodded. "If you have, then so have the rest of us. Maybe I should release your memories."

Della frowned and said, "Release my memories? What do you mean?"

Oksana looked oddly sheepish. "Yeah... that's a bit awkward. Sorry. We met a few days ago, but I had to wipe your memories so that we could get away safely."

"Hang on. You can *do* that? You can mess with my mind?" Della demanded, sitting up straighter.

Oksana nodded apologetically, and stretched her hand across the corner of the table to touch Della's knuckles. The beautiful vampire took a deep breath and closed her eyes, turning inward. Della felt a sensation like floodgates opening in her mind. Image after image bubbled up from her memory, leaving her reeling.

The gunmen on Canal Street. Dark figures emerging from swirling mist. Bodies strewn everywhere. Being shielded and protected by a terrifying figure who had just shaken off a bullet through the chest like it was *nothing*. Tré's hand accidentally brushing her skin. An electric shock of familiarity shooting through her.

Della gasped and clutched the table, feeling her heart thundering in her ribs. She felt disoriented, the combination of memory and wine making the world tilt alarmingly for a moment.

"I'm so sorry," Oksana said. "It's an uncomfortable sensation, I know, but I thought you ought to be able to remember the entire story."

"You were there, too! I recognize you now." Della pointed a shaking finger at Oksana.

"Yes. We were there trying to stop the attack. Not that it really helped things much in the long run," Oksana replied in a bitter voice.

"But the guy that freed me was hurt! He was shot in the chest."

"Mm-hmm," Oksana confirmed. "It happens sometimes. That was Xander. Don't worry, though—he's fine now. Or will be shortly, at any rate."

Della gaped at her "How?"

"Well," she said, "that's one of the differences between vampires and humans. We have an amazing ability to heal. Our blood and saliva have healing properties, so Tré just allowed Xander to… um… borrow some of his blood to heal the gunshot wound."

Della felt more than a little nauseous at the idea, but wisely decided not to comment.

Once her stomach had quieted enough to deal with food again, she and Oksana ate in silence for several minutes. Despite everything that had happened in the last two days, Della felt more centered and connected to her surroundings than she had in years. It was almost a disappointment when her thoughts drifted back to mundane matters.

"When can I go home?" she finally asked, her mind turning towards the future. She realized that all of her possessions had been lost when the men had attacked her. "I don't have anything with me. It's all back in that alley, or in a police station somewhere."

A new trickle of disquiet entered Della's mind, despite the aura of serenity that seemed to hover over the old house. She was surrounded by strangers—*vampires*, no less—with no phone, no money, and no way to contact anyone for help. She didn't even know where she was, exactly, or how to get back.

Would anyone even be looking for her? They wouldn't. Not until she failed to show up to work for a couple of days without calling in, anyway.

She was completely on her own.

EIGHT

A door behind Della opened abruptly. She jumped, nearly spilling her glass of wine.

Okay, obviously I don't feel as peaceful as I thought I did.

Tré walked through the door, looking cool and unruffled.

"You can't go home," he said in a flat voice.

Della blinked once, sure that he was joking. "What do you mean I *can't go home*?"

"Exactly what I said. You. Can't. Go. Home," he repeated.

Oksana shuffled some empty wrappers and stood up from the table, as if she suddenly wanted nothing more than to vacate the premises before the fireworks started.

"Of course I'm going home!" Della said, glaring at Tré as fiercely as she could manage while Oksana made a quiet escape.

"It's too dangerous," he said. "You need to understand that Bael is clearly after you, and I can't guarantee that we'll be able to swoop in and save you every time he decides to attack. *Think.* What if we had been two minutes later yesterday?"

"I never asked you to come rescue me," Della snapped, ignoring the twinge of discomfort as she remembered the way she'd been silently praying for someone... *anyone*... to save her.

Yes, it was true she'd been terrified and depressingly useless at defending herself. But the fact that Tré had played white knight for her twice now didn't automatically give him some kind of… *claim* on her. It didn't automatically give him control over her life.

Tré rubbed his eyes wearily and shook his head. "You didn't have to. I can't *not* come to your rescue."

Della's gaze narrowed as she stared at him.

"I can't just sit back and let it happen once I hear you," he continued, his voice growing quiet enough that she had to strain to make out the words.

"Hear me? How could you have heard me?" she asked, bewildered.

Tré looked like he would rather not answer the question and shifted his weight from one foot to the other. "I can hear you in my mind."

Okay, then. As if this day couldn't get any weirder.

Della blinked and opened her mouth, but no words came out.

Tré sighed and said, "When you screamed, I heard it in my thoughts, and I was compelled to fly to your aid."

She snapped her jaw shut and swallowed. "Is that normal for vampires?"

Tré hesitated before answering. "Not… exactly."

"Then how —?"

"Look, Della It's clear that you and I are connected somehow. I don't really understand it yet, but I will. In the meantime, you must stay here so that we can keep you safe."

"Absolutely not!" Della replied, crossing her arms defensively. "In the last couple of days, I've been shot at, punched, threatened with rape and murder, and had my memories wiped. *I want to go home*. I need to try to find my lost phone and I.D., change my clothes, and call into work to let them know what happened. I can't just hole up here like some frightened rabbit—"

"Here, you will be safe," Tré interjected.

She scoffed. "Yeah, not to be rude or anything, but I'm the only human in a house full of vampires. I think *safe* is kind of a relative term at this point, don't you?"

He was still burning holes in her with his eyes. She took a deep breath, and changed tack.

"Also, if I change how I'm living my life, doesn't it mean that this creature—*Bael*—has won? I'm not willing to let that happen, Tré, and you shouldn't be, either. I need to go home. And if you plan on keeping me prisoner here against my will, what does that make you? You'd be as bad as him."

Tré deliberated silently for long moments.

"Fine," he replied eventually. "*Fine*."

Della exhaled in relief, relishing the idea of simply being able to go home and take a *shower*. Strange, what seemed important in the midst of chaos.

Tré wasn't finished, though. "But I'll be going with you to protect you while you do whatever it is you need to do. After which, we'll return here."

Della's expression fell. She narrowed her eyes, studying Tré's determined features. Resentful but resigned to the inevitable, Della sighed in frustration before nodding and getting to her feet.

She just needed to get back to the city. To normal people, and familiar surroundings. Then, she could figure out what to do.

"All right, then. So, how are we going to get there from here?" Della asked, following Tré down the hall. She still had no real memories of arriving at the old house, but she felt confident that a bunch of vampires with super mind-controlling powers weren't exactly going to commute back and forth in a Prius.

"I suppose we'll have to be creative," Tré answered in a clipped tone. "Come with me."

He was clearly still irked at her stubbornness, but he led the way out of the front door and down a short flight of steps leading off the porch. Della glanced over her shoulder. The plantation house had once been a grand building, though it had fallen into disrepair. Nature was slowly pulling it back into the swamp, as it tried to do with all human structures in this part of the world. A proliferation of ivy grew over the walls and half of the roof, wrapping itself around the windowsills as though trying to find a way inside.

She shivered. Inside, the place might have been strangely peaceful, but from out here in the dark of night, it was creepy as hell.

She and Tre followed a dirt footpath that wound down a gentle slope and into a clump of trees. In the moonlight, Della could make out an old, run-down barn with shingles that were falling in through gaps in the roof.

"Er... what are we doing out here, exactly?" she asked.

"Nothing remotely as unsavory as what you're probably contemplating," Tré answered in a dry tone. He ushered her toward the old outbuilding with a light touch to her lower back. She almost missed the rest of his sentence, distracted by the warmth that lit up her insides at the simple touch. He continued, "This is where we keep the Jeep — Xander's current obsession. We don't generally have need of it, for obvious reasons. But if we didn't keep something around for him to tinker with when he gets bored, he'd lose his mind. What's left of it, anyway."

"He... works on cars when he's bored?" Della asked, confused.

Tré shrugged, the movement barely visible in the pale moonlight.

Della laughed; she couldn't help it. These vampires were immortal, had magical powers, and were battling a demon that was apparently intent on destroying the world. Yet one had an unhealthy obsession with junk food, and another was a closet mechanic.

Tré shot her a dark look from under his brows as he hauled the door open on rusted hinges. The screech sounded loud against the quiet backdrop of the bayou at night.

"Why cars?" she asked.

Tré grimaced and shrugged. "I've never asked. All I care about is that it keeps him out of trouble.

Mostly. He has to be doing *something*. Otherwise he'd spend all his spare time hunting drug addicts. As distractions go, this one could be much worse."

"Hunting *drug addicts*?" Della asked, appalled. They entered the old building, which smelled of mildew and engine grease. Something small scrabbled away from them in the darkness, and she jumped.

Tré took in the disturbed look on Della's face, and raised an eyebrow. "No need to look like that. He doesn't kill them. None of us do. We don't have to kill humans to feed. As for Xander, he just happens to appreciate blood that's been, shall we say, *adulterated*. Preferably with extremely strong mind-altering substances."

Della swallowed and nodded, still feeling more than a little queasy at the idea of blood-drinking, whether illegal narcotics were involved or not. Still, it *was* reassuring to learn that the vampires were able to feed without murdering humans. She wondered idly if any of them had fed from her while she was unconscious, and rubbed a nervous hand around her neck.

Tré's glowing silver eyes pinned her in place. "*Please*, Della. I can feel the fear pouring off of you in waves. You're perfectly safe from us, you know. You have my word on that."

"I'm sorry, this is all just so much to take in," Della murmured, and dropped her hand back to her side.

The corners of his mouth turned down. "Then let's get this over with, so we can both relax."

He walked over to a vehicle covered by a brown tarp, and pulled it off. The disturbance sent plumes of dust into the air, and Della sneezed, waving a hand in front of her face. She looked skeptically at the ancient Jeep, wondering if it would even *start*, let alone get them all the way back to New Orleans.

Tré yanked on the passenger side door, which popped open with an ominous creak of metal.

"Ladies first," he said, the words sounding decidedly wry, and gestured for Della to get inside. Despite the hint of self-deprecating humor at the state of their ride, his expression was still set in deep, worried lines.

As she slid into the passenger seat, Della could detect the faint smell of oil and gasoline. She didn't claim to know much about cars, but she thought that this was probably the oldest Jeep she had ever seen. It looked like something straight out of a documentary about World War II.

Tré climbed into the driver's seat and turned the key, which was already in the ignition. After only a brief sputter, the engine roared into life and settled into a steady growl.

"He must be pretty good to keep this thing running," Della commented.

Tré snorted. "Please don't ever tell him that, unless you want to be subjected to a three-hour lecture on engine maintenance."

Despite her misgivings, she felt a smile tugging at her lips.

It didn't last long, though. The journey to New Orleans was not exactly what you'd call a comfortable one. Having no memory of arriving at the manor house, Della was surprised to find just how remote the place really was. The road that they took back towards the city could hardly be called that. It was more of a track, littered with washouts and potholes that caused the Jeep to lurch and jounce, threatening to bang Della's head on the bottom of the hardtop every couple of minutes.

What seemed like a very long time later, Tré pulled out onto a smooth, paved highway, much to Della's relief. Her head was pounding from clenching her jaw, and she had a vice-like grip on the handle above the door. They had not spoken the entire time, not wanting to shout over the bumping of the car and the loud growl of the engine.

"You might suggest that Xander take a look at the suspension next time he's in a mood to tinker," Della said. "You know. Just saying."

"I'll pass it along," Tré replied, shooting her a sidelong glance.

Della looked out of the window and tried to get her bearings. She still didn't know where they were. The Jeep was traveling along a dark road surrounded by lush trees. She could see no sign of the approaching city.

"What side of New Orleans are we on, anyway?" she asked, trying valiantly to get a conversation going.

"Lakeside," Tré answered, not offering more.

Della watched him with interest. During the walk across the grounds of the plantation house, he had seemed cautious and reserved, but not unfriendly. Now, though, he seemed noticeably tense and watchful. His eyes were completely focused as he stared out of the windshield, maintaining a firm grip on the steering wheel. At frequent intervals, his gaze would flicker up to the rearview mirror, as if he was watching for someone behind them. When Della turned to look, she could see no sign of headlights.

Had she said something that made him withdraw? If so, what? They hadn't exactly been touching on deep topics. After a few more failed attempts at drawing him out, Della gave up and sat staring out the passenger window in silence.

Figures, she thought. *He's the hottest damn thing I've ever laid eyes on. Typical that I would be attracted to someone who isn't even human. 'Emotionally unavailable' probably doesn't even begin to cover it. Seems about on par for my life these days.*

Surreptitiously, Della glanced out of the corner of her eye and studied Tré's features. His dark hair, longer at the top, fell in tousled curls on the left side of his forehead. The rest was cleanly cut above his ears. Della could see strong muscles in Tré's neck and guessed that the same fit physique extended beneath the dark clothing that shrouded him in the blackness of the night.

By the time they reached her apartment, Della was ready for a break from Tré's gloomy presence, regardless of whatever wonders of male musculature might be hidden under those expensive, tailored clothes. It was bad enough being attracted to a vampire, but first he'd kissed her senseless and now he seemed aloof to the point of indifference.

Apparently mixed signals weren't exclusively the purview of human men. Who knew?

As they walked towards the front door of her apartment building, Della noticed the pale glow of predawn lightening the eastern horizon. She paused and glanced at Tré, who had followed her to the front stoop with silent footsteps.

He'll never have time to make it back before dawn, she realized.

She pulled at the door with one hand and paused with it partially open, a warm, humid breeze wafting out from the entryway beyond.

"Look," she said quietly, "it's going to be light out soon. You'd better come inside."

She made the offer before taking time to truly wrap her mind around what she was doing. Something niggled in her memory... something about inviting a vampire into your house. Was that one of the real superstitions, she wondered, or one of the stupid ones, like not having a reflection?

As Tré stepped into the pool of light cast by the lamp above the front door, Della was startled to see how exhausted and worn he looked. There was an edge to his eyes, and dark circles made him look drawn and pale under the orange glow.

Tré pinned his gaze upon her with such intensity that, despite his wan appearance, Della felt herself flush under his regard.

Jesus. He looks like he wants to devour me whole, Della thought with a shiver.

What she felt was not *alarm*, though. Not exactly. It was hotter than that. More primal. Because there was also tenderness in that tightly focused gaze. Tré moved closer to her, an expression of sudden, desperate longing behind his pale gray eyes.

Della felt her knees quiver under her weight, and tightened the muscles in her legs to lock them. The last thing she needed was to embarrass herself further in front of him.

"All right," Tré said. "Thank you."

She was momentarily confused, her higher brain functions once again caught up in the la-la land of raging hormones. She stared at him with parted lips, completely bewildered for the space of two heartbeats before something clunked back into place in her head.

Oh. You invited him inside. Duh. Real smooth, there.

Della turned around and pulled the door open further, leading Tré down a dimly lit hallway, counting the three doors to her apartment.

With fumbling fingers, she pulled her keys out of her pocket and unlocked the door. She'd been relieved to find them there, after losing her cell phone and purse in the assault.

When she pushed open the door, she felt a rush of air drift out, carrying the familiar scent of *home*. Finally, she relaxed. Everything in her apartment was still in place, the sweet smell of honey and lemon from a wax warmer standing on her kitchen counter tickling her nostrils.

With a vague gesture inviting Tré further into her apartment, Della dropped her keys on the table by her door and kicked off her shoes. She walked quietly across the living room before stopping by the fishbowl.

"Hey, Jewel," she said to the little creature inside, which swam around to regard her through the glass, its mouth opening and closing. She smiled. "Yeah, count yourself lucky that you're just a goldfish, and don't have to deal with the kind of excitement I've had over the past couple of days."

Jewel continued to make fish faces at her, and — predictably — did not reply. Della sprinkled a bit of food in the top of the bowl and went into the kitchen. She yanked open the refrigerator, suddenly ravenous despite the snacks Oksana had shared with her earlier.

She pulled out leftovers from a simple meal she had prepared a few days previously. After sniffing suspiciously at them, Della shrugged and dumped the rice, vegetables, and sweet sausage onto a plate. It still smelled all right, and frankly, on the list of things that seemed likely to kill her these days, food poisoning ranked pretty low. She grabbed an apple out of her fruit tray and started munching on it.

"Want some food?" Della asked, turning towards Tré with her mouth full.

He appeared more than a little amused, if the odd quirk of his lips was anything to go by, but he merely shook his head and said, "No. I ate a couple of days ago."

Della shrugged acknowledgement and began pulling out utensils and a glass for water.

A few minutes later, she was sitting at her table with a steaming plate of food in front of her.

Without glancing at the silent figure standing motionless in the corner—though she was still viscerally aware of his presence—Della began to eat.

I've got to find a way to get my phone back, she thought. She'd left her laptop sitting on the kitchen table and, between mouthfuls, she pulled it over and started jotting down a list of her missing possessions so she could file a police report. Next, she searched through her emails for a credit card and bank statement so she could freeze her accounts.

Damn. I'm going to need to have all of these account numbers and card numbers changed and reissued. Thank God I at least have a passport, otherwise I'm not sure they'd even let me do it. I'll need to get a new driver's license and buy another cell phone, too.

With her mental list growing, Della felt a crease of worry beginning to form between her eyebrows.

"Jesus. What if someone steals my identity?" she said aloud. She'd only been talking to herself, but Della saw Tré move towards her from where he'd been lounging against her counter. A look of concern clouded his face.

"Sorry," she said quickly, trying to wave it off. "I'm just thinking aloud."

Tré stopped next to her and leaned down until they were at eye level, resting his hands on the table. He captured her gaze and held it with his, effortlessly.

"Della," he said in a low, careful voice. "None of those things matter any more."

"They matter to me," she whispered, even as her body reacted to his nearness.

She could feel herself alternating rapidly between hot and cold, barely able to breathe. She wanted to dismiss his claim that her life had changed irrevocably; that she could never return to her normal day-to-day existence.

Yet, when he focused on her like this, she was also completely captivated by his presence. Not only was he the most amazing thing she had ever laid eyes on—she could also sense the power he held. It was shrouded, yes. Held under strict control. But it was there, and it made her tremble—everything else she'd been thinking about, forgotten in an instant.

In this moment, however, his eyes looked lost, as if he were searching for stable ground amidst a sea of crashing waves. All of the cold distance from earlier had vanished like smoke, replaced by this strange vulnerability. Her hand rose without conscious volition, stretching forward to gently cup his face. As before, the touch of skin on skin was like an electric shock, completing some circuit that flowed between the two of them.

Oh my God, this is so messed up, a voice whispered in the back of her mind. *What are you even thinking, Della?*

Della searched Tré's face, and found unmistakable hunger reflected back at her in his eyes.

She knew, on some level, that she was playing with fire. With elemental forces that she couldn't hope to stand against. He was a *vampire*, for Christ's sake. For all she knew, he had her under some sort of hypnosis or spell. She had already discovered that they could mess with her mind and alter her memories. What if they could take away her free will, as well?

What if what she felt... *wasn't really what she felt?* How would she know?

NINE

"Kiss me again," she commanded, in a fit of what might have been either bravery, or foolishness. "I have to know if what I'm feeling is real."

Tré's eyes darkened, growing hot. Intense. He straightened away from her touch on his cheek, and she thought at first that he was withdrawing from her. He wasn't, though. He circled behind her chair, his movements smooth as a stalking panther's.

He was so close that when he spoke, it sent shivers down her spine, the fine hairs on the back of her neck standing up. "It is real," he said. "It is also very, very dangerous."

She tried her best not to let her voice quaver. It *almost* worked. "A demon who can rip people's souls in half apparently wants me dead, and I live in a city that's trying to tear itself apart. Define *dangerous*."

He gave a low rumble of dark amusement that jolted something low in her belly. Fingers trailed over the line of her shoulder, drawing her heavy mass of curls to the side.

"This, *draga mea*." The unfamiliar words had the feel of an endearment. They tickled at some half-forgotten dream memory in the back of her mind. "*This* is the definition of danger."

His lips closed on the line of muscle his finger-tips had just explored, and she gasped. His hand tangled in her messy mane of hair; he used the grip to draw her head to the side, baring the side of her neck to him as well. He kissed his way up her shoulder and the column of her throat, lighting every nerve along the way.

Her eyes slipped close and her mouth fell open as lust slammed into her with a power she had never known in her life. She wasn't a virgin, by any means. She hadn't been for years, despite always being a little too short and a little too chubby. A little too awkward, a little too flaky, and with a stupid little black mole on her right cheek that she'd always hated, but never had the time or money to get removed.

Even so, she'd had boyfriends. She'd had sex, and it had always been okay. She'd liked it. It was nice.

But she'd never gone weak and lightheaded at the touch of a man's lips to the side of her neck. No one had ever gathered her hair into a tight grip and used it to hold her still while he suckled and nipped at her earlobe. No one had ever pulled the neckline of her stretchy top over her shoulder and then used his teeth to drag her bra strap out of the way.

She had never before in her life felt so hot and needy that she was afraid she would *die* if the kisses stopped.

The place between her legs ached and throbbed against the hard seat of the kitchen chair. She wriggled, searching for relief, only to go limp and pliant again as Tré pulled her head back, baring her throat to him completely. He kissed her temple... her cheek... her closed eyelids. His free hand roamed over her, skimming her sensitive breasts before sliding up her vulnerable neck to cradle her jaw — holding her face cupped between his hands like a chalice.

Della's heart pounded, her breath coming in little pants as he slowly lowered his lips to hers. She tried to strain toward him, but she was completely under his control. He teased her for long moments, kissing the sides of her mouth, brushing his lips to hers for only an instant, backing off between butterfly touches.

She was undone already... dizzy... unraveled... too far gone even to beg for what she needed. *What was he doing to her?*

When he finally took pity on her and sealed their lips together, plundering her with a hunger that matched her own, her sex clenched and clenched as if she might come from nothing more than the touch of his lips on hers, his strong hands holding her helplessly in place as he ravished her mouth.

When he let her up, she gasped for air like a drowning woman, immediately straining upward again, trying to chase him. Again, he prevented her, the hand tangled in her thick hair and the hand cupping her jaw keeping her effortlessly in place as he returned to teasing. The tip of his tongue outlined her swollen lower lip, and dipped inside to tease at her own tongue. Dueling with her. Playing with her. All of her senses honed with laser focus onto that tiny point of slick, teasing contact.

"*Please*," she begged, when his hand slid back down to cup her breast and he returned to kissing his way along her shoulder and the nape of her neck. "Please, please, I need you, I *need* this. Don't stop..."

She should have been humiliated. Appalled. Embarrassed beyond all thought at the idea of begging for sex like a cheap hooker, from a man she barely knew. Her scalp tingled as he rolled her head back again for another brief, fierce kiss.

"I couldn't stop now if I tried, *draga*," he said, the words low and hoarse. "May God have mercy on whatever's left of my soul for it."

She moaned and reached for him blindly, tearing at buttons until she could touch the flawless marble skin underneath. No, not flawless — a complicated pattern of tattoos was visible over his right shoulder as she pushed the tailored black shirt back, disappearing down into the sleeve.

He gave her lip a final nip and released her hair in favor of pulling her top over her head. She knew she was dirty, sweaty, and smelly after the events of the previous night, but it was the bruising over her ribcage and upper arms that made him suck in a breath and draw back.

She reached for him, needy and pathetic, and hating herself just a tiny bit for it. "No, please," she said, "don't pull away. They're... they're not important—"

"They *are* important," he replied, "but I have no intention of pulling away. Come."

He guided her to shaky feet and tucked her under his arm, pressing kisses to her hair as he led her with halting steps down the hallway. It took them longer than it should have to reach the apartment's uninspiring three-quarter bath with its pedestal sink and molded plastic walk-in shower — probably because she kept shoving him against the wall along the way to mouth at his exposed collarbone and run her hands over his hard chest.

"No bathtub?" he asked, looking around the cramped space in confusion for a moment before returning his attention to her. "Ah, well. No matter. Someday I will fill a huge claw-foot tub at the plantation house with steaming water and rose petals for you. And I will lay you down in it and pleasure you until water sloshes out onto the floor under the force of your ecstasy."

The noise she made sounded like it had been punched from her, and she probably would have blushed scarlet if she'd had any blood left above the waist.

"Now, though," he continued, "let me take care of you, beloved. Let me live here inside this beautiful dream with you for a little while longer."

"Anything," she breathed. "Anything, Tré... *please*."

He examined the shower for a moment and turned on the flow of water, letting it warm up while he turned back to her and tenderly removed the rest of her clothing, kissing the newly exposed skin as he went.

"So beautiful," he said, running his large hands over hips that were too fat, a waist that wasn't flat enough, thighs that rubbed together when she walked. "So beautiful, *draga mea*, in any lifetime."

She wasn't. She *knew* she wasn't. But... maybe, here and now, it would be all right to pretend that she was? A lump rose in her throat, and she returned to pulling at his clothing, wanting to see more. "Off," she said. "Get it all *off.*"

He was the beautiful one, and if some inexplicable moment of insanity meant that she got to experience that beauty for a bit, she was damn well going to relish every moment.

He chuckled and helped her shed the rest of his clothing. The tattoo wrapped around his right arm like a sleeve, vaguely tribal. His chest was smooth and hairless, but a line of dark hair trailed down from his navel to the thick patch framing his erect cock.

He was perfect. Mouth-watering. She wanted to devour him. Without conscious thought, she started to go down to her knees in front of him, but he caught her by the shoulders and lifted her back up.

"No, *draga*," he said. "Not this time, at least. I won't last, and there's only one place I want to be right now."

She was already wet between her thighs, but the words made her even wetter. Christ, she could *smell* herself. There was no question that he could, too. Again, the thought should have horrified her — but it only made her hotter.

"In," he said, and guided her into the shower, following her and closing the door behind them, enclosing them in the warm, wet, intimate space.

Warm water flowed down her body as he positioned her under the spray. It soothed her aches and bruises, but did *nothing* to soothe her need. He soaped up a washcloth and washed her, the movements slow and achingly tender. The nubby texture of the terrycloth swiped over her face and neck, her shoulders and arms, her collarbone.

She gasped and clutched at his shoulder for balance as it rubbed over first one tender breast and then the other, her nipples going hard and sensitive under the attention. He soaped her stomach and pulled her forward to rest against him so he could wash her back. His hard length nestled in the crease of her thigh and she rolled her hips, wanting to feel more.

He hissed out a breath and buried his face in her hair for a moment before pushing her back to lean against the shower wall.

"Still so impatient, after all this time," he said, though the words made no sense.

He returned to washing her, running the cloth down first one leg and then the other, lifting her feet one at a time and setting them back down carefully. Finally... *finally*... he threw the washcloth into the corner and slid his bare hand up the inside of her leg.

Della bit her lip and let her head fall back against the cool plastic of the shower stall. When he reached his destination, she was wet and dripping for him in a way that had nothing whatsoever to do with the spray of water playing over them. He *growled*, cupping her and letting his fingertips delve into her heat.

Della panted, balanced once more on the cusp of orgasm, dizzy with need. "Tré, *please…*"

Thankfully for her tattered sanity, he didn't make her wait any longer. Instead, inhumanly strong hands gripped the meat of her thighs and lifted her, still with her back pressed against the wall of the cramped shower stall. She clutched at his shoulders and wrapped her legs around his hips, feeling deliciously open and vulnerable as the tip of his hard cock slid against her folds, seeking her entrance.

She shivered and angled her hips to position him, relishing the groan that was dragged from his lips. The connection between them flared to new heights as she sank down on his length, impaling herself, her mouth open in a soundless *'oh'* of pleasure.

It was like slotting the last piece of a puzzle into place, only to find that the picture revealed was far more beautiful than you ever thought it could be. Warmth spread from her core outward, driving away the icy chill that had settled in her soul over the past few horrible, harrowing days. He flexed his hips, and she nearly sobbed with how perfect it all was.

She buried her face against his shoulder, heat surrounding her from within and without as water from the shower flowed over their bodies.

"So perfect," he murmured into her hair, echoing her thoughts. "*Draga mea…*"

She was helpless to do more than wriggle, held as she was in his sure, inhumanly strong grip. So she wriggled, circling her hips to feel him move inside her. He groaned and used those perfect, long-fingered hands to lift her and let her slide back down his length, over and over, each slow, deep thrust sending her higher and higher until she cried out, clenching hard around him as her ecstasy spilled over like wine poured from a jug.

He held her through all the little fluttering aftershocks, cradled against his muscular form, every last bit of tension flowing from her spent body for the first time in what felt like *years*. The feeling of complete and utter serenity was so divine — so *unexpected* — that a low moan slipped from her lips.

He was still hard inside her, but he merely murmured, "Rest, beloved. I have you." He held her like that for long minutes, pressing kisses to her temple and the wet mass of her hair, before carefully lifting her off of his hard length and helping her steady herself on her feet, still leaning against the wall.

She was beyond speech, beyond anything except gratitude as he turned off the shower and guided her out into the steamy bathroom. He rubbed a towel over her pliant body and led her, naked, to her small bedroom. The bed was still unmade after her frantic late-morning rush after oversleeping her alarm — had it really only been a day ago?

He pulled back the tangle of sheets and blankets, laying her down on her back in the center of the bed, following her to settle in the cradle of her thighs. Still drugged and mindless with pleasure, Della wrapped her legs around him and used the grip to pull him back inside her. He came willingly.

They rocked together for an endless, perfect stretch of time, the sky beyond the curtains growing gradually lighter as night released its grip on the world. Della's thoughts slowly reassembled themselves in the aftermath of the shattering climax she'd experienced, only to come apart again as Tré altered the angle of his hips and brushed against a new place inside her that sent her flying.

She wrapped her arms around him, stroking up and down his back, feeling the play of muscles under her hands. Feeling wild and wanton, she stretched down to splay her fingers over the perfect swell of his buttocks, using the grip to encourage him to go faster. Deeper.

He groaned low and latched onto her shoulder with his lips, his thrusts growing sloppy. She arched as the sensation pushed her over another peak. As she came back to Earth, panting and sweat-damp, it was to the sight of Tré tearing his lips away from her and rearing up, his fangs bared and his eyes glowing silver as he toppled over the edge, shuddering and pulsing into her.

A jolt of real fear punctured Della's haze of pleasure, and she caught her breath. The small noise seemed to penetrate Tré's awareness, and a look of horror creased his features. He disengaged and pulled away clumsily, staggering out of the bed and across the room, putting space between them. Obviously fighting for control.

Della gaped at him for a moment before scrabbling to pull a sheet over herself, as if that would make any difference to what had just happened. And... what *had* just happened?

"Tré?" she asked uncertainly.

"Don't—" he began, only to cut himself off with a shake of the head. His face was haunted. He angled it away from her and closed his glowing eyes. "Just... give me a minute."

She stayed very still and silent, caught between the flood of happy hormones from the *best freaking sex of her life*, and the realization of what he had—apparently—almost done to her.

He took a deep breath and let it out slowly. When he opened his eyes again, they were no longer shining with that eerie silver light.

"I should leave," he said in a hoarse voice.

She glanced at the muted light visible through the curtains with a look of consternation, and then back at him. "Don't be stupid," she said. "It's almost daylight out there."

He only shook his head. "You're not safe with me here."

Della took a moment to consciously relax her body and release her grip on the sheet. "Well, I'm over here, and you're way over there looking like you're about to jump out of your own skin, so..."

He still wasn't looking at her. "I almost—"

"But you didn't," Della said gently, sitting up and letting the sheet fall away from her breasts, unashamed. He hadn't, and right now he looked like he'd rather chew off his own arm than let his fangs get within two feet of her neck.

"Della," he said. "*I'm not safe for you.*"

She frowned. "I think we've had this conversation already. *I'm not safe*, period. A demon is trying to kill me. I thought you were the one who was going to protect me. Wasn't that why you came here in the first place?"

It was a low blow, she knew. And, indeed, she couldn't help the stab of guilt she felt at the expression of agonized uncertainty that flickered over his features before he could hide it.

She made a conscious effort to soften her tone. "Are you all right now? Your eyes aren't glowing any more."

She saw the bob of his Adam's apple as he swallowed. "I'm in control again."

"Then come back to bed." He drew breath to refuse, but she cut him off. "No, let me finish. It was the sex, right? So... no sex. Just come back to bed so we can hold each other. I trust you, Tré."

It was true. Ironically, it was the very fact that he'd freaked out on her and fled the bed when he'd felt himself start to lose control that had sealed her trust. If he hadn't allowed himself to harm her in the throes of passion, he would never allow himself to harm her, no matter what.

She had many things to fear these days, it seemed, but he was not one of them.

Tré appeared to be struggling with himself. Finally, he looked up and met her eyes. "You are foolish to trust me, *draga*. But I am also weak. I could never resist you. And you always knew it."

Again, he was talking as if they'd known each other before, somehow. But he approached the bed with cautious steps and climbed into it when she held the covers aside for him. When he was situated, she shuffled over and curled against his body, resting her head on his shoulder—eager to reclaim the sense of security she'd felt in his embrace. After a moment's hesitation, his arm curled around her shoulders, and she let out a sigh of contentment.

"That's the ticket," she murmured, happiness once more flooding her, making her feel warm and sheltered. "I'll take this over *safe*, any day of the week."

Tré shook his head, disregarding her words. "I lost myself. I must be better than that."

"'Better than that?'" Della craned up so she could look down at him, a wicked expression sliding across her face. "What... you mean you were holding out on me earlier? I find that difficult to credit..."

Tré gave her a despairing look, but eventually he softened—unable, as he had confessed earlier, to resist her. The knowledge made her feel even warmer inside.

"No," he finally murmured, scooting closer to her and pulling her back down so he could kiss her hair. "I would never have the strength to do such a thing, with you naked and wanting me. But I promised myself a long time ago that I would always, always remain in control of my instincts. I will never again be a bloodthirsty beast controlled by hunger and rage."

At first, Della did not know what to say. She reached out and traced her fingers along his shoulder, down finely chiseled muscles and across planes of soft, smooth skin.

"What does that mean?" she finally asked.

Tré went as still as stone, and Della looked up at him, worried. He was regarding her with a closed expression, as if debating something.

Finally, he took a deep breath and said, "Remember what you asked me earlier today? Back at the manor house?"

Della thought back. Everything from the last two days had seemed like such a blur that she struggled to place her finger on one specific conversation.

"Oh," she said, finally. "Yes. I asked you why you called me Irina."

TEN

"Do you still want to know?"

"More than ever," she said, meaning it.

"Are you certain of that?"

Della looked curiously at him. He seemed tortured again, his eyes flashing with old pain, as if from memories that should have been long forgotten.

"Why wouldn't I be?" Della asked.

"It will change what you think about me," Tré told her in a flat, dead voice.

Della scoffed. "I sincerely doubt that."

Tré shrugged as if resigned, pain still buried under his voice as he began, "I was born to a nobleman's family centuries ago, in a small village in what was then Moldavia — in Eastern Europe. At that time, relationships between a young man and a young woman were strictly forbidden outside of a betrothal."

Della listened silently. Tré's gaze wandered past her shoulder and into the middle distance, as if he were seeing things that she could not.

"I respected the laws that my father upheld, until the day I fell in love."

His softened in memory, as if warm sunlight were flooding across his pale skin.

"Her name was Irina and she was the most beautiful woman I had ever seen. She was the daughter of a local *voivode*, an administrative official. We spoke one day at a gathering both our families had been asked to attend. We fell in love that night, talking together in the moonlight beside a window. I will never forget how her hair shone in the pale light. How her eyes seemed to sparkle with life.

"I spoke with my father the next day and our families agreed to our union. That was the happiest day of my life. Not only was I getting a beautiful, perfect woman, but I would also be responsible for allying two powerful families."

Della lifted her eyebrows and gave him a wry smile. "You old romantic," she quipped.

"It wasn't the power that attracted me to her," Tré said, as if wanting to dispel the idea immediately, "but her beauty, her kindness, and her mind. She was perfect in every way."

Silence fell for several moments, and Della made no move to break it. It seemed to her that Tré was struggling with the memories. He shut his eyes and his face twitched as if in pain.

"The region was already on the brink of war. In the evenings you could feel it hanging heavy in the air, like electricity from a gathering storm. It was making everyone else uneasy, but not me. I defied the darkness because I was so happy and at peace."

Tré shook his head as if in disgust. "So young. So naïve. My disregard for the evil around me did not shield me from the coming violence. Instead, it drew the evil right to me."

Della looked at Tré in confusion, completely baffled by what he was saying.

"Bael," Tré responded to her unspoken question. "The demon of the underworld, ever present on this earth. He came for me one night."

"I thought demons were only a fantasy," Della said quietly, "or, you know, some kind of religious metaphor for humanity's dark side."

Tré smiled, but it was a sad expression. "You probably thought vampires weren't real up until today, too."

"That is very true," Della said. "So, this demon came and found you?"

"Yes," Tré breathed. "He could see the power I was gaining in my homeland. He wanted to enslave me, and take it for himself."

"How?" Della asked.

"The same way he created the undead men who attacked you. He would have done the same thing to me, or worse."

"But... *how*?" she said again, needing to understand.

Tré was quiet for a moment, considering her. He looked as if he did not want to say what was in his mind. Finally, he spoke again, the words emerging slowly.

"Bael has a terrible power—to rend the soul from the body. He surrounds his victims in blackness and tears the Light from their soul. Then, he casts it into the very pits of hell, leaving nothing but Darkness behind. They are not dead, but they are not truly alive, either."

"He did that to your soul?" Della asked, her eyes wide. The shape and magnitude of the danger in which she found herself was finally sinking in. She shivered. Tré drew her closer to him. If this was the danger she was facing, she understood now why he had been so on edge when they were traveling.

"Yes," he continued, "every person has both Light and Dark in their souls. Some people have more of one or the other, but typically the Light balances the Dark. What Bael does is to… tear those fragments apart and cast the Light into hell. All you are left with is the darkest parts of yourself, and he is free to exert his will over you."

Tears sprang into Della's eyes, unbidden. She laid her hand on Tré's chest, as if trying to sense his soul hidden within. "But you're not an undead puppet."

At this, Tre looked anguished. "No. I'm not."

He squeezed his eyes shut, as if the pain inside him had taken on a physical manifestation. Della wrapped herself around him, trying to ease his obvious distress.

His words were barely audible. "Bael lured me into the forest on the outskirts of my village, in the depths of night. I couldn't resist him; it was like a beacon that I was compelled to follow. I walked along the familiar paths in a sort of…trance. When I reached the end, Bael cast me into a pit. I was covered in mud and filth, and the blackness of his evil spirit settled over me."

Della ran a comforting hand over Tré's chest, feeling it heave beneath her touch. She wondered if he had ever spoken about this to anyone, or if he had carried the heavy weight of these memories around for centuries, with no outlet.

"The pain was unbearable. I remember screaming for death, begging Bael to just... *end my life* rather than tear my soul into pieces. We are supposed to be whole. What Bael does is a violation against nature."

"What saved you?" Della asked, although something was stirring in her memory. There was something familiar about Tré's words. She could not understand how or why, but she could almost see the place in her mind. It was like watching a video playing in a loop in her head, as Della saw him covered in mud and thrashing on the ground amidst a dark cloud.

"Irina saved me," Tré murmured, turning to look at her. "Her love saved me. I don't know how she knew to come, but she suddenly appeared through the trees, calling for me."

In Della's mind, she could feel herself running, branches scratching her arms, stumbling a little along a dirt path.

"I clawed my way out of the pit," he continued. "The surprise of it stopped Bael from tearing my soul out of me, although it was now in two pieces. It was like a knife had ripped me open while fire was consuming my flesh."

In her mind, Della could see Tré screaming, his hands tearing at his hair as he flailed around on the ground.

"I could feel burning in my throat, like the worst thirst I had ever experienced. All of my senses were heightened. I could hear ants crawling along the bark of the tree nearby. The veins of all the creatures in the forest around me were pulsing with blood, and the sound of it drove me mad with bloodlust. Then, suddenly, Irina was there."

The images in Della's mind were so strong that they blocked out her room and Tré's face. She could see herself falling to her knees, her hands trying to soothe the shuddering body in front of her.

"She smelled like the most delicious feast I had ever attended, and I could feel saliva welling up in my mouth. Instinct commanded me to bite, but I was too weak to move at first."

The smell of mud and stagnant water nearby choked her. An icy breeze bit at her exposed neck. She grasped her beloved's shoulders, trying to shake life back into him. His crazed eyes rolled wildly, burning silver from within.

"Sometimes I wish that I had done it," Tré whispered. Della could see that he was teetering on the edge of emotional control.

"Done what?" she asked, trying to follow his words despite the visions swimming in front of her eyes.

Tré closed his eyes and grimaced. "Killed her while she begged for mercy. That would have been the final death knell for my soul. Bael could have had it, and there would have been nothing left of me."

Horror flooded her. As Tré was speaking, memories were pouring into her—memories she had long forgotten, or never even knew she possessed. "But you didn't?"

A flash of brilliantly white fangs.

"No," Tré continued, shaking his head. He didn't speak for some time, but lay next to Della, breathing deeply, still trying to maintain control. "Bael surrounded us, laughing. He glories in destruction and desolation. He delights in ruining lives and ripping families and loved ones apart. It's almost as though he gains power from it."

Della could hear the horrible cackle echoing in the back of her mind, as if it reverberated across the centuries. Feeling sick, she asked, "Then what happened?"

"The bloodlust and thirst threw me into a feeding frenzy. I was out of my mind, and the longer I laid there in her arms, the stronger I became, as Bael's bitter venom poured through me. I think Irina knew what was happening. I remember hearing her yelling into the night, trying to fight off Bael, but I was already sinking into the Darkness in my mind."

"No! Stop! Leave him alone!"

Della could hear herself shrieking. She closed her eyes and she could see herself turning to face the Darkness, defiant.

"He will destroy you," a voice crooned in her ear. "Your childish insolence will not save you; then your soul will be mine forever."

"No," she replied, in the calmest voice she could muster. "You are a thing of evil, a damned spirit of the underworld. I will not bow to your darkness or violence. You will spare his life."

"Who are you to command me?" The voice answered, simultaneously like ice and fire. "What will you give me in return?"

"I will give my life for his."

The evil spirit seemed to consider this, swirling and taking shape around her. Finally, a face loomed at her through the mist, bodiless as it floated along, ever closer. To her astonishment, she saw that she was speaking with an ancient and wrinkled toad. All around her there was the sound of skittering legs, and she felt as if bugs were crawling up her skin as he moved closer and closer.

"Your love cannot save him. He's been turned and has already forgotten. He will destroy you in your insolence. And yet, you will give me your pathetic life?"

"For his," she said again.

"Then you will suffer for all eternity, knowing that it was your beloved who drained every last drop of your life blood."

Tré's voice seemed to shatter the darkness of Della's mental images.

"Irina bared her throat to me. All I remember is sinking my fangs deep into her jugular and drinking as if my life depended on it. In her last breath, she told me that we would see each other again. That our souls could not be kept apart."

Della couldn't help herself, she recoiled in horror. Tré, intent upon recounting his memories, seemed to hardly notice.

"When I came to, I was... myself again. Bael was gone and Irina was dead at my feet. Before I could even fully take in what I had done, there was a noise in the trees nearby. I could see men crashing about, torches in their hands. I ran. I ran and I wept tears of blood for my lost love. I did not understand at first what had happened to me, that I had been changed into a creature of the night, forever condemned. I have wandered the world all these long years, trying to offer penance for my actions. I have long considered Irina's dying words to me. I thought that she meant in the afterlife, but upon meeting you I realized I was wrong. She meant we would see each other again in the mortal world."

Shock rooted Della to the spot. The full meaning of Tré's words finally hit her. She realized, now, that when Tré looked at her, he wasn't seeing her at all. He was seeing the reincarnated spirit of his lost love.

But how was that possible? Della was *Della*, not some woman from medieval Europe. This *Irina* person was dead, and had been for centuries.

She opened her mouth, but found no words to speak.

And yet, she had these memories. Was it possible that she *had* been reincarnated? Could she truly be Irina, reborn?

"It was not mere chance that we met each other a few days ago," Tré said, looking into Della's eyes intently. "It is my belief that Bael has tracked you here and that he is surrounding you with violence as… a sort of *punishment* for his failure."

"But—" Della stammered. "But that can't be possible! How could I be her? And why would Bael hunt me down? *I haven't done anything!*"

"You represent one of his greatest failures, and his greatest weakness."

"Weakness?" Della demanded, sitting up in bed. Fear and anger were burning in her stomach, making her head spin. "How is an evil spirit with the power to tear apart souls concerned about me being his weakness? That's ludicrous."

Tré shook his head. "We aren't completely sure, I'm sorry to say. It's possible that..."

His voice trailed off. Della turned and looked at him, willing him to continue. She needed to know the worst.

"*What?*" she finally asked, as Tré continued to stare into space. "It's possible that... *what?*"

"There was a prophecy that one of us located, saying that a Council of Thirteen would convene, and that it would mean the destruction of Bael. These thirteen, so the prophecy goes, would be his greatest failures."

Seeing Della's bewildered look, Tré continued, "Vampires are Bael's greatest failures."

Della struggled to picture the vampires she'd met or been told about when she was at the old plantation house. "But... there are only six of you. Are you saying I'm the seventh?"

"I don't know," Tré answered. He looked deeply unnerved as he considered her.

Great, she thought, with more than a touch of hysteria. *I just fell into bed with a powerful supernatural creature who thinks I'm the reincarnation of his lost love, destined to join him in an eternal battle against evil. Suddenly, that psychotic break is looking way more attractive than it did a few hours ago.*

Tré and his friends had saved her life twice now. But it wasn't really *her* they were saving. It was the memory of a dead woman from centuries ago.

She'd fallen into bed with Tré, a powerful, immortal creature. But he hadn't fallen into bed with Della, the insurance agency receptionist who loved jazz and kept a pet goldfish.

No. He'd fallen into bed with Irina, a ghost from the distant past.

-o-o-o-

Tré felt Della go still next to him. He could hear her heart rate speeding up. The expression on her rapidly paling face was growing distant. Cold, almost. He could smell her sudden disquiet, pungent in the small bedroom.

Why the hell had he blurted out those things in the way that he had? Tré mentally cursed himself, already regretting his decision to be completely honest with the woman next to him. Why had he told her about the prophecy? If it wasn't alarming enough to discover that there are vampires in the world, he had to essentially outline centuries' worth of a bitter war that had nearly torn the heavens and earth apart forever.

All he had succeeded in doing was to terrify her before she even had a chance to process everything. He reached out a hand, desperate to soothe away Irina's—

No, not Irina. Irina was still dead, as much as he might delude himself otherwise. This was Della, and he owed it to her to remember that. He tried to soothe away Della's growing horror, palpable around them. To his dismay, she pulled away from him and rolled onto her back.

"It's just so much to take in," she whispered quietly, still looking deeply troubled.

"I know. I apologize for springing all this on you at once, but I feel compelled to be honest with you."

Della smirked at the ceiling. It was not a pleasant expression. She scrubbed a hand over her eyes and said, "Yeah, not that it matters anyway, right? You could simply wipe my mind blank, like before."

Tré sighed. "Della, you have to understand—"

But she interrupted him with a harsh laugh. "Don't worry, Tré, I understand just fine. I was an inconvenience to you at that point. Oksana explained everything. You needed a quick getaway and I had already seen too much to attribute it to shock or trauma."

Tré remained silent. She was completely correct, of course. Yet, Della could have no idea of the mental anguish he had gone through in the moment that he recognized her spirit. Not only had his body responded to her presence, as though he had touched a live wire. His tattered soul had started calling to her, as well, desperate for recognition. He wanted to be known and to know her, learn everything about her again.

He would never grow tired of seeking out the deepest parts of her soul.

Della lay silently next to him, not speaking. Her eyes were closed, but Tré could see the tension in her shoulders. Despite his centuries of experience, he was at a complete loss on how to respond.

"Della, what Oksana did to you is... not a practice that we use often," he said in a low voice.

She snorted derisively.

"It's true," he continued.

"So I guess I was just lucky, then?" Della asked. Her eyes were burning with a fire that Tré recognized. It was the same intense look that Irina would use when he was being particularly pigheaded about something.

Her expression was so endearingly familiar that he almost smiled. *Almost*. But...

"No," he said. "You are, by far, the unluckiest soul I've ever met. Even centuries ago when we fell in love. You managed to find the one man within an entire continent that was being hunted by a spirit of the underworld."

His attempt at levity seemed to go completely unnoticed, as Della didn't even crack a smile.

"So, this *Bael*. He's like the devil or something?" Della asked.

"That's a good question," Tré replied, growing thoughtful. "On the whole, I would say not."

"You keep answering in riddles. What does that even *mean*?"

Tré shook his head. "What you have to understand, Della, is that we have spent years studying Bael. Decades. *Centuries*. Eris, in particular, has been most studious, and has sought a deeper understanding of the spiritual realm present on Earth. He is one of the most renowned—though unknown—scholars of his age, yet even he doesn't fully understand Bael."

"It all sounds like some crazy religion," Della observed. "Or maybe a cult."

"Where do you think your various religions came from?" Tré asked, raising an eyebrow at her. "They are all inspired by the truth, it's just that different humans from different areas during different times have given their gods different names, and put different interpretations on events."

Della looked interested almost in spite of herself. "It's all the same?"

"Yes, of course. There are aspects of it that all the major religions have correct. And, no doubt, aspects that they have wrong."

"So, this *master religion*. Does it start with 'In the Beginning, God created the heavens and the earth…'" Della asked, somewhat sardonically.

Tré snorted a laugh. "I suppose you could say that. Untold aeons ago, the Light and the Dark lived in balance with one another. One never overpowered the other until something happened to offset that balance."

"Something?" Della asked curiously.

"That's one of the things that Eris is unclear about."

"How convenient," Della retorted with an eye roll.

Tré frowned at her, but continued, "When the balance was thrown off, there was a disturbance throughout time and space. The Void, which is where the Light and the Dark had existed mutually, began to coalesce in a ball of energy as the

Light and Dark pulled apart. Then it exploded, forming the universe which is still expanding to this day, propelled outward by the force of the explosion."

Della remained silent, taking everything in.

"Our reality," Tré continued, "is literally driving apart the Light and the Dark."

He had struck a chord in her. He could tell.

She frowned. "But... that's *horrible*. Can the two halves ever be reunited?"

Tré shrugged, thoughtful. "Maybe one day, at the end of time."

Her frown deepened.

"Well, that all sounds dead depressing to me," she said. The idea that her world would end in a fusion of the Light and the Dark seemed to really bother her, but she tried visibly to shake it off. "So, where does Bael come into this picture?"

"The Light and the Dark are made up of a multitude of beings—humans included. Bael was once an archangel, of sorts. He helped bridge the gap between the two forces. He became fascinated by the Dark, though, and soon fell into corruption. When the Void was destroyed, he was hurled from his place of neutrality into the clutches of the Dark. Instead of fighting back, however, he fully surrendered and allowed himself to be transformed into a thing of base evil. Stripped of all the good that had helped balance his soul, he grew in power in the Dark. Like a parasite, I suppose, growing fat on power not his own."

Della wrinkled her nose and looked away, as if disgusted by the mental picture. "Sounds like he deserved what he got."

Tré felt anger possess him at the memory of all that Bael had done to him, and to the others. He clasped his hands together, the knuckles growing white. "Yes, he deserves everything he has gotten... and more."

"Were there others like him?"

"Other archangels, you mean?" he asked.

"Yes."

"Of course. Eris believes that the Biblical figure of the Archangel Michael is based on Israfael, for instance."

"Who?"

"She was the balance to Bael. The other half of the bridge. When the Light and the Dark were ripped apart, she was weakened in the great battle that ensued. Israfael is the Bringer of Light. I believe you are filled with her spirit and her goodness."

Della looked taken aback. "Me? You're kidding, right?"

"Not at all," Tré answered calmly. "How else would you have been able to use your love to bind the fragments of my soul together? Israfael can cast out evil from within and without. She has the power to heal any wound, physical, mental, or spiritual. Or, at least, she had that power once. Now she's a shell of what she was. Our greatest hope is that the Council of Thirteen will, as the prophecy suggests, restore Israfael to full power and cast Bael into the pit of Darkness forever."

Della remained silent for long moments. Tré looked at her, apprehensive—still not at all sure that he should have been completely honest with her. Yet, he could find no real regret in his heart.

She needed to know. Even if she didn't truly understand, she was Irina reborn, and she was cursed to be hunted by Bael until the end of her life.

The thought chilled Tré to the bone. He was sickened by the idea that he would lose her again. Though it was perhaps foolish of him to do so, he vowed to prevent it this time.

Somehow.

He had the ability to control himself now, at least. He had spent centuries developing the discipline not to take human life when he was forced to feed. He no longer fell victim to the terrible blood-lust that possessed his mind. He no longer let his vampiric instincts control him, turning him into a beast.

Not even, he finally acknowledged to himself, when he had been sorely tempted by passion and lust earlier. He had stopped himself before he'd tasted Della's blood, though it had been a close-run thing.

Tré lay completely still, watching Della silently. He knew that he had frightened her badly with talk of the spiritual war in which she had inadvertently become embroiled. He could practically hear the confused thoughts whirling around inside her head.

"I do have bad luck," she murmured after a moment.

"Yes," Tré breathed.

"And now he—Bael—is after me?"

"So it would seem."

"And the only way to bring back this good angel, Israfael, or whatever, is to unite thirteen vampires together? That will somehow give her back her power?"

Tré grimaced. "Much of this is conjecture. But... that is what Eris has been able to gather from the prophecies."

There was another long stretch of silence.

"I need a shower before work," Della said, rolling out of bed. Tré blinked in confusion at her abrupt departure.

ELEVEN

Della walked out of the bedroom without another word. Tré followed her with burning eyes, but did not attempt to stop her from entering the bathroom and shutting the door with a solid click. His heightened senses allowed him to hear her quietly slide the lock closed on the door and knew that she needed privacy more than anything at that moment.

And who wouldn't? It was a lot to take in. Especially all at once.

Outside of the questionable sanctuary of Della's apartment, Tré knew that the sun was rising above the horizon. He could feel the heat on his skin, even through the walls. As long as they were under shelter, the warmth was not unpleasant or too intense.

Yet, despite long centuries of practice, he had never quite adjusted to the inability to step into direct sunlight. When he had been mortal, one of his favorite sensations had been the sun on his face and a cool breeze in his hair. Now, though, he would scorch as if being lit on fire. He could survive direct sunlight, and had—but it was intense agony every time.

Bael was surely aware that the sun was rising, too. As a creature of the dark, his power would wane in the sunlight and wax by the moonlight.

It was clear to Tré that Della intended to return to work. He scowled, knowing that it would be very difficult for him to follow her. And, of course, if she knew, she would try to prevent him regardless. He did not need to read her thoughts to know that she was pulling away, trying to distance herself from the horrors he had laid at her feet.

Tré sighed and stared at the ceiling, imagining he could see Bael floating above Della's apartment, waiting for her to emerge again. Perhaps he was unwilling to attack while Tré was present. Tré had been completely unnerved when Bael had allowed the two of them to pass through New Orleans without harassment earlier, even though the demon could hardly have been unaware of their travel.

Tré listened to the sounds of Della showering, and tried to decide what to do. He could hear the quiet snap of her shampoo bottle and the sound of water dripping off her beautiful hair. He could feel love and desire swelling inside him. His soul was completely convinced that this woman was Irina, who had managed to find her way back to him despite all odds. He would do everything in his power to protect her, even if it meant sacrificing himself.

He would never forgive himself for betraying her centuries ago. He knew, intellectually, that no mortal could withstand the terrible power of being turned into a vampire, and the insane bloodlust that followed. But still, he could not forgive what he had done.

I will make this right, he thought with quiet determination. *Come what may, this time I will not fail her.*

-o-o-o-

An hour later, Della walked the last stretch of road leading to her office. She'd been set for a fight when she emerged from the shower, armed with an argument Tré couldn't refute. Bael was a creature of darkness, he'd said. Just as he was. Tré couldn't emerge into the daylight. And judging by the fact that most of the craziness these days kicked off after dark, neither could Bael.

But she could. And she would—just long enough to check in at work and let her boss know she was okay, but that she needed some time off. Then she would run a couple of errands, like getting a new phone and ID, and come right back.

She rounded the street corner a block from the agency and stared in horror.

It looked as if a bomb had detonated in the center of the street.

She moved forward with slow steps, staring at the blown out buildings surrounded by police tape, many of which had clearly been burned in vicious fires. Her gaze was drawn toward a car, blackened and empty, little more than a metal shell of its former self.

Hurrying now, Della sped up and found that the insurance agency was still, miraculously, standing.

She picked her way along the sidewalk, stepping over broken glass spread all over the concrete.

As she approached the building, she noticed that a maintenance worker was boarding up one of the front windows to the left of the door. She murmured a distracted good morning to him, staring with wide eyes at the destruction. He nodded back solemnly, but did not speak.

When she stepped through the door, she found Rich — her boss — standing in the center of the demolished office, looking around. His arms were hanging limp at his side. His eyes were wide and blank with horror.

Della saw that her desk, which stood several paces straight through the front door, was one of the few that were still standing. All its contents had been strewn on the floor nearby. Filing cabinets were overturned, the manila files full of white paper regurgitated into heaps all over the place. Ugly slash marks marred the top of her desk, and the picture she kept of herself, her parents, and her sister before she'd died was stomped into shreds near her chair, which was on its side.

"Oh, my God… *Rich*. What happened?" Della whispered.

Rich, who appeared to have not heard her enter, looked around at her voice.

"Riot. Last night." They were the only words he appeared able to speak. He covered his eyes with one hand and took several steadying breaths.

A loud exclamation sounded from the doorway, and Della turned to see Alice standing framed against the light. Her expression mirrored the shock and disbelief that seemed to have settled in Della's stomach like a cold, dense ball of lead.

Bael, Della thought savagely, then shook herself. How could she believe that a demon from the underworld had anything to do with this mess? Catastrophes had been happening all over the city for months, there was no reason to suddenly start blaming everything on an evil spirit, just because a vampire had told her a scary story that morning. *Pull yourself together*.

She brushed past Rich and leaned over, placing her hands underneath a small, overturned filing cabinet. Lifting with her legs, Della set it upright with a soft thump that made Rich flinch and come back to himself a bit. His lost expression softened as he watched Della riffling through papers that were hanging out of files and sorting them into stacks.

She looked up at him, where he was watching her without moving.

"*What?*" she asked, more sharply than she intended. "We can't just sit around and let them win. So let's get this office back together and open for business."

Her words were apparently enough to shake Rich out of his reverie. He blinked. "Yes," he said slowly, "you're right, of course. Let's get to work."

Della and Alice set about finding all the scattered documents in the lobby of the office, placing them in piles on Della's desk.

"What happened?" Alice whispered after Rich slunk into his office, looking ill, and closed the door behind him.

"I guess there was a riot down here last night," Della whispered back. They cleared an area on the floor and sat down, sorting through the stacks of creased and trampled papers — organizing them as best they could.

"Do you know what it was about?" Alice asked.

"Who knows," Della murmured back. Suddenly, Della felt a shift in the air around her, almost as if a fluttering wing had rubbed lightly across the back of her neck. With a shiver and a jump, Della looked around, but saw nothing. Distantly, she thought she heard the sound of cold laughter, and a chill ran through her.

"Della?" Alice asked, staring at her friend with concern. "What is it?"

"*Nothing*," she snapped, the word coming out harsh.

Alice frowned. "Are you sure?"

"Yes!" Della said. "I'm... just a little on edge with all these horrible things going on. That's all."

"You and me both, honey," Alice said, and went back to her stack of invoices.

-o-o-o-

Several hours later, Della stood and brushed bits of dirt and lint off of her clothes. She and Alice had worked straight up to lunch and Della, completely famished, decided to walk a few blocks down to a small deli to buy a sandwich.

If the place is still standing, Della thought bitterly. She went to grab her purse, only to realize that it had been lost in the alley the day before. All she had was her apartment key and the pitiful wad of emergency cash she'd pulled out from under her mattress and stuffed in her pocket that morning.

She lifted a hand in a goodbye wave to Alice and Rich, both of whom looked a bit less shell-shocked after the progress they had made cleaning things up over the last few hours. With a final deep breath, Della headed out the door.

After purchasing a cheap turkey sandwich from the thankfully-still-standing deli, Della crossed to the opposite side of the street and started meandering back towards the office by an indirect route. When she was about two blocks away, she noticed a small door to the side of the main entrance of a building. It stood in the shadows, completely sheltered from the sun, set in a dark frame.

A plaque on the front read *Madame Francine's Voodoo Shop* in ancient, scrawling letters. Della rolled her eyes at the blatantly clichéd kitschiness of it — yet another tourist trap where visitors could buy 'authentic New Orleans merchandise' to send home to their families during Mardi Gras.

After a moment of hesitation, however, she felt the strangest compulsion to enter the shop, which suddenly seemed to offer respite from the madness of the outside world. She wondered vaguely what the titular *Madame Francine* might have to say about all the horrible things occurring in her city.

Almost without realizing she was doing it, Della opened the door and stepped inside. The smell of burning incense tickled her nose, threatening to make her sneeze. It was complex and sweet, in sharp opposition to the briny smell that always seemed to hover over this part of New Orleans.

Della's eyes flitted around the profusion of merchandise in the shop, only to fall on one of the oldest women she had ever seen. Madame Francine had coffee-colored skin, soft and deeply wrinkled. Around her head, she wore a beautiful red head-scarf with shockingly white hair peeking out from underneath. Her dark eyes were clouded with cata-racts, but Della had the distinct impression that Madame Francine could see more of the world than most.

Her very presence eased the tension in Della's shoulders. The old woman was like a deep foun-tain, overflowing with spring water.

These realizations flashed through Della's mind so quickly that she did not have time to speak. Madame Francine beckoned her with an im-perious wave. Obediently, Della shuffled forward, a glass case standing between them.

"You are troubled, my dear," Madame Francine said in a grave voice.

With furrowed eyebrows, Della stared back and nodded silently. She had no idea what to say.

"The deepening darkness is swirling around you, taking shape, coming ever closer. Have you sensed it?"

Della thought back to all the horrible things that had happened to her in the last few days. It did feel as if she were hurtling towards a point, like she was balanced on the brink of a terrible battle for her soul.

"I… don't know what to do about it," Della breathed, feeling her eyes well up with tears. "I've tried to run away from it, but I can't. It's following me."

Was it possible that all the people in New Orleans had suffered because Bael was after her? Had all the bloodshed and destruction somehow been her fault?

"Running away is never the answer, child. Follow me," Madame Francine said, and led Della into a back room. The tiny space was crowded with deep-cushioned furniture and smelled even more strongly of incense than the rest of the shop. Madame Francine settled herself in a chair and gestured Della to take the one opposite from her.

Della sat, feeling a deep sense of unease.

"Tell me your story," Madame Francine said in a voice like warm molasses.

Without conscious volition, Della opened her mouth and the story of the last few days came pouring out, the words practically tumbling over each other. She did not know why she trusted this complete stranger, but something about Madame Francine gave Della the feeling that she held answers to at least some of her questions.

Della described the first shooting; the man that had died in front of her. She told Madame Francine about the frightening people with extraordinary powers that had rescued her, but wiped her memories. She spoke about being attacked in the alley and taken to the manor house where she met the coven of vampires. She told Madame Francine everything, and was only able to stem the flow of words when she got to the part about sleeping with Tré that morning.

She poured out the soul-deep fear that she had barely acknowledged to herself—that she had finally lost her mind and imagined all of it from start to finish.

"It's just so farfetched," Della said, winding down. "How can I be expected to believe that vampires and demons and angels and the mortal struggle between good and evil is taking place around me? Everything in our world says that these things are all fairy tales! How? I can't just change my entire thinking in one day!"

Madame Francine sat back and observed Della over her folded hands. They sat in silence for a long time while the old woman regarded Della, deep in thought.

"I am very old, child," she finally said, "and I have learned to see beyond the physical world. I sense a great struggle in you as the Darkness settles over this city. And I can tell you that humans are not the only beings that inhabit this world. The ones you call vampires are merely another facet of the battle between Light and Dark. Another reflection in the mirror of humanity."

"But they're so..." Della's voice trailed away for a moment as she strained to find the right word to describe her interactions with the vampires. "They are so *scary* in a lot of ways. They give off this cold and calculating vibe, but then they put themselves at great risk to rescue humans from danger. Tré—their leader—told me it was their eternal battle. And yet — being around them makes the hair on my neck stand up at the same time."

Her treacherous memories returned to the morning's events — lips trailing over those fine hairs on the back of her neck, drawing every nerve to attention.

Not helpful, damn it.

"Perhaps you are sensing the damage to their souls — or the threat of a predator?" Madame Francine suggested.

She sighed. "Maybe."

"You have the same awareness of the spiritual world as I do, child. With time and observation, you will be able to open your eyes further and see into their realm. I believe that you will become very powerful in your own way, if you can survive this coming Night. But you are in grave danger now, child."

Della shivered at her words.

"What do I do?" she begged. "How can I survive a war that I have no part of? This isn't my battle — I didn't do anything wrong! I just want to live my life the way I choose!"

"Do you think that we have sole control over our destinies?" Madame Francine asked, pointing a knotted finger at Della. "Do you think it is up to you to decide your fate?"

Della did not respond, terrified that the answer might not be what she wanted it to be.

"You do not have the power to choose your life," Madame Francine said. "You were given these experiences, this path to walk. It is your job to do the best you can with the circumstances before you, but you cannot flee from the coming storm. None of us can. Things will come to a head very soon, and you will have to face the truth—or be destroyed."

"So you're saying I should go back to the vampires?" Della asked after a long moment.

"You should take any help that is offered to you. These creatures are halfway between our realm and the spiritual realm. They are uniquely able to guide you and protect you from harm while you are preparing for the fight ahead, Della."

-o-o-o-

It was only later, as she was hurrying back towards her office, that Della realized she had never actually told Madame Francine her name.

She shivered, not sure if she felt more or less afraid than she did before going into Madame Francine's shop. The old woman's words were alarming in more ways than one, but on the other hand, the advice she gave seemed sound.

At least in theory, Della thought. She wondered about the pronouncement that she supposedly had the ability to sense the spiritual realm. Part of her wanted to reject the idea as absolute nonsense, but another part of her had always known that her awareness was greater than that of most of the people around her.

With time and observation, you will be able to open your eyes further and see into their realm, Madame Francine had said. What did that *mean*? How could she become more powerful? She wasn't a vampire; she was just a human.

Della rounded the corner towards her office and immediately felt a chill skitter down her spine, making her shudder. Della glanced behind her and saw nothing. Then, unable to help herself, she scanned the skies above her, looking for... what?

Perhaps it was her imagination, but she thought that the sky had darkened as the midday winter sun passed its zenith.

Pushing the disturbing thought out of her mind, Della reached for the door handle of the office. As soon as her hand touched the cold metal, it was as though she was being wrapped in a suffocating cocoon. Her skin prickled uncomfortably and her breathing grew labored. She distinctly felt the sensation of ants crawling up her legs. She brushed her ankles against each other, trying to dislodge the feeling, and pulled the doors open.

A terrible scene greeted her. Alice was lying sprawled on the floor in a heap, clearly dead. Her body was limp... broken... like a rag doll tossed away by a child.

As Della inched closer, her mouth falling open in horror, she noticed the slowly expanding pool of blood surrounding her friend. A gaping wound was clearly visible in the middle of her back.

Alice had been shot.

The feeling that ants were crawling up her body intensified. Della clawed at her arms, trying to relieve the terrible sensation even as silent tears coursed down her face.

As if in a trance, she made her way deeper into the office. The door to Rich's office was ajar. Her boss lay slumped over his desk. Blood was dripping steadily off the polished wooden surface, and his skull had been blown apart at the back. Brain matter was flung everywhere on the floor and wall behind him.

Reeling, Della stumbled backwards, tripping over a trashcan. She landed hard on her back and scrambled away from the horrific scene as fast as her arms and legs could carry her.

Bile filled her mouth and she gagged once, feeling her stomach trying to propel its contents upward. Laughter rang again in her head and she scrambled unsteadily to her feet, barely breathing.

What do I do? What do I do?

Panic flooded her mind. A small part of her knew that she was supposed to call for help. She was supposed to contact the police and give them a statement, but that very small voice was quickly silenced by a crushing presence descending on her mind.

She was like a crazed thing as she flung herself out the door and landed on her hands and knees on the sidewalk in front of the building. She heaved several times, emptying the contents of her stomach onto the ground in front of her with a sickening splatter. The smell made her gag again. She tried in vain to draw breath, desperate for untainted air.

There was none. There was nothing but death and rotting flesh around her. She could smell it as she scrambled to her feet again, the bitter taste of bile still coating her mouth. Della staggered down the road in a stumbling run, falling over curbs and crashing into parked cars. The world around her was spinning and swaying before her eyes. She tripped and fell hard against a concrete retaining wall at the end of the street.

Dimly, Della was aware of pedestrians staring at her open-mouthed, hurrying to get out of her way. She must have looked like a madwoman, stumbling down the street, her eyes flitting wildly from side to side, fresh vomit staining the front of her shirt.

A woman cried out in alarm and pulled her small child closer, shielding him from Della as she stumbled past. A man cursed at her and darted off the sidewalk to avoid her. Others crossed to the far side of the street as they saw her coming.

For well over an hour, Della alternated running, walking, and crawling her way towards her apartment, which was more than three miles from her office. At long last, she collapsed in front of the building, thrashing around on the ground, convinced that spiders were crawling in her hair and clothes.

She dry heaved, having lost the last of her stomach contents long ago. Evil laughter surrounded her, further confusing her. She was almost home, but she could no more have risen to her feet and walked the final few steps to her door than she could have sprouted wings and flown.

The din of cold, hysterical laughter was deafening, and she clasped her hands over her ears. Curling up into the fetal position, she closed her eyes and prayed for help, or for a quick death.

I can't fight anymore, I can't! Oh God, please! Help me. Please, somebody help me. Tré!

TRÉ!

TWELVE

Moments later, Della felt gentle hands touching her face. She cracked open an eyelid, even as she continued to claw at the skin on her arms.

Relief flooded her as she saw Tré standing over her, blocking the bright sunlight from her eyes. He was wearing a black t-shirt and effortlessly slid his arms under Della, pulling her against him.

As she was lifted up, Della struggled wildly, feeling like she was about to fly off the earth and into space because of the tilting motion in her mind.

"Della, be still," Tré said urgently.

His voice was tight, and Della knew, in the corner of her mind that still maintained a tenuous grip on sanity, that something was wrong. There was some reason why he shouldn't have been able to come for her... what was it?

Carrying her as if she weighed nothing, Tré whisked Della up to her apartment building. As soon as they were in the cool shade of the entry-way, Tré breathed a sigh of relief, hurrying along the hallway to her unit.

Still cradling Della against his chest, he used her key to open the door and slip inside. Della could sense the familiar surroundings, but the evil presence was still curling through her thoughts, wrapping around them like a serpent and *squeez-*

ing. It was like a toxic substance creeping in her soul, and it made her feel like black oil was pumping through her veins and filling her mouth. She retched again and sobbed into Tré's shirt.

He lowered her onto her bed and brushed tangled hair out of her face. Madame Francine's words came back to her again, as if they were crackling through a badly tuned radio. She remembered that the shop proprietress had said she could gain power against the Darkness.

Pressing her fingers to her head, Della concentrated as she had never done before, trying to imagine the toxic oil being siphoned out of her body. She mentally pushed at it and found that, unlike real oil, it had density that she could grasp, although it cost her a huge amount of energy to do so.

"Yes, that's it," Tré encouraged, covering her hands with his own. "Fight back against him, Della. *Push him out.*"

Della shoved and kicked at the blackness, feeling it recede with each surge of effort. Sweat broke out across her forehead and under her clothes, but Della did not give up. She imagined herself as a powerful angel, able to banish Bael with a simple thought.

Suddenly, a brilliant light shone in her mind, the most intense radiance she had ever experienced. With a jolt of recognition, Della sensed that the expansive spirit was Tré, filling her mind with his, and flooding her with his love. She realized in a daze that she was immersed in the Light side of his spirit, being shielded and protected from the evil that had surrounded and violated her. Mentally, Della reached out to Tré, feeling his warmth like balm creeping through her heart, expanding outward through her body.

She could sense him within her. His emotions were open to her—his thoughts and feelings. She could feel his heart swelling with a depth of love for her that she could never have imagined. There was recognition and honor of Irina's soul within that love, it was true, but there was also delight and enjoyment in *her*. He sensed the connection she shared with his long lost love, but it was *Della* that he saw when he looked at her.

It was *Della* he had acted to save.

This realization was such a profound shock that Della actually jerked in surprise. Her heart swelled, threatening to break free of her ribcage as a surge of love for him in return flooded her spirit. He had come for her. He had fought... *for her*.

With that, Bael's grip on her mind loosened, slipped, and was gone. The emptiness felt strange after sharing her mind with a demon for more than an hour.

Exhausted, Della slumped back onto the bed, turning her face so that it was hidden against Tré's neck. The last vestiges of Bael's dark possession had not yet worn off, and Della still felt as though ants were crawling on her. She flinched, wanting to scratch at them, but she was too weak to do much more than moan.

"Shhh, it will fade, *draga mea*. Just try to rest. You've been through a terrible ordeal today.

Breathe deeply and slowly," Tré murmured, kissing her forehead.

Della took a slow, deep breath and nearly gagged as the smell of bile assaulted her senses. "Oh, my God." The words were a bare whisper. "I smell horrible!"

Tré chuckled and held her tighter. "Well, to be fair, I've smelled worse. But, yeah, you definitely stink."

Della made a weak sound, midway between a laugh and a sob, as reaction set in and made her tremble. She let Tré release his grip on her so he could carefully pull the soiled shirt over her head. He threw it onto the floor in the far corner of the room. She breathed more easily, then, relieved to be free of the noxious smell from her clothing.

Tré settled her more securely against him, and she sighed with contentment as he wrapped his arms protectively around her. As he started to rub her back, though, Della's vision cleared enough that she could see angry burns blistering his skin.

"Oh, my God, Tré—is that from the sun?" she exclaimed, trying to sit up.

"It's of no importance," Tré assured her, pulling her back down to lie against him.

She was too weak to resist, but she scowled. "The hell it isn't. You're hurt!"

Tré shrugged with evident indifference and started rubbing gentle circles on her exposed skin. Della, exhausted from her struggle with Bael, felt her eyelids droop despite herself. She leaned more heavily into him, even as she struggled to stay awake and maintain focus.

"I would do it again," Tré said quietly. "A thousand times, if necessary. I made a grave error of judgment today, Della, and I almost lost you."

Della shivered again, despite the warmth of his embrace. "What happened to me?"

Tré did not answer for a moment, prompting Della to glance up at him. His expression was grave. His normally pale face, even paler.

"I thought you would be safe enough, in the daylight. But Bael is growing in strength. You were possessed by him. I'm quite sure he would have destroyed you, given a bit more time."

"He wouldn't have just turned me into a vampire?" Della asked, swallowing hard.

"I... don't believe so. No."

"Why not?"

"Revenge," Tré answered simply.

Della fell quiet, contemplating his words. It all made a twisted sort of sense now — the reason she was continually being tortured for *nothing*. Bael was getting back at her for sins she'd committed against him in another lifetime. For Irina's interruption of the atrocity he'd been attempting to perform on Tré's soul. Her argument with Madame Francine rose in her mind.

"This isn't my war," she said, hearing a plaintive note creep into her voice.

But that was a lie, and she knew it now. It *was* her war. She'd been a player in the battle against Bael for centuries without ever knowing it. Was it possible she'd lived *other* lives since then? Had her soul passed by Tré's before, like two ships in the night, each never knowing that the other was near?

Madame Francine was right. She could not choose which path to walk, but she could choose how she reacted to the demon bent on her destruction. Della pulled Tré closer and trembled against him as her thoughts turned towards Alice and Rich.

"The people at my office..." Della started to say, her voice quivering.

Tré placed a comforting hand on her cheek. "There's nothing you can do for them now, Della. It's over."

"You know what happened?"

"I saw it in your mind when I joined with you to fight Bael."

"Is it my fault?"

"Did you pull the trigger of that gun?" Tré asked.

"Of course not."

"Then how could it be your fault?"

Della looked at him with wide eyes, feeling tears burn behind them. "Bael is attacking this city to get to me. Everyone is suffering because of my presence."

Tré tightened his arms around her. "I won't argue with you that he has his focus here because of you, but Bael's plans are far grander and more ambitious than mere revenge against one soul."

Della made a skeptical noise, but Tré continued, inexorable. "He wants to turn the Earth into his realm, made into darkness in his likeness. It doesn't matter to him where he attacks, just as long as he is consuming souls and creating an army of the undead. If it wasn't here, it would be somewhere else."

"But, it's my fault that Rich—" She swallowed hard, unable to finish the statement.

"No, it's not." Tré insisted. "Della, listen to me. Your employer was not possessed by Bael when he took his life. That's not how Bael works. He would rather have turned the man into a pawn to use against you. I believe that Rich already struggled with the darkness inside himself, and saw no way back to the Light."

Della tried to digest the words. It did not absolve her from her grief and guilt, but it made sense that if Bael wanted to inflict the maximum damage against her, he would have been more likely to turn Rich into one of his puppets. He would have been perfectly positioned, close to Della.

"I never knew," she murmured quietly. "I never knew he was struggling so much."

Tré shrugged again. "Those in most need of help are often least inclined to seek it."

Della stared at the angry skin on Tré's arm, tears trickling down her cheek, lost in thought.

Everyone who gets close to me is in danger, from within and without. When is this going to end? How can we possibly survive this? Is everyone around me going to die? Am I… going to die?

-o-o-o-

Tré was suppressing the pain on his arms, head, and neck with some considerable difficulty. The sun had eaten at his exposed skin from the moment that he had stepped out of the building and run to scoop Della into his arms, until he had whisked her back inside. The depth of his fear for her when he heard her mental cry and realized what was happening meant that he did not feel the scalding pain until afterward.

Now, however, he felt it. Felt it to his very bones. He clenched his jaw in an effort not to show it, feeling the sharp points of his fangs scrape at the inside of his cheeks. Della was still staring at the burns with wide, liquid eyes. The intensity of her gaze made the hair on his scalp prickle.

"You must be in agony. What do we need to do about this?" Della asked.

Tré could tell that she was using worry for him as a distraction from her own pain. Which was fair, he supposed, since he'd been using worry for her as a distraction from his. He mentally shook himself and attempted to concentrate.

"It will heal," he said, which was true as far as it went.

"Do you need medicine?"

"No," he admitted after a pause. "I... need Xander, or one of the others."

Della's finely drawn brows drew together. "Another vampire, you mean?"

Tré nodded, feeling his skin pull and seep fluid onto his shirt. "Yes, I'll be able to heal much more quickly with help."

As much as Tré might want to keep Della to himself, curled together in her bed with the illusion that the outside world was safely held at bay, doing so would be a poor tactical decision on several fronts.

He exhaled quietly and shut his eyes. It was harder to concentrate on sending a mental call when his pain was so acute. After a moment, he felt Xander's mind brush against his, and tasted the concern permeating the response.

He pushed a small part of his pain towards the other vampire to communicate that he was injured and needed help. Immediately he felt Xander spring into action and then disappear from their mental connection.

"Xander is coming," he said, noting that Della still looked worried.

Worry gave way to confusion. "How — ?"

"Our minds are connected," he explained. "I just called to him and conveyed that I was injured."

Della looked intrigued. "Okay. That's interesting. Like telepathy?"

Despite his pain, Tré felt the corner of his lips rise in a smile at her obvious curiosity.

"Not quite like what you might read in science fiction, or see in the movies," he said. "We didn't... think words at each other. It's more along the lines of sharing impressions, I suppose. We can communicate in more detail if it becomes necessary, but it requires considerable concentration and energy expenditure. Xander and I are very close, so I'm confident he understood the gist."

"Handy," Della said, lifting a hand to scratch at her scalp through her tangled hair. "So, what is he going to do?"

"Come here, I would assume."

Della looked alarmed and clambered out of bed. He was relieved to see that, although she was a bit shaky still, she seemed to be recovering from the attack.

She rummaged around in the chest of drawers sitting across from the bed. "*Shit*. I need to brush my teeth and clean up. Change clothes—"

"You've got time," Tré assured her, glancing out of the window. Dusk was starting to fall around them, but he knew that Xander would not risk movement during daylight hours while he was still recovering from his own injury. He would have been able to tell through the link that Tré was not in immediate danger.

Della gave him another searching look. "You're sure you'll be okay? There's nothing I can do to help until he gets here?"

Tré's face softened. "I told you, *draga*," he said, the endearment rolling from his tongue in Romanian and leaving a sweet taste in its wake. "It's of no real importance, and it will heal."

Della bit her lower lip uncertainly and nodded. "If you're sure. I'll just be down the hall, though, if you need anything. All right?"

With a final searching look, she turned and disappeared into the bathroom, leaving Tré alone. He heard the shower turn on a moment later, and let out a pained breath of amusement at Della's protectiveness. She had no real conception of how much more fragile she was than he. *She* was the one in need of protection, here.

Tré bit down on his lip to control the pain as he examined the skin on his arms. It was worse than he had thought at first. Without blood from one of the others, it would take a very long time to heal, and would probably scar.

Still, it truly was no matter. Tré leaned back onto Della's pillows and stared at the ceiling. He felt reasonably confident that the attack today had finally convinced Della of the danger she was in. Would it be enough to persuade her to return to the plantation house, though?

Bael would surely think twice about trying to attack her there, with all the vampires united under one roof. They had already proved their ability to stand against his undead forces in the various skirmishes they'd engaged in over recent months.

Though they numbered six and not thirteen, it was clear that Bael was already wary of them. If Della were under their direct protection, would he give up his desire for revenge against the soul she carried?

Deep down, though, the pessimistic part of Tré knew that there would be a final battle over Della's soul—and very soon. But he still hoped to whisk her away to the closest thing he could offer to safe haven before that time came.

His worries must have chased him down into an uneasy doze, because before he knew it, Della was standing over him. She was wrapped in a towel and smelled sweetly of shampoo, along with an intoxicating scent rising from her skin that was all her own.

Despite the pain of his burned flesh, Tré smiled up at the perfect vision hovering above him, and she smiled back.

"How are you feeling?" she asked softly.

"Better, with you standing there looking down at me," Tré replied. "How are you?"

Della paused, as if assessing herself. "Honestly? Shaken. I'm also hungry and a little lightheaded. I really need to get some food in me at some point."

"That's easily remedied," Tré said, glancing at the falling darkness outside. "Xander will be here shortly, I'd imagine."

Della nodded and began to dress. She slipped into a comfortable pair of jeans and a t-shirt that clung to her waist, accentuating her delectable curves. Tré's eyes feasted on her, feeling desire building up inside him again in spite of everything.

At that moment, he heard a soft whoosh in the hallway outside of her apartment, heralding Xander's arrival. He reached out with is mind and found that Eris was with him.

"They're here," he said to Della, who nodded and went to the front door. He remained where he was on the bed, finding it much easier to lie still than try to get up in the state he was in.

He heard her say, "Come in, please — he's in the bedroom." An indistinct murmur of voices followed, and three sets of footsteps approached.

A moment later, Xander and Eris entered the bedroom behind Della, both of them towering over her petite frame. She straightened her spine and turned to look up at them, but Tré could tell she was still intimidated by their presence.

Xander raised an eyebrow at her. "Apparently your mother never warned you about inviting vampires across the threshold?" he asked. Only someone who knew him well would be able to see the hint of amusement playing around his green eyes.

Della swallowed, but glared up at him gamely. "Bit late for that now, or so it would appear," she said.

The amused crinkle around Xander's eyes deepened, and he expanded his gaze to include Tré, sprawled in her bed. "Evidently," he agreed.

"*Xander*. Enough," Tré said, summoning a severe expression.

Perhaps it fell short of the mark, because Eris stopped his curious perusal of Della's apartment and shot him a deeply unimpressed look.

"If we're going to list off tales from vampire lore, perhaps we should start with the part about *not going out in the sun*," he said, raising a dark eyebrow.

Della shifted her feet, looking uncomfortable.

Tré scowled. "Or, for preference, we could fast forward to the part where someone gives me some damned blood before any more of my skin sloughs off."

"Your wish is our command, oh fearless leader," Xander answered with a brief, mocking half-bow. His eyes cut to Eris and back again. "That's actually why I dragged this one along. I'm still a bit weak, and he's already used to acting like a milk cow."

"Yes, *thank you*, Xander," Eris said, clearly past done with the banter. He turned his attention to unbuttoning the cuff of his white shirt and rolling the sleeve up past his elbow, baring the olive-tinted skin of a well-muscled forearm.

"Della," Tré said, "as you've probably gathered, these are Xander and Eris, two more of my fellow vampires. Try not to hold them against vampire-kind in general."

"Uh... nice to meet you both," Della said, seeming a bit taken aback by the interaction.

"Likewise," Eris said, giving her a brief once-over before crossing to Tré. Eris had been tight-lipped after the incident with Snag in the alley, and Tré wondered what their resident scholar made of her.

"It's a pleasure to meet you when I'm not bleeding out from a gaping chest wound," Xander said pleasantly. His expression morphed into a frown. "Or do you not remember that part?"

Della caught her lower lip between her teeth for a moment before letting it slide free. Tré found himself unable to look away from her full, perfect mouth, his pain momentarily forgotten.

"No," she said, looking up at Xander. "I remember it now. Thank you. You... saved my life."

Xander's return smile was charming, for all that it did not touch his eyes. "Oh, it was nothing," he said. "All part of the service, I assure you."

Eris had foregone the extended introductions in favor of looking over Tré's injuries with a practiced eye.

"You've really done a number on yourself," he said with professional interest. "This is going to take some serious transfer of life force to heal properly."

"But, hey—look on the bright side. At least you didn't get shot," Xander told him, flopping down into the room's single chair to watch.

Tré raised an eyebrow at him, covering the flinch at how much doing so hurt his face.

Eris started rolling up his other sleeve, and eyed Della curiously. "So, you are the embodiment of infamous and much-mourned Irina, then? This whole situation is fascinating, I must say."

"So I've been told. But my name is Della," she replied, lifting her chin defiantly.

Rather than being offended by her hard tone, it seemed that her attitude pleased Eris in some way. He nodded with satisfaction and gave her a brief smile. "So it is," he said. "And rightly so. My apologies for the presumption."

To Tré's relief, he finally proffered his wrist, returning his full attention to the reason they were there in the first place.

Tré barely contained a moan of longing as he sank his fangs deep into Eris' arm. With a rumble of satisfaction, he drew the sweet, healing blood from Eris' punctured vein and felt it course through him, adding to his own blood supply. His life force had been pulsing angrily along with the flashes of pain from his skin, but Eris' gift was like a balm that soothed and cooled the angry storm.

He had not realized just how tightly he was holding himself until he relaxed and allowed the breath to flow out of his lungs, taking much of his tension with it.

"That's better," Xander said in encouragement, rising from his borrowed chair to stand over Eris' shoulder while Tré fed. He grasped Tré's hand from where it was clasped around Eris' wrist, and used it to lift his arm so that the light from a lamp nearby illuminated the blistered, peeling skin.

As they watched, the skin grew lighter, the red patches fading to pink and then back to their normal pale coloration. The pain vanished over the course of several minutes while Tré fed from Eris' arm.

As he did so, he felt the bond between them strengthen, and could more clearly sense the other vampire's mind and mood. Tré could discern a deep feeling of concern underneath his facade of calm.

He could even taste the relief seeping through Eris' blood as he continued to drink. The rich taste of it eased the bone-deep thirst that had been growing in him since his injury.

Allowing his eyes to slide away from Eris, Tré's gaze found Della, who was standing in the corner with her arms folded. She looked fascinated by what was taking place in front of her, but the faint tinge of green in her face told Tré that she was also disturbed by what she was seeing.

After he drank his fill and his skin was no longer blistered and throbbing, Tré leaned back with a deep sigh of relief.

"Just rest for a few more minutes," Eris said, his voice emerging raspy. The process of sharing blood with an injured comrade was both draining and intimate. As Xander had said, Eris was more familiar with it than most of them, given his odd, one-sided relationship with Snag. Nevertheless, it was clear that his own strength was sapped after the generous gift he'd offered.

Tré patted him on the arm and ran a hand over his eyes. "Take your own advice, *tovarăş*."

There was a huff, and the mattress dipped as Eris settled on its edge. Meanwhile, Xander returned to his borrowed chair and flopped down in it again, lacing his hands together across his stomach.

"So," he began, "are you going to tell us how this happened, or are we going to have to start guessing?"

When Tré didn't answer, Xander said, "Fine. You can tell me when I get close. Tré, you let Della here out of your sight because you thought it was safe during the daytime. But it wasn't, because our lives are doomed to be fucked five ways from Sunday, and so you ended up getting nearly turned into a pile of ash in a—thankfully successful—attempt to keep her alive."

Tré leveled a hard stare at Xander, who returned it without backing down. It would have been easier to maintain the severe expression if the other vampire hadn't hit on nearly the exact truth with his very first guess.

"It wasn't Tré's fault. It was mine," Della said, looking rather ill.

"Nonsense. The only one at fault is Bael," Tré said into the ensuing silence. He let his head fall back to rest against the headboard, and closed his eyes. "He caught you in a moment of weakness and tried to possess you, Della. I've honestly no idea how you managed to make it back here without succumbing—and on foot, no less."

Della's reply was very quiet. "I had to get back here. I knew, somehow, that I had to get back... to you."

Tré's eyes flew open. He straightened away from the support of the headboard to meet her gaze, an unaccustomed lump rising in his throat even as something large and warm swelled in his chest.

"And so you did," he said after a beat, their eyes locking for a long moment as the others looked on curiously. With an effort of will, he broke away from her to glance at Xander. "Unfortunately, I had to rush out into the sunlight to get her inside. It's... been a bad day for everyone involved."

"It has," Della agreed in a whisper. She cleared her throat. "I got to work this morning, only to discover that a riot had broken out on my street and the rioters had trashed our office. A couple of us were trying to get everything cleaned up. I left for lunch, and when I got back, Bael tried to take over my mind. I'd just discovered that..."

Her voice trailed away and Tré saw her bite her lip.

"You'd just discovered... what?" Eris asked, rousing enough to rejoin the conversation.

Della took a deep, shaky breath. "My boss had a gun. He killed one of my co-workers. She was a friend of mine. He shot her, and then turned the weapon on himself. I... found their bodies, and that's when I felt Bael's presence."

"He used that moment of shock and despair as a way to enter your mind?" Eris clarified, glancing from Della to Tré, who nodded.

"And all this, during daylight?" Xander asked, his face deadly serious. They all knew that Bael's power waned significantly during the daytime hours. It was unusual for him to strike while the sun was high.

"Yes," Tré answered.

"Well, that's certainly ominous," Eris said, his voice deceptively mild. He blinked, returning his full attention to Della. "But you managed to get back here, and against all odds, you fought him off. How?"

Della glanced at Tré, and her face colored. "It was Tré. He... helped me somehow. Lent me his strength, so I was able to push Bael out of my mind."

Eris' dark eyebrows lifted in clear surprise, and he sent Tré a speaking look. "Did he, now?"

Xander was staring at him, too. "You joined mentally," he said, "with a human." The words had the form of a question, but the delivery was flat.

"I didn't even realize that was possible," Eris said, looking at Della with new interest. "And you were aware of this mental joining, at the time? He didn't just tell you about it afterward?"

Della frowned. "Well, of course I was aware of it. It was kind of a hard thing to miss. I could feel what he felt and he added his strength to mine. Why do you both look so surprised? I thought you vampires could muck around in human minds with no problem." She paused. "Which, by the way, is *creepy as hell*, in case no one has ever mentioned that before."

Xander snorted.

"It's not something we do often, or lightly," Eris said. "But the human mind isn't really designed to process such things. It's not so much the fact that Tré gained access to your mind, but rather the fact that you were aware of it and able to make sense of what was happening. That's a vampiric trait."

"Oh," Della said. She looked taken aback.

"Were you aware of it when Oksana wiped your memories, the first time we crossed paths?" Eris continued.

"No," said Della. "I had no idea what was happening. I thought I must be going mad, but the EMTs convinced me it was just a natural reaction to severe trauma."

Eris nodded, still obviously fascinated. "Which lends credence to the idea that you and Tré were able to join in such a way because it was your soul that shielded his, all those years ago when Bael turned him. You saved him, and that connection still persists to this day."

The unexpected mention of that darkest of times sent a sliver of ice through Tré's chest. But Della was staring at Eris, shaking her head.

"I really didn't, you know," she said. "You all keep talking about me being this person… this Irina… but I'm a twenty-six year old receptionist from New Jersey. I didn't do any of these things you think I did."

Tré could understand how hard this must be for her. But her safety rested on her willingness to accept the dark realities life had dealt her.

"Do you deny the connection between us, *draga mea*?" he asked.

She looked so lost and confused for a moment that he longed to chase the others away so he could take her in his arms—but now was not the time. After the space of several heartbeats, though, she seemed to deflate.

"No," she said quietly. "I don't *understand* it— but I don't deny it. I feel it, too. I felt it from the moment your skin first brushed mine. Like an electric shock, straight to the heart."

"Bael will not rest until he has revenge on her, Tré," Xander said. "You have to realize that."

"I concur," Eris echoed.

Tré nodded and closed his eyes for a moment, thinking. He knew that Della possessed a stubborn spirit, identical to Irina's. He hoped she would not fight them on this.

"So what does this mean for me?" she asked into the silence.

"It means," Eris said, "that your life will never be the same again."

She blinked, tears pooling in her eyes, but not spilling over. "I can't stay here, can I? This place has always been my sanctuary from the outside world—but it's not any more, is it?" The words were wistful. Sad.

Tré didn't want her to be sad.

"No," he said, before either of the other two could speak. "At the house in the bayou, you would be under our combined protection. I can't imagine that Bael would dare attempt a full attack on the place, with so many of his own failed creations gathered in one place, and spoiling for a fight with him."

Della let out a slow breath, growing resigned. "I guess I've got no choice, then. God knows, if I'm going to survive this, I need the help. You six are the only option I have."

The ice in Tré's chest stabbed a little deeper. "You *will* survive this, *draga mea*," he said, intense. "I will lay down my life, if necessary, to ensure it."

Rather than look reassured, she clenched her jaw and looked away. Wordlessly, she started walking around her room, gathering a small bag's worth of clothing and personal items with angry, efficient movements.

"I don't want you to lay down your life," she said, still not looking at him. "I just want this… not to be happening, I guess."

She stowed a couple of foil-wrapped energy bars in the bag's front pouch, and slipped on a pair of hiking boots. Pulling her honey-colored hair back off her neck, she tied it up and slung her bag over her shoulder.

"But it is happening," she continued, glancing around the room at the three of them. "So let's move. Tré? Are you strong enough?"

"Yes," Tré said, already rolling off the bed despite the echo of his injuries still draining his vitality. "Of course I am. Let's go."

THIRTEEN

Della took a deep breath and followed the three vampires out of her bedroom.

I should be terrified right now, she thought, remembering the way Eris' deep brown eyes and Xander's cold green ones had studied her intently when she had opened the door, as if sizing up her possibilities. *Voluntarily giving myself over to a coven of vampires, for God's sake. What the hell is wrong with me?*

But she could still feel the security of Tré's arms around her. She could remember the fierce protectiveness of his mind as it swirled together with hers, like water and wine mixed in a glass. Those things could not be faked. They were *real*.

When they reached the front door, Della glanced around her beloved little apartment and wondered if she would ever see it again. She knew that she was fleeing for her life, and there was no time to linger over physical possessions. Yet she still felt tears sting her eyes as she scanned the familiar walls. This place had been her own. Her retreat. Her safe haven. Leaving it now felt like she was leaving a part of herself behind.

Tré must have sensed her turmoil, because he was suddenly *there*, by her side, gently taking her hand in his own.

"Della?" he asked, looking down at her.

Get yourself together, girl,, Della thought savagely. *Now is not the time to show weakness or fear. Bael can get you that way.*

Della didn't know if that was exactly true, but the demon had seemed to slip so easily into her mind when she was distraught over the loss of her coworkers. She squeezed the strong, callused fingers wrapped around hers and tried to wrap herself up in every good feeling of hope and happiness that she could muster, as if doing so would shield her from the threat of an oily, malignant presence in her mind and the sensation of spiders crawling over her body.

Della shivered, but looked steadily back into Tré's pinched, worried face.

"It's okay," she said. "I'm just going to miss this place. That's all."

Tré's expression softened with understanding. "I know. Hopefully it won't be for very long."

Della laughed, though it was not a happy sound. She doubted very much that this battle would be a quick or easy one.

"Yeah. Now, how are we getting back to the plantation house?" Della asked.

Eris had stepped out into the hallway of her apartment complex. He glanced up and down the hallway, clearly checking for anyone who might take note of their presence.

"We'll have to take the Jeep," he responded. "Unfortunately."

"I have a car," Della said quickly, pulling out her keys. "I almost never use it, though. Easier to take the tram to work and errands than try to find parking."

She passed the keys to Xander, who took them from her hands, his eyes lighting with interest.

"What kind of car is it?" he asked.

"Xander," Tré said in exasperation. "Does it really matter?"

Xander gave Tré a withering look. "You really don't get it at all, do you? Of course it *matters*."

Eris cleared his throat. "As charming as this little domestic argument is, I think we should probably stick with the Jeep. The road to the manor house isn't exactly conducive to a small car."

"Agreed," Tré said, and gestured them all forward.

A thought occurred to her, and she started rummaging through her bag.

"Did you forget something?" Tré asked, a furrow forming between his brows. "We need to get moving."

She came up with a little pad of Post-It notes and a pencil stub. "Just a minute. I need to write Mrs. Carpenter down the hall a note. Someone needs to take care of Jewel if I'm not here."

Xander frowned. "You have a jewel? Bring it with you. It might come in handy if we need untraceable money on short notice."

She stared at him. "Jewel is my pet fish. She'll die if no one takes care of her."

She thought she saw a smile tug at Eris' lips in her peripheral vision, but he covered it when she leveled a glare at him.

"Do it quickly, then," Tré said, his eyes scanning their surroundings as if he expected an attack at any moment.

She nodded and jotted a note for her neighbor, who had watched her apartment on several occasions when she'd been out of town. Confident that Jewel wouldn't become an unintended casualty of her bad luck, she hurried back to the others and readjusted the bag on her shoulder as they headed for the main entrance.

Once they were outside, Eris led them around the corner to the little parking lot in the back, where the Jeep was squeezed between two large trucks. Della glanced up at her car, four spaces down, to make sure it was still okay. She usually tried to drive it once a week, just to make sure that the oil and gasoline did not become stale in the engine, but otherwise it was saved for trips back home to see her family. Would she ever drive it again?

"2011 Nissan Sentra," Xander said, walking around the vehicle with an appraising eye. "Standard package?"

Della stared at him and shrugged one shoulder. She had known some of the specifications when she bought it, but at the moment it did not seem very important.

"Just get in the Jeep, Xander," Eris said with a groan, motioning towards their beaten up vehicle. "We've got a long drive ahead of us."

Xander rolled his eyes. "Right. Fine. Tré, give me the damn keys. And before you ask—yes, I'm sober. *Painfully* so."

"Wonders never cease," Tré said, and tossed him the keys. Eris slid in the front seat, leaving Della and Tré to sit in the back.

Xander positioned himself behind the wheel and started the vehicle with a low rumble. "So. I bet that car of yours gets about thirty-two miles to the gallon, am I right?"

"Something like that, I guess," Della answered. She glanced over at Tré in consternation, and he gave her a look in return that clearly said, *humor him*.

They drove through the cramped roads of the Garden District and got on the highway to cross the river before heading southwest, toward Lake Salvador. It seemed incredible to Della that there could be people out here with them, just driving around—going about their daily lives without a care in the world.

In the past few days, everything in Della's life had been upended and turned on its head. She'd seen people die. She'd been attacked. Terrorized. She had no job, and she'd just left her home behind, carrying nothing but a small overnight bag slung over her shoulder. Her future was bleak, with a demon of the ancient underworld hunting her down and a group of eccentric vampires her only hope.

The irony was enough to make her choke.

"Are you all right?" Tré asked, his voice pitched for her ears alone, breaking into Della's musing.

"Yeah," she answered, turning back towards the window on her left. "*Great*."

He took her hand, which had been resting on the seat next to her, and gently squeezed her fingers. At his touch, Della felt herself relax a bit, reassured by his steady presence, almost despite herself.

They had been driving for nearly thirty minutes when Della — still lost in memories of the life she might never be able to return to — felt the car slowing down. She glanced around and saw that Tré, Eris, and Xander all seemed to be on high alert. The three vampires were leaning forward in their seats, looking out through the front windshield with matching wary expressions.

"What is it? What's going on?" Della asked, her heart starting to race.

"It's a roadblock of some kind," Tré answered without taking his eyes off the line of flashing red and blue lights in front of them.

"Oh," Della answered with considerable relief, "it's probably just the police setting up a DUI checkpoint or something like that."

Tré's gaze swiveled in her direction. "A DUI checkpoint?"

"Yeah," Della said encouragingly. She felt giddy with relief that it was nothing more frightening. "You know — *driving under the influence.* There's usually one of them somewhere in the city. It keeps drunk driving down when folks know that the police are out looking for them."

"You're quite sure of that?" Tré interrupted, his eyes still staring fixedly at the flashing lights ahead.

Della faltered and glanced back out of the window. "Well, I mean... *yeah*. I — I think so. What else would it be?"

"Roll the windows down a crack, Eris, just to be safe," Tré said quickly. "And Xander, if you're lying about being sober, so help me — "

"*Nice*," Xander said. "Thanks for that."

As soon as the back windows were cracked an inch or two, Tré's nostrils flared, as if scenting for something.

"Look, you three," Della said, trying to put them all at ease, including herself. "Think about all the craziness that's been happening around New Orleans recently. It only makes sense that there would be a greater police presence. They probably just... don't want the violence and problems to spread, or something."

No one answered her. Tré had his head cocked towards the cracked window as the line of cars in front of them proceeded through the checkpoint. Della watched red brake lights fade into the distance, after winding their way through the heavy, plastic barriers.

Xander inched to a stop and rolled his window down completely. A state trooper wearing a blue uniform and one of those vaguely ridiculous Smoky-the-Bear hats sauntered over to them. He held his hand up to shield his eyes from the headlights and Della frowned. He was wearing sunglasses, which seemed rather unusual after nightfall.

The officer stepped up to the side of the car, his hand resting casually on his utility belt.

"License and registration," he said in a flat voice. Something about his lack of inflection made Della's neck prickle.

Xander, never taking his eyes off the officer, dug around in his back pocket for his wallet and slipped an ID into his hand. Eris, who had been rummaging around in the glove compartment, passed over the registration papers.

The officer examined them slowly, a hint of a leer playing around the corners of his mouth.

"That all seems to be in order," he said, passing them back through the window.

He paused, glancing into the backseat. She couldn't tell because of the man's dark shades, but she felt certain that he was staring right at her. Nonplussed, Della shrank back, trying to melt into the shadows of the vehicle. She made herself small, which seemed to stiffen Tré's spine with additional tension. She saw him lean forward and lay a warning hand on Eris' shoulder.

"Anything else we can do for you, officer?" Xander asked, his British accent lending a lazy drawl of challenge to the words.

The state trooper considered Della for a moment longer before his gaze turned back to Xander.

"Yes," he said in the same flat drone, "you can all step out of the vehicle for me, please."

At that moment, he lifted his hand to his sunglasses and pulled the frames off his face. The strobing lights surrounding the traffic stop illuminated his features, and what Della saw made her gasp out loud. His eyes were flat and dead.

Inhaling, she caught the same whiff of decay that had surrounded the undead men who attacked her in the alley near her apartment building. An identical scent surrounded the officer's body like a cloud as his eyes continued to stare blankly at each of them.

At that moment, several things happened at once. Tré gripped her arm so tightly it hurt, Xander swore loudly, Eris jerked back and covered his nose, and the Jeep's tires squealed as Xander stamped on the gas.

Before she could do or say anything, the tires found traction and her body was slammed backwards into the seat behind her as Xander crashed through the flimsy portable barricade. A loud scraping of metal and plastic told them that the plastic barrier had dragged their bumper off as it was flung aside by the vehicle.

"*Shit*," Xander snarled, spinning the steering wheel madly as he tried to avoid a tree on the side of the road.

"What was he?" Della asked loudly as she and Tré were flung to the side of the car. Xander had evidently decided that their best means of escape was an off-road chase through the bayou, and she scrabbled for purchase.

It felt like her heart had frozen inside her chest, and she massaged her ribs with one hand while she tried desperately to cling to the door handle with the other.

"One of the undead," Eris spat back, sounding furious—his mild, bookish demeanor vanishing in the space of a moment.

"One of Bael's puppets," Xander clarified.

Della spun around and saw that red and blue lights were following them. Through the misty darkness, it was impossible to tell how far away their pursuers were.

"So they're after us now?" Della asked, terrified. "How did they find us? How did they even know to *look* for us?"

"A good question, and one for another time," Eris said, his voice low and dangerous.

"Shouldn't we have stayed on the highway?" Tré called to Xander over the roar of engine noise. "We could have driven faster!"

"Those police cruisers would have smoked this old wreck," Xander snapped in reply. "This was the best option at the time."

"*Brilliant.* I imagine you're having second thoughts right now?" Eris countered. Della could practically hear him gritting his teeth. "You know, when I woke up this evening, I really didn't think this was how my night was going to go!"

Della could see that Eris was gripping the handle above his head with white knuckles.

"There seems to be a lot of that going around," Tré shot back. "*Xander*—"

"Would you both just *shut the hell up*?" Xander yelled over the howl of old machinery pushed past its limits. "I'm a bit busy trying not to wreck us!"

Tré and Eris fell silent as Xander reached over and killed the headlights. They were plunged into total darkness as they continued bumping and juddering along, broken only by the flashing red and blue lights behind them, occasionally filtering into the cab of the vehicle.

"Maybe we should stop and talk to them?" Della asked half-heartedly. "We could try to explain what happened. Surely they're not all undead, right?"

"If only that were true," Eris answered her.

"This is insane, though!" Della shouted. "Isn't there a chance that some of them would be normal that could help us? Whereas, this is basically guaranteed to kill us!"

Della gestured to the pitch-blackness in front of them, even though she doubted that Eris could see her.

Xander didn't answer but spun the wheel to one side and then the other, barely missing a large tree that loomed out of nowhere in the darkness.

Della and Tré hung on for dear life, occasionally cracking their heads on the roof of the vehicle when they were pitched upwards by an unseen hole in the trail they were forging through the bayou. Mud and loose dirt slapped against the windows as the tires tore up the boggy ground. All the while, police cruisers followed, slowly but surely gaining on them.

Della could see one cruiser just a few car lengths off the Jeep's left rear bumper, jouncing along just as badly as they were on the uneven track. She imagined, although she could not be sure through the chaos and darkness, that she caught a gleam of dead eyes in the driver's side seat, watching her.

Of all the terrible things that had happened in the last few days, Della was more frightened in this moment, more convinced that she was about to die, than at any other time. She was abruptly certain they were about to crash into a swamp where she would meet an ugly death by drowning or being eaten by alligators. Horrible images of her own neck being snapped as they were propelled head first into a tree filtered across her mind's eye as she fought to remain upright while being tossed around like a rag doll.

"We need a plan," Tré finally barked. "Crashing through the swamp in the dark does not constitute a plan! Our luck is going to run out sooner rather than later!"

Xander laughed, wild and derisive. "Yeah— sorry, boss. I've been trying to think of something in between dodging rocks and huge holes that could swallow this Jeep completely. How about I concentrate on not killing us? Piece of cake, right? Here's an idea, though! Why don't *you two* figure out someth—"

Xander's words were cut off by a scream of metal as the vehicle dropped suddenly, the ground beneath falling away. For the space of one breath, the Jeep was suspended in the air before smashing into the wet earth. Della flew forward, the safety mechanism on the ancient seat belt snapping without slowing her forward momentum.

Tré's arm came out of nowhere, stopping her body before she could smash into the back of the driver's seat. It felt like running into a solid steel guardrail, chest first.

Feeling as though she'd been hit by a bus, Della groaned and clutched at the back of her neck, which was throbbing with pain.

"Are you all right?" Tré's frantic voice cut through the gloom and the sound of sirens as the Jeep came to rest at an angle. "Della!"

Della coughed once, feeling aching ribs protest at the movement. "I think so," she croaked.

They moved around, feeling for each other in the darkness as Tré called to the other two vampires. "Xander? Eris? You're all right?"

In response, they heard the engine grinding as Xander cranked the key in his hand.

"Come on," he growled as he pumped the gas pedal, trying in vain to turn over the engine.

"Even if you get it started," Eris said in a strained voice, "I don't think we're going anywhere. We're stuck in the bottom of a ditch, you clod."

Della felt horror punch her in the stomach, even as Tré's hand closed around her wrist.

They were trapped. The vampires could fly away if they had to. But for her, there would be no escape.

FOURTEEN

"Everybody out, don't let them flank us!" Tré ordered, pulling Della towards the door on his side. The window on her left had smashed as the car landed against the roots of a large tree. The impact to the trunk had caused leaves and sticks to fall from the branches overhead onto the top of the disabled vehicle.

Tré threw his shoulder against the door pulling on the handle at the same time. "Damn it. It's jammed."

He spun easily onto his back and gripped the seats on either side of him. With immense strength, he kicked the door, which popped open partway and stuck again.

Xander and Eris were clambering out of the passenger side as Tré carefully pulled Della through the gap. As soon as she landed in the mud, Della saw flashing lights creeping closer to the edge of the ditch.

"What do we do?" She asked, shrinking against Tré's side and quivering as reaction to the crash set in. For all her talk earlier, she held out no real hope that these officers drawing ever nearer to them were not a part of the undead uprising led by Bael.

"*You* are going to run," Tré told her. With a sound of metal scraping against metal, Tré pulled a wicked looking knife from a hidden sheath at the small of his back. "*We* are going to fight."

Ignoring her open-mouthed stare of disbelief, he pressed the handle of the dagger into the palm of her hand and pushed her forward.

"Go," he commanded, uncompromising.

Della took a single stumbling step and balked, looking up at Tré in consternation. Her gorge rose at the idea of leaving him there, surrounded by the undead they could already see gathering at the edge of the embankment.

"Go!" Tré ordered. "Della, you have to run now. Don't worry — I'll find you. I'll come back for you, I promise." He surged forward and pressed his lips to hers for a bare instant before pushing her away again.

"I — I — " Della stammered, unable to articulate the horror rising in her mind. She was terrified at the idea of leaving Tré behind — it would be like leaving part of herself behind. The bond between them stretched, pulling at her heart. She was damned well not going to allow an army of Bael's servants to destroy that connection.

She would run, but only far enough to get out of the vampires' way as they fought.

"*Go!*" Tré bellowed.

Della stumbled backwards at the unexpected shout and tripped. Flipping onto her knees, she scrambled forward until she was sprinting into the darkness without the slightest idea where she was going.

Once Della made it several yards away, she darted into the trees. She peeked out from behind a trunk to see Tré and the others illuminated by large spotlights wielded by police officers on the track above them.

As she watched, panting for breath, she saw Xander pull a gun out from his waistband and cock it with a practiced movement, holding it securely in his right hand. Eris pulled out two daggers, flipping one to Tre, handle first. He caught it with a sharp nod of thanks. Together, the three men turned towards the large group of cops gathering nearby. The breeze lifted Della's hair off her neck, prickling the skin, and she could detect the smell of rotting flesh in the air. Choking back a gag, Della realized the three of them were about to be overrun by the undead.

-o-o-o-

"We need backup," Xander said as he pulled the 9mm Makarov out of his waistband. "Much as I hate to admit it, having Snag's batshit crazy super-strength here right now would be *really* helpful, assuming he aimed it in the right direction."

"Yeah, I'm on it," Eris muttered as he flipped his extra dagger to Tré.

As the three vampires turned towards the army of undead scurrying around the police cruisers, Tré felt Eris send out a strong call for help to the others back at the plantation house. The power of the summons echoed through the depths of his divided soul.

Would they get the message and respond in time? Were they close enough to sense it? Tré knew that they were still quite a distance from the house.

Sometimes mental messages went astray in the heat of a moment, especially across long distances.

"*Drop your weapons and put your hands in the air.*" The flat voice resounded through a bullhorn's speaker. Spotlights from above were blinding them, so they could not see who had spoken.

"Hmm," Xander said philosophically. "He sounds very unfriendly, doesn't he? You'd almost think we were criminals or something."

"You just drove through a police barricade," Eris reminded him. "You *are* a criminal."

"They weren't real police! Besides, you don't have much room to talk. You're an art thief!"

"*Former* art thief, if you please. Don't be crass when we're about to be attacked by undead minions, Xander."

"Shut up, both of you," Tré snapped. "We're in a bit of a spot here, in case it's somehow escaped your attention. They hold the high ground."

"Drop your weapons, now! Get on the ground!" The voice bellowed again.

"So, which is it? Put our hands up or get on the ground? Your instructions seem very unclear to me," Xander called back, making no move to relinquish his gun.

"Are you two ready?" Tré asked, running a quick gaze over his companions.

Eris gave a curt nod, and Xander grinned, showing fangs.

"You kidding, Tré? I told you days ago that I'd been getting bored lately," Xander drawled.

"Then let's do this." Tré closed his eyes and pulled his life force deep into his center. He felt his physical body dissolve into mist, swirling in the night air. He could sense Xander and Eris next to him, their forms mingling with his. Their power united, and they hurtled towards the police cars.

They formed into a dense cloud, flying through and around the crowd of undead, disorienting them and slamming them against their own vehicles. Several yelled and waved their guns around, but with nothing to aim at, they did not fire their weapons.

Tré separated from the other two and materialized behind two sergeants crouched by a large SUV, their weapons pointed into the air. Before they had a chance to turn, Tré slammed his fists into the backs of their heads before pulling himself into a mist again.

Both undead men bashed their faces against the glass of the window and crumpled to the ground for a moment, blood spraying out of their noses as they recovered themselves and staggered to their feet. It looked oily and nearly black in the dim light.

One opened fire, aiming at Tré. He dematerialized, sensing the passage of the bullet through the place where his body had been. He darted through the cracked windows of a patrol vehicle and found Eris on the other side, fighting in his physical form with a very large, burly man.

Eris, a much leaner figure, was losing his advantage over the undead man. A cut above his eye was already starting to swell as he twisted around his attacker. Tré, exploding into physical presence right above the undead man, dropped onto his shoulders and knocked him to the ground, grabbing his neck and twisting with a fierce jerk until the vertebra snapped.

Eris wiped blood out of his face and gave Tré a hand up. They turned to stand back-to-back.

Before either of them had a chance to speak, a blow to the side of Tré's head knocked him to the ground, temporarily stunned. Tré could see people moving around him in the darkness, but their voices sounded far away and dull, as if he were listening to something underwater. The world swam hazily and, for a moment, he wondered where he was and what he was doing. There seemed to be a fight in front of him but he could not remember why.

Then he blinked as the body of an undead man fell on top of him, and everything came rushing back into harsh focus. He scrambled against the man, who had wrapped his putrid hands around Tré's neck and started to squeeze.

Tré brought his left hand up above his head, breaking the grip of the undead, and flipped him over using a defensive roll. Anger boiled inside him as he pummeled Bael's minion into the dirt.

Another dark body crashed against his. As they slammed onto their sides, Tré twisted violently in the man's arms until they were facing one another. The attacker gasped in surprise as the heel of Tré's hand connected with his chin. Tré, using momentum from the blow, launched himself to his feet and stood over the dazed police officer. With a single smooth movement, he stamped a booted foot down, shattering his opponent's face and jaw.

Tré felt a sharp summons echo through his mind and looked up to find Xander. He and Eris had become separated as he battled the last two men. To his dismay, he found his fellows back to back a few yards away, on the far side of the police cruiser, surrounded by twenty or more undead who seemed to have popped up from nowhere. Many were wearing police uniforms, but others were dressed in gray, dirty rags.

The stench from their bodies was overpowering, the reek rising into the night.

Hope flickered and began to die in Tré's heart at the sight. They were surrounded by undead now, badly outnumbered. Della had disappeared into the darkness, but she had not left, as he'd hoped. Her human scent lingered nearby. It would not take this army long to find her, and all three of them had already been wounded in the brief foray.

Something grabbed at Tré's ankle and he stamped down on a hand before even looking at the source. He felt the bones snap and a snarl of fury sounded from the ground. It seemed that one of the corpses had crawled through the darkness, over the bodies of his fellows, and reached Tré's feet while he stood assessing the situation. Both of its legs were missing below the knee.

Another undead corpse sprang at Tré, and he grappled with it, trying to toss it away and get to the others' sides. Although the thing's right arm hung useless, it still landed several hard blows to Tré's ribs with its left.

Pushing forward, Tré used both his hands to gain an advantage on his opponent. Several well-placed strikes to the face caused the thing to stagger and fall into the darkness. A piercing cry startled Tré, and he looked down.

The thing had fallen on another of the corpses, which had been gripping a knife in its lifeless hand. The knife had pierced the man's back, the tip protruding obscenely through its chest. The undead creature struggled for a minute and then fell still.

Tré turned back and saw that even more of the things had surrounded Xander and Eris, who had created a low wall of bodies in front of them in hand-to-hand combat. Yet the group creeping forward grew ever larger.

We can't win, Tré thought. *We won't be able to stop the darkness coming for Della.*

He could sense the endgame approaching, even now. He could feel Bael's presence drawing ever closer, looming over the battle in hopes of a feast. His greatest mistakes, his centuries-old errors, were finally being rectified. Tré wavered, on the verge of ordering the other two to flee. Only the thought of Della held him back.

"Don't be an ass, Tré," Xander called, and he realized that he must not have been shielding his thoughts. "We're not going anywhere."

Shouts and harsh, lifeless laughter rose up from the army as they closed in around his friends.

With a surge of strength, Tré transformed into mist and flew to their sides. They would stand together, in the vain hope that their sacrifice would mean that Della could get away. If there was the slightest chance that she would live, Tré was willing to take it.

Xander looked grim and battered as he raised his gun, shooting fruitlessly into the oncoming hoard. Eris' normally unflappable demeanor was slipping, his face smeared with mud and blood as he hacked at anything within reach of his dagger.

As he took his physical form inside the ring of undead corpses already dispatched by the others, Tré pressed his shoulders against theirs and let them feel his flash of regret at dragging them into this mess.

Xander snorted derisively, and glanced around at the leering faces and flat, bloodthirsty eyes surrounding them. "And where else would we be, Tré? Still, it's one hell of a way to go."

From out of the darkness, the cry of a hunting owl rent the night air. It was echoed by two others. Tré felt Eris catch his breath in surprise. He expanded his awareness to the trees around him and sensed Oksana, Duchess, and Snag, all swooping low to their rescue.

The three huge birds crashed into the crowd of two dozen undead, clawing at faces, and puncturing eyes with their sharp talons. Pandemonium broke all around them as the undead broke ranks, turning to face the new threat.

Eris and Xander sprang forward into the fray, knocking heads together and tearing at limbs. Tré's attention was drawn towards the far left of the battling crowd. He could see two undead men, their heads turned in the direction of the abandoned Jeep, making their way further down into the ditch.

Della! A shock of horror seemed to stop Tré's heart for a beat.

With a cry of rage, Tré leapt forward, bowling over anything that got in his way, hot in pursuit of the two creatures that were hunting his mate. Hurtling after them, he caught up to the closest one and tackled it to the ground. His victim, who had turned at the last minute, only had time to raise a bloody knife in one hand before Tré slammed against him.

As their bodies landed together in the mud, Tré felt his hands sliding against rotting flesh, and the bite of the blade against his chest.

Placing both hands on the sides of the undead's face, Tré wrenched the thing's head to the right, feeling a satisfying snap as its neck broke. Instantly, the struggle went out of it. As always, Bael's power abandoned the animated corpse immediately — the moment it was no longer useful to him.

Tré struggled to draw breath into lungs that felt... *wrong*... and looked around for the second undead. He found his target roughly seven yards away from him, a look of triumph on its pale, ghastly face.

Ignoring the explosion of pain in his chest, Tré planted one foot firmly on the ground and attempted to lunge forward for another tackle. But, for some reason, his body was no longer cooperating. He propelled himself forward by force of will, only to crash back to the muddy ground as violent tremors shook his arms and legs.

Looking down, Tré saw the handle of the knife that his last victim had been holding. The blade disappeared straight into his chest, directly through his heart.

-o-o-o-

Della screamed in denial as Tré attempted to rise and collapsed back to the ground, the hilt of a knife protruding from his chest. "No! *Tré! No!*"

She had not fled when she had the chance. Instead she had observed the arrival of the other vampires from her position behind the tree, transfixed in horror by the brutality of the battle.

As her cries filled the night, she saw Xander look towards her, then follow her gaze to where Tré was lying on the ground, the blade lodged in his chest.

The sound also attracted the attention of the undead man still standing near Tré's body. He spotted Della, who had stumbled forward without thought into the illumination of the spotlights.

Xander swore and wrenched his right arm free of the two undead he was fighting. With one of his precious remaining bullets, he managed to fire off a shot that caught the creature advancing on Della in the thigh.

Della saw the thing lurch at the impact of the bullet, but it continued to shamble forward as if nothing could stop it from achieving its goal. Oily, black blood seeped out from under the man's rags, further staining them along with the filth of centuries. Della gripped the knife that Tré had given her and looked into the thing's face.

His eyes were completely blank, glossed over with a white film. His mouth was pulled wide in a ghastly grimace that showed teeth rotting out of his decomposing skull. Knowing her death was only seconds away, Della's eyes fell onto Tré, still crumpled on the ground in a lifeless heap.

A firestorm of righteous anger flared in Della's chest, and she tightened her hold on the handle of the blade Tré had given her. With a yell like a banshee, she flung herself forward towards the creature. Perhaps she caught it by surprise, if the thing could even feel surprise. Whatever the case, it did not raise its arms in time to fight her off. She plunged the knife deep into the undead's stomach, black blood spurting all over her hands and torso.

The thing let out a loud *oof* noise as putrid air was forced out of its lungs in a rush. Della twisted the handle and the man staggered against her. His momentum propelled them both towards the ground.

Della landed flat on her back in the mud at the bottom of the ditch, still holding the knife tightly in her hands. The heavy body landed on top of her, forcing the knife even deeper into the man's gut. Della continued to snarl and scream in rage, wrestling against the dead weight on top of her.

To her horror, the thing began to move again with a raspy groan, its eyes still lifeless as it pressed itself up, away from the blade.

"You'll have to spill more blood than that to finish me, pretty little piece of meat," it rasped, leaning forward to whisper in her ear. Della shrieked again in rage, trying to wrestle the knife out from between them.

The thing let out a cackle of cold laughter and ground her down further into the mud. It leaned forward to run its cold, slimy tongue up Della's face as she struggled fruitlessly to free herself, and she knew that she going to die now. Bile rose in her throat and tears sprang to her eyes.

Still fighting like a madwoman, she screamed for help one last time and tried to knee the thing in the groin. She twisted and writhed beneath the creature, unable to break free.

Suddenly, Della felt its body fly off her as if jerked away by a puppeteer's strings. She struggled upright and saw Duchess crouched above it in the mud a few feet away, a look of disgust on her beautiful face.

She, too, held a blade in her hands, and she slashed the sharp edge across the thing's throat. With a gurgle, more blood sprayed everywhere and it finally went limp.

Panting heavily, Della dragged her filthy sleeve across her face. She tried in vain to wipe the stench of the man off her skin as she rolled over and clambered onto her knees.

"Thanks," she gasped, unable to say more. Duchess nodded tightly in acknowledgement and stood up, looking around for a moment before rushing back into the fray.

Sounds of the battle filtered through Della's sluggish mind and she pushed herself unsteadily to her feet.

She had to get to Tré.

Her mind seemed stuck in a horrific loop, replaying the moment he fell over and over again.

With faltering footsteps, she stumbled towards the body of the man who had loved her for centuries, still lying prone on the ground. The knife remained firmly lodged in his chest.

Tripping over a twisted root protruding from the ground, Della fell, landing in a muddy puddle and sinking up to her wrists. It barely slowed her down, as she yanked her hands free and crawled the remaining distance towards Tré.

"Tré!" she cried, grabbing his shoulder with filthy fingers and shaking it. He did not stir. His eyelids did not so much as flicker. Della lowered her ear towards his mouth, trying in vain to hear the sounds of life coming from his lungs.

A final death shriek from one of the undead police officers filled the night air, and silence fell. Della listened with all her might, but all she could hear was her own pounding heart and the blood in her ears rushing back and forth.

"*Tré*! Come on, wake up!" Della begged, tears spilling over and running down her face as she shook him again.

The splatter of boots in mud made her look up in time to see Xander running toward them. He slid on his knees next to Tré's other side and put a hand on Tré's chest.

With a quick, one-handed motion, he ripped Tré's shirt so they could see the wound exposed under the floodlights that had illuminated the battle.

The blade had clearly pierced his heart.

Della stared at Xander, whose left arm was dangling uselessly at his side, dislocated at the shoulder.

A hand on her upper arm made her jerk in surprise and look around wildly. It was only Eris, lowering himself slowly to his knees next to her, a grave expression on his face. Blood was streaming from a wound on his head, and he seemed to be moving carefully, as if he had broken several ribs.

Oksana and Duchess hurried up, both looked shaken and muddy, but unhurt. Oksana's eyes fell on Della, worry and grief shining from their dark depths.

Della looked up at her, pleading. "He can't die! He's a vampire! That... that means he's immortal, right?"

Oksana's lips flattened to a thin, unhappy line. "We can still be destroyed. It might not be death as you know it, but things can be done to us to end our existence in this realm."

Della thought about Oksana's missing leg and choked down bile.

"We've got to get him back to the house," Xander said in a strained voice, drawing her attention back. He reached forward and jerked the knife out of Tré's chest, examining the dark metal blade. "Iron. *Fuck*. He's going to need a huge infusion of blood and life force to survive this. It would have been worse with a wooden stake, but we've still got to hurry. We have very little time."

"How? How can we get him there?" Della whispered, feeling as though her terror was strangling her. The air around her seemed far too thick and heavy. She choked on it, trying to fill her lungs in spite of the crushing sense of doom that was pressing on her heart.

"*Snag.*" Eris said quietly. He stood up and stepped away, pulling Della back with him. She looked up at him, confused, then towards the darkness where the others were looking.

She had not noticed the sixth vampire standing in the shadows, but she could see his outline now, moving slowly towards them. He stepped into the light, blinking sunken, red-rimmed eyes in the glare from the police lamps.

His features were chiseled, unyielding as ancient stone. He looked around the scene with eyes that held a permanently haunted look, as if he had lived through eons of suffering. The aura of barely restrained power around him was truly terrifying, and a chill slithered down Della's sweaty back.

He walked forward towards Tré, his mouth a flat, narrow line.

"What's he going to do?" Della whispered to Eris.

Eris looked at her for a long moment. "Help. I hope," he said.

FIFTEEN

At Della's words, Snag's gaze rested on her. They stared at each other for the stretch of several heartbeats. A jumble of images bubbled up from Della's memory—a powerful, shadowy figure descending like a hurricane on the alley where she was being assaulted, tearing her undead attackers limb from limb, blood spraying the walls. She lifted a hand to her mouth.

Something flickered in the depths of Snag's eyes. Eris, standing behind Della, stirred as though he, too, noticed a change in the old vampire.

Snag lowered himself to the ground in a movement that was oddly graceful. After a brief hesitation, he reached out and drew Tré into his arms. Although the ancient vampire was whipcord thin—almost skeletal—he seemed to possess immense strength. He lifted Tré's heavy form effortlessly into his arms and stood.

"What are you doing?" Della demanded, unsure if he would answer.

He remained silent, staring at her with a depthless expression. Despite her terror for the one she loved... despite the fact that she was exhausted, sore, and had just had the fight of her life... Della felt a wave of peace steal over her. Peace that she could not understand.

"I—" she stammered, but was unable to finish.

Della felt sure that somehow, the ancient vampire was using his power to communicate with her without words. He was tempering her anxiety. She felt a deep sense of reassurance from a source she could not identify. She lifted a hand to her head and blinked rapidly, trying to make sense of the sensations.

"Don't fight him," Duchess advised in a wry tone. "He'll put you in a coma if you don't calm down."

Drawn up short, Della nodded and lifted her hands in a gesture of peace, still staring at the vampire in front of her. "All right. I'm not fighting. Just... help him. *Please*."

Snag gave a silent nod in return, and shut his eyes. Immediately, he and Tré dissolved into mist and swirled away. Movement out of the corner of Della's eyes told her that Eris and Oksana had followed them, floating into the night sky and away from the scene of the battle.

"Can we do that?" Della asked, gesturing towards the now empty space around them.

"No," Xander said with a grimace, as Duchess moved towards him with a determined look in her eyes. "Snag is the only one powerful enough to transport anyone while in the form of mist. We'll have to get back some other way."

Duchess circled him, examining his shoulder from all angles.

"The joint is out of its socket," she said.

Xander lifted an eyebrow. "Gee. You think?"

Duchess raised a brow right back at him. "Don't get smart with the only one here strong enough to put it back in for you," she said. "Now sit down. *Mon Dieu*, you're tiresome when you're sober."

Xander flopped down, clearly exhausted. Duchess sighed and placed a small, elegantly shod foot against his side, dragging his useless arm up into a raised position.

"Do it," Xander commanded through gritted teeth.

With a wet pop that made Della's stomach turn, Duchess jerked his shoulder back into place.

Xander swore creatively in at least three different languages. Duchess straightened and stepped away from him, brushing mud and dirt off her hands as though she performed such tasks on a regular basis. Xander, however, massaged his shoulder with his uninjured hand and gave her an aggrieved look.

"Vicious hellcat. You could have reset it without half that much force," he said in a dark voice. A sheen of sweat was visible across his forehead, and his skin looked clammy.

Duchess gave a short bark of laughter and started towards the Jeep, still wedged against a tree.

"This thing is never going to run again," she said, turning back towards Xander.

Still massaging his shoulder, Xander walked up and looked at the battered vehicle with a mournful expression. Della knew that he had spent many hours working on it.

With a sigh, Xander said, "We'll use one of the police cruisers instead."

In the end, they found an SUV that was more or less undamaged by the battle. The keys were on the ground, clasped in the loose grip of a beheaded undead cop. Xander delicately removed the key ring with a wrinkled nose, clearly disgusted by the pungent smell.

As they drove towards the manor house, Della sat in the back and tried not to imagine Tré's lifeless body with the knife sticking out of it.

How long before Snag reached the manor house? What could the vampires do to heal Tre? Surely he would be dead after a knife pierced his heart? But… *could* vampires even die? Oksana had made it sound like they could…

Disturbing thoughts swirled through Della's mind, yet her body remained still and calm. Even though there was a storm going on inside her, it seemed that her brain was overloaded. She had seen too much violence, blood, and death to take in anymore, and her body simply remained in a state of shock.

When they reached the old house, she slid from the leather seat and landed with a soft thud on the ground. She followed Duchess and Xander up the front steps and inside in a daze. Wearily, she climbed the stairs up to the room in which she had awoken the previous day, though it seemed like a lifetime ago.

Snag was standing in one corner of the room, a silent specter. He appeared calmly unruffled by the scene before him. Oksana was sitting in the chair by the bed, holding her wrist over Tré's parted lips.

He was completely still and did not appear to be breathing.

Della watched, not even flinching as Oksana sank her teeth into her own wrist, drawing fresh blood to the surface. She wiped the blood over Tré's lips, pulling his jaw open a little more.

"He won't drink," she said, as the three newcomers walked in, an undertone of desperation coloring the words.

Della saw that Eris was standing next to Oksana, rubbing Tré's neck near his jawline.

"I'm trying to stimulate his feeding instinct," he explained, glancing up at her, "and Oksana has been wiping blood in his mouth. He should be able to sense it and allow his body to take over and drink it."

"He's too far gone to bite down," Oksana said, still visibly upset.

"Is he dead?" Della asked, as tears started rolling down her muddy face.

"Not exactly," Eris said. "I can sense his life force, but it's very weak, flickering in and out. He needs to feed, or we'll lose him."

The others glanced around helplessly.

Oksana stood abruptly and glared at Snag, who had made no move toward the others, or the man on the bed. "Your blood would heal him, Snag."

Snag blinked slowly at her and did not respond. Instead, his eyes moved to Della, who stood paralyzed under the mesmerizing stare. He seemed to be beckoning to her somehow, because Eris looked up at her with a snap of his head.

"*Oh,*" he said in surprise, a troubled expression flickering across his handsome face as he looked from her to Snag, and back again.

Xander, Oksana, and Duchess all fell completely silent, turning towards Della in unison.

"There's only one person in this room whose blood can heal Tré's heart," Eris said quietly.

Della glanced around wildly at all the vampires now staring at her. "Wh-what? You mean... me?"

Eris nodded without speaking.

Della stood frozen in place, sure that these vampires had lost their minds. How could her blood save Tré, when she wasn't a vampire? They all had a close bond already from sharing blood, because vampire blood had healing properties. Hadn't that been what Tré had told her?

Doubt flooded her, followed closely by alarm. She barely knew any of these people — these *vampires* — and here she was, trusting them with her life. They had acted to save her, yes — but, what they were asking of her now was...

She swallowed.

"*He's going to need a huge infusion of blood and life force to survive this,*" Xander had said.

They were asking her to sacrifice her life for Tré's, just as Irina had done centuries ago.

"I don't know if I can do this," she said in a tiny voice. "You're asking me to — "

"Della. I know this must be terrifying," Oksana said in a quiet voice. Della glanced at her face and was startled by what she saw reflected in Oksana's eyes. There was no deception there, just empathy, coupled with desperate hope. "But your soul is connected to his in a way the rest of us can never be. You can *save him*. I know you can."

Della's feet carried her closer to the bed as if she was in a trance. She looked down at Tré, who was rapidly losing the last color remaining in his face. Although his features had always been pale, Della thought he looked waxen now, like he'd already departed from his body, and what lay before them was now merely a lifeless corpse.

Are we too late? Della wondered, as grief possessed her heart again. *Can I really save him? Do I have the courage to even try?*

Della remembered how Tré had risked his life to rush to her aid when she was in Bael's clutches, and love surged inside her breast. She remembered his skin blistering and searing under the bright afternoon sun. He had ignored it in the face of her need for him, and not only had he carried her to the safety of her apartment, but he had lent her his strength and power to drive the demon out. A demon that he hated with every fiber of his being—the one who had nearly torn his soul in two.

She could see now what a sacrifice that had been. He had injured his body and put his soul at risk yet again by exposing himself to the same demon that had ripped his life into pieces and destroyed her in her former life.

Tré had flung himself into deadly danger time and time again to rescue her. During their last battle, he had tried to fight off the second undead creature coming after her, even with a jagged knife protruding from his chest. He had been mortally wounded saving her life, and here she was, questioning whether or not she should sacrifice herself for him?

He loved her, and she loved him. There was no doubt in her mind. From the most carefully guarded depths of her being, Della could feel his arms wrapping around her, cradling her as they made love. She had felt like the most precious thing on the planet as his hands had caressed her. Her body sang under his touch, coming to life as if for the first time.

Heart thudding madly, Della exhaled the breath she'd been holding and took a step forward. Without a word, Oksana and Eris stepped away from Tré, making a path towards the bed. Della could feel her blood rushing through her head and ears. It sounded like the ocean. She tried to swallow, but her mouth was completely dry.

Will it hurt to die?

The thought made her feet stumble, but only for a moment. She kept moving forward. It seemed to her that she had always been destined for a horrible end—even when she was Irina, centuries ago. And now, again, as Della, walking calmly towards her own destruction. She was never meant to survive, and all Tré and his fellow vampires had done was to delay the inevitable for a few days.

She breathed slowly, trying to calm the instinctive, animal impulse to flee from the room and never look back. She might be demon-cursed, but she was *better* than that, damn it.

Each step, each thud of her muddy hiking boots on the floor, seemed to take an age to filter into her mind. It was like a death march, playing slowly in the background of her final moments.

Even as everything inside her screamed for survival, the love that had woken in her heart kept her moving forward, towards the man who had sacrificed everything in a doomed attempt to save her from the inevitable.

I will give my life for his. He is my soulmate, the one I was destined for. And… the world needs him more than it needs me. He and the others are all that stand between humanity and chaos.

As she walked past Oksana, their eyes met. Della could see sadness there. The lovely vampire reached out and touched Della's cheek, as if imparting strength to her. Della felt bolstered by the gentle brush of fingers, confident that she was making the correct choice.

She reached the bed and climbed onto the mattress, settling next to Tré, whose eyes flickered at the movement on the bed, a tiny furrow forming on his brow. She caught her breath at the nearly undetectable sign of life.

He opened his silver-gray eyes slowly. They almost slipped shut again several times, as if he was being dragged down by weakness and exhaustion.

Eris was right, his life force was nearly spent.

Tré gazed up at her with a distant, dazed expression. Della wondered if he could even see her, and if he was aware enough of his surroundings to really understand what was happening.

"I love you," she whispered hoarsely. She had to lick her lips with a parched tongue before she could make any sound at all. "Take what you need of me, Tré. I give it freely. Perhaps…"

Della's voice trailed away as tears welled in her eyes. She knew what to say next, even though she could not clearly remember her life as Irina as anything more than a dream. "…perhaps we will meet again in another lifetime."

Tré's unfocused eyes sharpened—a final burst of strength. Air rattled through his damaged chest as he attempted to speak. "I won't… take your life… Della. Not… again. Never… again."

Della smiled through her tears. "You're not taking it, Tré. I'm giving it."

She leaned forward, pressing a kiss to his cool forehead. She could smell the wonderful scent of his hair. She closed her eyes and breathed in, wanting his smell to be the last thing she would ever know.

A sudden thought came to her, though, and her eyes flew open. She looked up, meeting the others' eyes one by one.

"Don't let him punish himself over this. You have to promise me—all of you. And…" she hesitated, suppressing a shiver. "… don't let me become one of those… undead *things*. Burn my body afterward, if that's what it takes. I don't want Bael using me like that."

Oksana made a pained noise and stepped forward, reaching for her. "Della," she said, "*ti cheri,* no! You thought we were asking you to sacrifice your life for his?"

Della blinked in confusion. "What else?" she asked, barely a whisper.

"Snag believes Tré can turn you," Eris said, also appearing taken aback. "Make you one of us."

Della straightened in shock, looking around at the vampires assembled in the bedroom. She thought about her unfulfilling life and how she seemed to have screwed everything up as a mortal.

"Is that even possible?" she asked.

"If Snag thinks it's possible, then he's probably right," Xander answered. "But you should understand what that means first. We thought you already did."

She stared at his green eyes and handsome face, her mind whirling. "Which is what?"

"Your soul is complete right now," he said. "If you surrender to life as a vampire, it would mean that your soul will be ripped into two pieces. You would be a physical shell for both the Light and the Dark, but they will no longer be in balance inside you."

Della frowned, trying to understand. "Well," she said, "given my track record as a human, that doesn't sound so bad right now."

"Also," Duchess said, "It will be the most exquisite agony you have ever experienced."

"Oh," Della said, feeling as if all the air had been punched from her lungs.

"Think carefully before you do this," Xander said. The serious tone of his voice was in stark contrast to his normal shallow demeanor and sarcasm. His pale face was pinched with worry — for her or for Tré, she wasn't sure.

Della felt Tré's fingers brush her wrist, and the now-familiar swoop in her stomach that followed.

"Will it save his life?" Della asked, staring down at Tré, her eyes filling with tears again.

"Yes," said Eris. "At least, Snag seems to think so. And he is seldom wrong about such matters."

She bit her lip. She didn't know what to do, and time was running out. She looked at Eris' brown-eyed, olive-skinned face with its finely sculpted Mediterranean features. She thought of all the undead that he had destroyed to protect her, and the efforts he put into saving her life.

She glanced over at Xander, Tré's closest friend and comrade. She glanced next to Oksana, whose soul-deep kindness surpassed that of most humans she had known. At Duchess, who was brave and beautiful and brilliant and calculating in a way that made Della's heart burn with jealousy.

Finally, her eyes fell on Snag. Ancient, withered, and haunted, he stood silently against the wall behind the group gathered around the bed. Their eyes met, and she felt as if she were falling into that tired, pain-filled gaze.

What do I do? Is this really the right thing? she thought, not sure if he could hear her.

Snag cocked his head in slow motion, as if listening. For a moment, they stood staring at one another in a frozen tableau. Then, without warning, Della felt the same sense of calm steal over her that she had felt after the battle earlier. It felt to her as if Snag was reassuring her that her sacrifice would, in fact, save Tré's life. That it would save both of their lives from Bael's bloodthirsty desire for revenge.

She took a deep breath and nodded her understanding. A moment later, he tipped his chin in acknowledgement—a bare hint of movement.

Della turned back to Xander and the others, new determination flooding her.

"I'll do it," she said, reaching out for Tré's hand as she spoke. She gripped it tightly, even though he could manage no more than a weak twitch of the fingers. "I'll become a vampire. Please, help me save him. Tell me what to do."

"All right, then," Xander said, relief audible in his words. "First, let him bite you."

She shivered, unable to stop herself.

"Okay," she said, and turned back to Tré, her heart pounding. "Okay…"

Their eyes met for the briefest of moments, and she kissed him, a chaste brush of lips. She slid her cheek along his, feeling him press weakly into the contact, burying his face against her neck and shoulder.

She felt the butterfly brush of his eyelashes against her skin, and closed her eyes. Clearly using the last of his strength, Tré surged forward and sank his teeth into her throat.

Della gasped in shock, feeling his fangs slide into her neck. She felt Tré draw on her blood; heard his groan of hunger… of need. Strength seemed to flood back into his limbs. He reached up and gathered her into a tight embrace, holding her to him as he suckled at her neck.

At first, there was no pain, and Della wondered in one tiny corner of her whirling, spinning thoughts if Duchess had been wrong about it hurting. There was only a deep, drawing sensation that seemed almost... *sexual*, pulling at her depths as Tré demanded that she give herself over to him, and something in her responded, surrendering to his need.

Then, an awful tearing sensation began to grow in her chest, as if her heart and lungs were being ripped from her rib cage. She cried out in pain as her eyes flew open, seeing nothing but a swirling fog of red and gray. She could dimly feel Tré continuing to drain blood from her neck, but also felt herself falling into a pit of fire, flames licking across every nerve.

She screamed and flailed, losing track of her surroundings. Everything was confusion—she knew the bed was just beneath her, but she seemed to fall a great distance, burning all the way. With one last agonizing shudder as her soul burst apart at the seams, Della slipped into merciful unconsciousness.

-o-o-o-

With the first infusion of Della's blood, Tré felt his flesh begin knitting itself back together. The pain lessened, and the fog that had clouded his vision lifted.

He drank deeply, instinct taking over as he tasted the sweet nectar of her life force entering his, strengthening him, bolstering his body and spirit. He sat up, cradling Della in his arms as he pulled more of her essence into himself.

She whimpered and cried out in pain, struggling weakly before collapsing against him. Still, he drained more and more blood from her, feeling the worst sense of *déjà vu* he had ever experienced wash over him like a wave.

Outside the sanctuary of the old house full of vampires, Tré could sense storm clouds gathering in the sky as Bael hovered nearby, convinced that his terrible vengeance against Irina's spirit—and Tré's—was imminent.

An evil voice whispered in his mind, full of hate and glee. *She will die at your hands once again, my beautiful abomination. Her soul will be mine forever.*

The words seemed to permeate the room. Tré was aware of the others' reactions as they flinched and set themselves as if for battle. Yet all Tré felt at the threat was a strong surge of defiance.

He would not allow Bael to take his beloved from him. Not again. *Never again.*

The first time he had drained Irina's life to save his own, he had been weak, crazed, mad with pain and horror after his turning at the demon's hands. He'd had no control over his instincts, and had simply latched onto the first living thing that crossed his path, which happened to be Irina.

Waking to find her lifeless shell laying at his feet and his hands covered in her blood had been the worst moment of a lifetime that now spanned centuries.

But he was no longer that crazed and desperate beast.

As the storm raged outside, Tré focused everything on the fragile form in his arms, stretching out all his powers to surround Della, to hold her life force together as her soul split in two. He could sense that the transformation was almost complete. Her blood began to taste less and less like a human's blood, and more like a vampire's. Her smell changed, growing less musky and more coppery.

"Careful, Tré. She's nearly there," Eris said. Tré could feel him standing poised next to the bed next to Xander, both of them prepared to spring at Tré and tear him away bodily before allowing him to take Della's life.

I know. I have control.

The mental message spread through the group, one by one. Possibly, it was undercut by the hint of a growled warning at the idea of anyone trying to pull his mate from him… but even so, he felt them all relax marginally.

"It's not that we don't trust you Tré," Oksana said, worry woven through her sweet voice. "It's just that you were almost… *gone.*"

The way she choked on the last word told Tré clearly that his life force had nearly been spent when Della provided the sacrifice necessary to save him.

He owed this beautiful, amazing woman everything. He owed her the integrity of his soul after her sacrifice when she had been Irina, and now he owed her his very existence. She had given up her humanity to save him, despite her fears. He vowed, then and there, that he would spend the rest of his life protecting her, shielding her from harm.

Tré wrapped his life force around Della's more fully, sheltering her from the wild storm of Bael's rage beyond the walls of the old house. He felt the last vestiges of her soul rip free under the strain of her draining blood. With a bone-deep shudder, Della jerked and seized as the Light and the Dark finally separated inside her. In that instant, Tré released her neck and cradled her securely in his arms like a child.

Oksana stepped forward cautiously and tilted Della's chin back, as the windows rattled in their frames. Tré fought an irrational stab of territorial aggression, unable to stem the protective instincts surging through him.

"Easy, Tré, I'm just trying to help," Oksana reassured, keeping her voice soft and her movements slow.

Tré nodded and clenched his jaw, trying to maintain control over his instincts. He raised his own wrist to his mouth and sank his teeth into the flesh.

Blood spurted around his fangs. He lowered his wrist over Della's slack mouth and rubbed it onto her lips.

"Drink, *draga mea*," he whispered. He could feel her life force flickering feebly and mentally willed her to accept the blood. "Come. You must drink now."

Long seconds ticked by as Della remained seemingly lifeless, unmoving in Tré's arms.

Drawing on all his mental power, he reached for the familiar contours of her mind and thrust a single command into its flickering depths.

Drink!

SIXTEEN

She was nearly gone, and the weakness of her divided spirit chilled him to the core. Outside, the wind grew even wilder, tearing at the trees and dragging loose shingles from the roof.

Icy fingers of doubt assailed him. *Had he made a mistake? A second terrible mistake in his miserable, endless existence? Had he drained too much life from her? Was she too weakened by the events over the past few days to withstand the transformation process?*

After a terrifying moment of mental silence, Della's tongue darted out to capture the blood lingering on her lips. With a feeble groan, she closed her mouth around his proffered wrist and began drawing blood. Tré could feel her gaining strength from him, and relief flooded his body, leaving him shaking.

She would be all right. If she was strong enough to feed, she had survived the change.

Once more becoming aware of the others' presence, Tré looked around at the solemn faces surrounding them. Oksana was still supporting Della's head, holding her in position to help her feed. She stroked Della's hair out of her face tenderly.

"That's it. Keep going, *ti cheri*," she said in a soft voice, the beginnings of a smile playing at the corners of her full lips. "You're both going to be just fine."

Eris looked thoughtful. "A new vampire has just been born—for the first time in over two hundred years."

Something crashed downstairs—a window shattering under the force of the storm, perhaps. They ignored it, secure in the strength of their bond against the creature that had created them.

Duchess frowned. "And is what's been done to her any less horrible than what was done to us? We've condemned her to a half-life spent in darkness."

"She consented," Oksana said, frowning up at her blood-sister. "We didn't."

"And it seemed unlikely that she could have survived Bael's attentions for much longer as a human," Eris said pointedly as something—a tree branch, perhaps—crashed against the outside wall.

A flash of mental pain and a faint *whoosh* of departing mist told Tré that Snag had left the room.

"What's eating him, anyway?" Xander asked, no doubt picking up on the same surge of disquiet from the ancient vampire that Tré had felt. "This was his idea in the first place!"

Della, oblivious, continued to suckle at Tré's wrist like an infant on the breast. Her brow furrowed as if she were concentrating. Oksana relinquished her supporting grip, and Tré tucked her more securely against his body.

"Della?" he asked. "*Della*?"

She didn't answer, but drew harder at his wrist. Her hands came up to grip his arm, and he felt the same spark between them, the same soaring sensation in his heart. The same electric connection with her as he had when his fingers had first accidentally brushed her skin.

Her eyelids flickered open, revealing a golden glow radiating from behind her soulful hazel eyes. At that moment, the house shuddered on its foundation, making the others jump in alarm. Tré was aware of the disturbance, but it was unimportant. He could not take his eyes off the beautiful face before him.

Della released his wrist and blinked slowly up at him, her mouth stained red with his blood. As the storm howled even more loudly around them, Tré lowered his lips to hers and kissed her with all the tenderness he possessed. The sweet smell and taste of her surrounded him, filling the empty places that had languished within him for centuries.

As they pulled apart, the wind that was making the house quake died down, the storm's strength finally spent.

It was over. They had won.

"Tré?" Della asked, sounding sleepy and dazed. "Did it work? Are you okay now?"

Her voice was like music to his ears. Love for her swelled within him until he thought his body would not be able to contain it. "Of course I am, *draga mea*. You are here with me, are you not?"

"And… Bael?" Della asked.

As soon as she had spoken, a distant, unearthly wail sounded over the dying wind. It made the hair stand up on Tré's neck. Duchess drew in an audible breath, while Eris and Xander looked around sharply. Yet the sound was mournful. Defeated.

Bael was fleeing before the immense power held within the old, abandoned house. The power of two united, unconquerable souls, joined at last after centuries apart.

The power of love, in the face of death.

-o-o-o-

Hours later, Della's eyes drifted open. A muted hint of sunlight was filtering in through heavy drapes across the window. Oddly, she could feel it on her skin, even though the dark crimson curtains kept the room itself in shadow—a prickling sensation that, while not precisely unpleasant in and of itself, hinted at danger for the unwary.

She and Tré were alone. She vaguely remembered that the others had been present, at first—all except Snag, who left earlier, smelling of old pain that could not be assuaged. Xander and Eris had offered Tré blood, both to speed his healing and, she presumed, so he would have enough to offer her throughout the first night of her turning.

In the end, though, it had been Oksana and Duchess who had nourished him. Though they were like brothers to him, with his mating instincts roused, Tré had been unwilling to allow the other males close to her. Something about the idea sent a delicious shiver through her, for all that she knew it was a temporary side effect of what the two of them had shared.

She stretched, exploring the changes in her body as she recovered from the turning. She felt... *strong*. Stronger than she had ever felt in her old life, where she had always secretly thought of herself as weak and a bit useless.

Confident. It was as though she had always been meant for a life of immortality. But she could also sense the damage done to her soul. Perhaps it should have bothered her more, but she had seen how the others acted with nobility and love—how they valued honor and the bond of friendship.

The Light and Dark halves of them might have been torn asunder, but they were still present. She would simply chose to draw her life force from the Light, rather than the Dark, she decided.

The sun, too, interested her. She could see the weak rays not blocked by the drapes and even feel heat on her skin through walls of the house. She knew that it would blister and burn if she were to step directly into it, and she felt a strong aversion. This alone troubled her about her new life, as she had always loved the feel of the sun on her skin when she was mortal.

The benefits, however, far outweighed the costs, and a secret smile twitched at her lips. Della stretched again, like a cat, feeling strong new muscles pull across her back.

"Good morning, *draga*," a velvety voice whispered in her ear.

The smile widened, and she turned to Tré, still lying next to her. He was propped up on his elbow, staring down at her as if he had never seen anything like her before in his centuries-long life.

"Good morning," she murmured back, craning up for a kiss.

"How do you feel?"

Della turned inward for a moment, taking stock. "Hungry," she decided.

Tré laughed—a low, rumbling sound that did interesting things to her insides. "Is that so? Don't tell me that you're going to be the next Oksana in the house," he teased.

"Ha. Very funny," Della said, and flicked him on the arm. "I'm going to tell her you said that."

He smirked, the expression far more attractive than it should have been.

"I didn't say it would be a bad thing if you were. But… there will be a lot about this that you'll need to get used to," Tré said, growing serious. "Don't hesitate to ask one of us if you have any questions."

Della chewed on her lip, feeling the unaccustomed prick of pointed fangs pressing hard against the inside of her cheek. "I do have one question now," she said.

"Yes?"

"How do you read each others' minds?"

Tré looked at her with a considering gaze. "That's a rather interesting question, actually. I'm not sure exactly how to answer it. I suppose that it's like… pressing your awareness outside of your body. Like remaining motionless but reaching for something across the room. It takes considerable concentration, but it becomes easier with time. Though some of us are more skilled than others."

Della frowned. "So, just reach out with my mind?"

Tré nodded, still looking at her as if he never wanted to look away. A new flood of warmth suffused her. She closed her eyes and tried to imagine herself with invisible fingers, reaching out for Tré. She concentrated so hard that she felt a prickle of sweat breaking out across her forehead.

"Did I do it?" she finally asked, unsure of what she was supposed to be feeling if she succeeded.

Tré chuckled and shook his head. "No, I'm afraid not. At least, I didn't feel anything. You might've reached for someone else by mistake, though."

That was interesting. "Would I know it if I did?" she asked.

He was obviously still amused. "Yes, it's pretty unmistakable."

Della tried again, closing her eyes. She strained and strained until Tré cupped her face with a callused palm.

"You're trying too hard. It's a matter of *allowing*, not *making*. Don't force it so much. You'll break something important." He tapped the furrow in her forehead lightly. "Or your expression might freeze that way. Didn't your mother ever tell you that?"

"You're making fun of me," she accused with a mock scowl.

The devilish gleam in his pale eyes belied his expression of innocence. "I would never do such a thing."

She tried on a glare, but it collapsed into a sappy smile in short order. She snorted in wry amusement. "Yes, you would."

"Well, perhaps I would," Tré conceded. "But only a little. Now, try again, but relax this time. Allow your mental awareness to expand with your breath."

Della flopped down flat on her back, pushing a rolled-up pillow under her neck. She took several deep breaths and tried to relax, letting her muscles go loose and pliant, one by one.

She concentrated on the life force she felt inside her. It seemed to swirl and undulate within her body, and she imagined for a moment that she could control the rippling waves. Channel them, and bend them to her will. Without warning, it was as if she could see everything in the entire house within her mind's eye.

She could tell that Oksana was wandering around the kitchen, digging into a bag of cookies as she hummed a sad tune. Eris and Duchess were in the living room, talking quietly to one another. Snag was holed up in the back bedroom, his thoughts hidden behind a featureless shield that she could not penetrate. Xander was still asleep down the hall. She looked towards Tré. She could see him clearly, both with her physical eyes and her newly awakened mental awareness.

Murmured thoughts tickled her awareness like whispers against the shell of her ear, and she drew in a breath.

You are so beautiful. So flawless. You were truly made for this immortal life, draga mea. How could I pos-

sibly be so lucky that my soul's true mate would find me, all these endless centuries later?

Della blinked in shock, and the awareness faded as quickly as it had come. She was astonished, knowing that she had just seen inside Tré's mind.

"I felt that," he said quietly. "Your mental touch was light as a feather."

She was still breathless. "Was it? I didn't feel like I was touching you."

"No?"

She shook her head. "It was more like… looking at you. Looking *inside* you."

"Interesting," Tré answered, lifting an eyebrow. "I've never heard it described that way. For me it's like reaching out and touching the mind of another person."

"Oh. Was I… doing it wrong? Do you think there's something wrong with my new powers?" Della asked, old fears and insecurities already trying to creep back into her heart.

"You," Tré said in a stern voice, "are absolutely perfect as you are. Remember, Della, there's great diversity in our experiences, even as vampires. Your powers will grow, and you'll be able to control them better very soon. I know it."

Della nestled against his neck, feeling reassured and very much in love. "Thank you."

Tré hummed in contentment, wrapping his arms more securely around her. "Why are you thanking me? I'm only telling you the truth."

Della thought for a moment, unable to put her complicated emotions into words. "You didn't have to save me that first night, you know. You could have let me die in a hail of gunfire along with the others in the street. I was nothing to you—just another faceless victim of the violence spreading over the city. But… you didn't let me die, even though it put your closest friend in harm's way. And from that point forward, you were protecting me."

Tré nodded, but did not speak; he seemed strangely lost for words.

"I don't know what I would have done," she continued. "I'm sure that Bael would have destroyed me without your protection. Now, you've put me beyond his reach forever."

"I wasn't really thinking about it like that," Tré admitted.

Della blinked up at him.

"You make it all sound so… chivalrous," Tré said, "but it was pure selfishness on my part, *draga*, I assure you. I simply *couldn't* leave you alone. It was like a stab of mortal pain, to think about you by yourself. I watched you, you know—even when you didn't know who or what I was."

Something stirred in Della's memory. It was hard to draw the images forward, as though she were wading through murky river water, searching for a single stone.

"Wait a minute," she finally said, sitting up in surprise. "The owl! You were at my apartment! You were sitting in the tree that night, watching over me!"

The realization hit her out of the blue. One of them had told her, early on, that vampires had the power to transform into owls, and she had seen it for herself during the last, awful battle with the undead.

"You were there, protecting me, even then," Della accused, looking down at her fated mate.

Tré gave a small shrug of concession. "You have a fantastic ability to get yourself into trouble, Della. I... needed to be close by, just in case."

Della smiled at him, rueful, but unable to dispute his words. She curled up against his side once more and began to daydream what her owl form would be like. After a moment, Tré gently nudged her with his shoulder.

"Does that not upset you?" he asked.

She craned to look at him. "Why would it upset me?"

"Some random vampire in the form of an owl, sitting outside your window all night watching you?" he asked. "That's not upsetting?"

She laughed—she couldn't help it. "Tré, do you honestly think that's the creepiest thing that has happened to me in the last several days?"

This argument seemed to sway him, and he pressed a kiss to her forehead. "Maybe not."

Della, who felt wide awake and suddenly far more interested in physical pursuits than talking, rolled on top of Tré's broad chest, now thankfully whole and unscarred once more. His silver eyes darkened, and she smiled down at him, feeling playful.

"You know," she reminded him, "I told you awhile ago that I was hungry. Aren't you supposed to be seeing to my needs during my period of transformation?"

A furrow of worry grew between his dark eyebrows. "Forgive me, *draga*," he said. "Do you need more blood? Or should I get Oksana to bring you something from the kitchen—?"

Her smile turned wicked, and she rolled her hips against his, drawing a nearly imperceptible gasp from his lips. "I said I was hungry," she repeated innocently, and repeated the movement just to feel him shiver beneath her. "I didn't say for what."

"Minx," he accused, swiping the pad of his thumb over her lower lip. "You realize that we're both still completely filthy from the swamp."

"Yup," she said, nipping at his thumb and looking down at him intently. "But you know what else I've realized? I'm *alive*, when I didn't really expect to be. And so are you."

"Good answer," Tré said. "Perhaps we could remove some of this dried mud from the bed by removing the clothes it's attached to."

"I *do* like the way you think," Della said. She reared up to straddle Tré's hips so she could pull her t-shirt over her head and toss her bra away, unsure where this new sense of brashness was coming from.

The way his silver eyes darkened made her body tingle, and she decided that maybe brashness was a pretty terrific thing after all. A strong male hand came up to cup her left breast, as if assessing the weight, and her eyelids flickered closed. The hunger she'd teased him about earlier roared to the fore, startling her with its intensity.

"I can feel your need, *draga mea*." The words were a low growl. "Can you feel mine?"

He thrust up against her and, yes, his stiff, hot length told her just how hungry he was for her in turn. "Too many clothes!" she managed on a gasp, though the barrier of fabric between them didn't stop her from grinding back down against him.

He flipped her smoothly off of her perch and shrugged out of the torn remains of his shirt. When that was done, he tugged her legs to the edge of the bed so he could pull off her hiking boots and socks. She hadn't even realized she'd still been wearing them—the others must have been too worried about setting off Tré's protective instincts to dare remove any of her clothing, no matter how innocently.

Della scrabbled at the button and zip of her jeans, lifting her hips to help Tré pull the mud-stiffened denim down and off. Finally, he leaned in and nipped at her inner thigh, sending her heart pounding madly as he slowly tugged her cotton panties off and flicked them away.

Tré rose to a standing position in the space between her parted legs, looking down at her as he deliberately unclasped his belt and let his tailored trousers—ruined, now—slide down his muscular legs. He wasn't wearing anything underneath, and Della's mouth watered at the sight of his bare flesh.

This time, she decided, she would not be denied. No sooner had he kicked his discarded clothing away than she clasped his hips, holding him in place so she could bend forward and lick a stripe up his length. He hissed and wove his fingers through the thick tangle of her hair.

"*My beloved,*" he whispered, as she kissed and laved the tip of his cock, reveling in the smell and taste of him. She looked up at him from under her lashes, wanting to see his face as she took him fully into her mouth.

He looked… *undone*… with his lips parted and his pupils blown wide. She wanted to put that look on his face over and over, for the rest of eternity. Della swirled her tongue and sucked, watching and smiling around the thick length in her mouth as his eyes fell closed in ecstasy.

She was no great expert at this, but seeing her effect on him gave her the confidence to experiment. The hand he still had wrapped in her hair seemed, quite honestly, to be more about steadying himself than guiding her. She got the impression that, short of not minding her fangs, there was very little she could do to him that he would not find pleasurable.

It was a heady feeling, that realization.

She continued to play with him, pulling him deeper and sliding back until she could flick her tongue over his tip, over and over, losing herself in the feel of him, grinding her aching sex against the edge of the mattress with small, instinctive movements to ease her own need.

"Enough," he grated eventually, using his hold on her mass of hair to ease her back, despite her mewled protest. She panted up at him, knowing that she must look debauched—lips swollen and wet, eyes dark with desire.

Without a word, he pushed her to lie back on the bed, her bare legs still hanging over the edge. He knelt smoothly between them, dragging her toward him another few inches and resting his head on her belly. His breath came in warm puffs against her cool skin as he collected himself.

"I will have you in every way it is possible for a man to have a woman, Della," he said into the crease of her thigh, and she shuddered with need, writhing under him to try and get him where she wanted him.

He didn't leave her waiting, trailing soft lips down to her inner thigh. From there, he lifted one of her legs over his shoulder and kissed her outer lips before brushing the tip of his nose along the seam, breathing her in.

She moaned—she couldn't help it. The sound turned into a whimper as his tongue parted her folds and dipped inside, tracing complex runes against her sensitive flesh. She wrapped her legs around him to keep him in place, feeling need coil tightly in her belly, growing and growing, ready to explode.

One of her on-again, off-again boyfriends had gone down on her a handful of times—always acting like he was doing her a favor. No one had ever attacked her sex with his tongue as if trying to devour her whole… as if she was water in the desert, and he was dying of thirst.

It only took moments before she was bucking, crying out her release as Tré's strong hands held her in place and made her take everything he could give. Made her feel every last nerve overloading and shorting out in a single, drawn-out wave of euphoria.

"So beautiful," Tré breathed against her, drawing another trembling aftershock from her body.

He slid two fingers inside her, making her keen and twist her hips restlessly.

"*More*," she begged.

She thought she felt him smile against her thigh, and then his clever tongue was teasing the sides of her oversensitive clit, working her toward another peak as he stroked over the front wall of her passage with insistent fingers. He sucked her throbbing nub between his lips and worried at it, sending her flying again.

When she came down, his fingers were still working her, even as her body fluttered around them.

"Tré, *please*," she whispered. "*Please!*"

Before meeting him, Della had never begged for sex in her life. She would have expected to find the idea embarrassing. Pathetic. But as Tré gave her a final kiss and rose gracefully to his feet, saying, "Anything you desire, *draga* — you already have all of me," a new wave of heat washed over her, and somehow *she* felt like the powerful one.

Tré grasped her by the ankles, lifting her legs and curling her body up until her knees nearly touched her shoulders, leaving her dripping sex deliciously exposed to him. She had always been flexible — a memento of a childhood spent in gymnastics classes. Thanks to that flexibility, coupled with the new strength and dexterity bestowed by vampirism, the position was not uncomfortable.

Still, it made her feel as though she was completely at Tré's mercy — under his control — and she instantly loved it. His cock was still rock hard as the tip brushed over her entrance, teasing. She tried to wriggle — to hurry him — but she could barely move. Her sex clenched over and over, trying to grasp at his length as he pressed the tip inside and backed off.

"Are you ready for me, Della?" he asked, sliding in an inch or two and back out again.

She wriggled again, needing him inside with every fiber of her being. "You know I am! You're just being cruel now…"

His thumb rubbed along the tendon of her ankle. "Cruel? To you? Never," he rumbled, and thrust inside her to the hilt.

She gasped his name, her vision whiting out as the most perfect feeling of fullness she had ever experienced flooded over her. Tré rocked into her, effortlessly controlling the pace. Della floated along on the waves of sensation, the angle keeping her riding the edge without *quite* being able to tumble down into another orgasm.

It was divine.

She couldn't have said how much time passed, but eventually, Tré's thrusts slowed until he was merely rolling his hips against hers. She whimpered when he pulled out, but it was only so he could release her legs and reposition her on her back in the center of the bed. When he settled himself in the cradle of her thighs and re-entered her, it was even better than before.

She wrapped her arms and legs around him, pulling him down into a kiss. The taste of him—and of her own juices still clinging to his lips—awakened a new kind of need in her, a hunger every bit as fierce as the one she'd teased him about earlier.

She pulled back, trying to force herself under control as saliva flooded her mouth. Her fangs itched to pierce his flesh. He slid his stubbled cheek along her smooth one, even as he gave a sharp thrust of his hips that drove her lust for him even higher.

"I can feel your hunger," he whispered in her ear, lips brushing. His hips snapped forward again. "Give into it, *draga*. You can't hurt me."

She moaned, powerless to fight it as her instincts propelled her forward the last couple of inches. Her fangs sunk into Tré's jugular, and the coppery taste that had quickly become wrapped up in feelings of *life love safety* poured into her mouth.

Their souls twined together as Tré's blood and life force flowed into her. Della stiffened and came harder than she ever had before, swallowing and swallowing as visions flashed through her mind like vibrant scenes from a film.

She was a boot maker's daughter in Germany, hurrying home from the market with a loaf of bread and some turnips, too worried about being out past dark to notice the handsome stranger walking on the other side of the street.

She was a nun in a Transylvanian abbey, too pious to look up from her prayers when a group of travelers arrived, begging sanctuary from the Mother Superior until nightfall.

She was the youngest sibling in a family of Mexican cattle ranchers…

She was a factory worker in Manchester…

She was a staff leader in the Women's Army Corps during World War II…

The circle of her life turned and turned, until it eventually landed here, in this bed in an old house in the Louisiana bayou.

She pulled away from Tré's neck, shaking, clinging to him, tears running down her cheeks. "So many lives… Tré… I didn't know there could be so *many!*"

Tré cradled her, still joined with her both physically and mentally. "Della," he said. "Della, my beloved. If I had only known to look for you sooner—"

She squeezed him tighter, the truth finally clear in her mind. "It doesn't matter. You're here now. *We're* here. We finally found each other."

He made a sound like the breath had been punched out of him and pressed deeper inside her. His teeth nipped at the side of her throat, the feeling sparking down her spine to the place where they were joined. She rolled her head to the side, baring her neck, *wanting* it, and he obliged— piercing her skin with two sharp pinpricks of sensation. Drawing her essence into himself as he shuddered and came inside her.

She held him, feeling strong and powerful and wise for perhaps the first time in her entire life. *This* was what she had been meant for. She and Tré were two parts of a whole. Without each other, they were incomplete.

But together, they were perfect.

SEVENTEEN

For almost a full day, Della stayed hidden in Tré's bedchamber, feeding from him whenever a new wave of hunger came over her. For some reason, she felt unaccountably nervous about joining the other vampires, and delayed her return into the wider world beyond their cloistered bedroom. Instead, she and Tré had wrapped themselves in a hazy cocoon of passion, and she sensed that he, too, was unwilling to shatter the peace around them after such a chaotic time.

Finally, during a quiet moment as she stood to one side of the large picture window, holding a corner of the drapes to one side so she could stare outside at the setting sun on the horizon, Tré came up behind her and wrapped his arms around her waist.

"Are you ready to go downstairs and talk to the others?" he asked, lifting a hand to play with her hair. She could feel the words rumble through his chest and into her back where their bodies pressed together.

Della hesitated, unsure. "I don't know. I could still turn out to be a horrible vampire, you know."

She felt his unhappy huff of breath tickle the top of her head, and turned to face him, pasting on a sly grin. "Or—who knows? I guess I could turn out to be a better vampire than even you."

Tré traced his fingers down the side of her face and hooked a stray lock of tangled hair behind her ear. "I wouldn't doubt that for a moment. You have always been the better part of me."

A lump rose in Della's throat. She wrapped her arms around him, and felt him press her more tightly against his chest.

"Everything seems so perfect right now," Della murmured.

"Everything *is* perfect right now," Tré corrected. "But I do know what you mean — the feeling that if we leave this room, terrible things will start happening again."

They stood in silence, wrapped up safely in each others' arms for several moments longer before Della eventually stirred.

"There's no use delaying it anymore, is there?" she said. "Let's go see what the others are up to."

Della's t-shirt was completely ruined. Her jeans had dried, stiff with mud, but she scraped it off and shook out as much of the resulting dust as she could before donning them and one of Tré's old button down shirts. It came down to mid-thigh on her, surrounding her in a cloud of his reassuring scent.

Muck from the swamp had soaked into her bra as well, so she went without. The material of the shirt was delightfully soft, and her nipples hardened as they brushed against it.

I will not drag Tré back to the bed and ravish him again, she told herself firmly. *I will act like a grown-up and go talk to the other nice vampires who risked their lives to save me so Tré and I could be together.*

Tré shot her a smoldering look that also managed to convey amusement, as if he knew exactly what she was thinking. Which, to be fair, he may well have done.

I will not drag Tré back to the bed and ravish him... yet, she amended. *I will go talk to the other nice vampires like a grown-up, then drag him back here and ravish him again afterward.*

He was still looking at her, the corners of his eyes crinkling nearly imperceptibly. "You will be the death of me, *draga*, I can tell already. And I will enjoy every single moment of it."

She couldn't help it. She grinned, joy suffusing her like the sunlight she would never feel again.

They walked through the old house together, hand in hand. Della found that, as a vampire, her senses were much sharper, and she could detect very subtle scents on the air. Their footsteps seemed overly loud, even when muffled by the moth-eaten carpet under their feet.

A low murmur of voices down the hallway greeted them. Della could tell immediately that all the vampires were gathered in the kitchen, with the exception of Snag.

When they pushed open the door, four pairs of eyes lifted to greet them.

"Well, now," Xander said, his eyes going wide an innocent in a way that was wholly unconvincing. "We were beginning to think you two would be holed up in Tré's room, going at it like rabbits for the rest of the century."

"Charming as always," Duchess said dryly. "What *would* we do without you, Xander?"

Della blushed, but she couldn't work up any real embarrassment. Perhaps being shameless was another side effect of vampirism.

"Tempting," she said. "But the bed will still be there in an hour. We came to see what the rest of you were up to."

Oksana laughed gaily, and popped open a bottle of wine that had been standing on the table. "Celebrating your turning, of course!"

Della could smell the sickly sweet scent of the wine all the way across the room, and wrinkled her nose at it. "Um, that's great."

Oksana poured herself a glass, not bothering to offer any to the other vampires in the room, and toasted her.

"Wow. Yesterday, I would have joined in with you in a heartbeat. Now, I don't think I could swallow a drop. That's so weird," Della said, looking on with a faint sense of queasiness as Oksana took a large sip.

"We've been telling her that for the last century," Tré said with a shake of his head.

Oksana smiled a bit sheepishly. "What can I say? Everyone needs a hobby. Cheers, eh?"

Looking around at the others, Della noted that the only person who did not seem pleased by the recent turn of events was Eris.

Della watched him surreptitiously for a few moments. He seemed lost in thought. Troubled, even. Thinking now was as good of a time as any for a bit of mental practice, Della concentrated on looking inside Eris with her mind. She had absolutely no illusion that her clumsy attempt would go unnoticed, so she was unsurprised when he looked up at her.

"What is it, Eris?" Tré asked, easily catching Della's concern and tracing its path back to the other vampire.

Eris blinked back to the present. "I've just been thinking."

"Well, that's never good," Xander said, not moving from his relaxed slouch against the far wall.

Eris ignored the jab, studying Della with his dark, intelligent eyes, lit from within by a hint of gold.

"Come now. You might as well spit it out, Eris — whatever it is," Oksana coaxed. "Della is one of us now, after all."

Eris sighed and shook his head, focusing his attention on Della. "I was just reflecting on how we stumbled upon you, Della. It was as though we followed the trail of destruction right to your door."

She sobered, the reality of the last few days puncturing the bubble of happiness that had surrounded her since she woke, safe and whole in Tré's arms, after their ordeal.

"Don't remind me," she said.

Eris gave her an apologetic look. "I am sorry, Della. It wasn't my intention to make you sad during what should be a happy time for the both of you. Honestly, I was just…wondering if that approach could work again for us."

Tré cocked his head, looking curiously at Eris. "Explain."

Eris rustled around under a stack of papers on a table in the corner and pulled out an ancient book with brittle, cracking pages. Della could smell dust and old ink when Eris flipped it open, and she breathed in, entranced.

He brought the book over to the large kitchen table and placed it down carefully, dropping into a chair in front of it.

"I've been rereading passages foretelling the fall of Bael," he said.

The others gathered around, intent. Della scooted closer, trying to read over Eris' shoulder but found that the text was written in an alphabet she did not recognize.

"The prophecy clearly states that the Council of Thirteen will unite, and the power of Bael will be cast from the land into eternal darkness," Eris said, running his finger along a line of strange shapes. Della frowned. Maybe it was Cyrillic?

Tré put a hand on Eris' shoulder. The older vampire leaned back into the contact and scrubbed a hand over his face, looking weary.

"We've been over this many times," Tré said. "There aren't thirteen vampires in the world. We would have found the others, if they existed."

"No. There are not thirteen vampires," Eris agreed, before gesturing towards Della. "There are, however, *seven*, whereas a short time ago, there were only six."

Oksana looked back and forth between the two of them, understanding dawning. "You think that we were the first half of the council, and the other half is out there somewhere, waiting to be turned?"

"I think it's possible," Eris replied, looking towards Della again. "We found you, Della, didn't we? Against all odds…"

The room was silent as they pondered Eris' words.

"So, if there are others out there like me — reincarnated souls of those you've lost — how do we find them?" Della asked quietly.

"We follow Bael, I suppose," Tré answered. He glanced towards Eris, who nodded and shrugged.

"But how did Bael know where I was and who I was?" Della asked, dragging up another chair and sitting down next to Eris. "*I* didn't even know who I was."

"That, Della, I do not know," he answered gravely. "He is a very powerful being, and also a very angry one. Vengeance appears to be one of his driving motivations."

"But why not just come and kill me when I was a kid? Or at any one of the thousands upon thousands of moments in my life when I was completely vulnerable?" Della asked. "Why take out his anger on an entire city?"

"His desire for vengeance is not merely against you," Eris said. "It's against all of us."

"His *failures*," Xander said, and Della was startled by the depth of bitterness behind the words.

"It's as we discussed before," Tré said. "Bael is attempting to change this world into his own. Trying to remake it in his image. He doesn't care how much he destroys in the process. He will not be satisfied until the living are nothing more than meat for the undead, and entertainment for his cruel desires."

Della shuddered, appalled anew by the evil that had located her so easily. She knew on a gut level that she was lucky to be in one piece, and sane. Her life as a human suddenly seemed as fragile as a butterfly's wing.

"You've overlooked one small detail," Duchess said. She had been very quiet during the discussion, leaning against the edge of the marble countertop with her arms crossed. Della could feel defensiveness rolling off her in waves, and wondered at it.

"What's that?" Xander asked. He looked tired. Drawn. She could tell that he, too, found something deeply disturbing about the conversation, and wished that her mental acuity were more developed so she could make sense of the undercurrents swirling throughout the room.

Duchess let out an unhappy breath.

"Let's just say for a second that Eris is right, and we can all locate our reincarnated mates, those who sacrificed themselves so we could survive Bael's turning," she said. "Let's just, for one second, assume that we can follow Bael's trail of destruction to each of them, and save them before they become his victims. The last time I checked, six vampires and six reincarnated mates do not make a Council of Thirteen."

Eris folded his arms and stared back at her.

"Yes, Duchess—I am, in fact, capable of performing basic arithmetic. But I'd still much rather have twelve of us than six if we have to do battle again. Which we almost certainly will. My instincts tell me that Bael will be enraged by his defeat here. It's possible that the next encounter will be far worse."

"And aren't you just a ray of sunshine on a cloudy day?" Xander asked, flashing a brief, brittle smile at Eris that came nowhere near his eyes.

"Pot, kettle," Eris shot back, looking sour.

"It will work out somehow," Tré said firmly, putting an end to the debate. "Whatever may come, we will face it together as we have done for centuries."

He reached over and clasped Della's shoulder, the gentle grip reassuring. Regardless of what lay before her, no matter what furious battle she was facing with Bael in the future, she felt serene, knowing that Tré was at her side.

She would never again have to fight her demons alone.

-o-o-o-

A week and a day after Della left her mortal life behind, she soared and dipped alongside Tré's owl form, feeling the night air ruffle the beautiful white feathers of her wings.

To her delight, her avian form had turned out to be a snowy owl — swift and nimble, with a smattering of black flecks across her wing coverts. She loved flying. It had already become by far her favorite thing about being a vampire. It was like a dream made real, and even better when Tré's large gray form flew silently next to her, the tips of their flight feathers brushing affectionately now and then as they drifted along the air currents rising from the city below.

Tonight, her heightened senses were nearly overwhelmed by the swirl of color and noise below them as Tré led her downriver through New Orleans' Garden District, where the Bacchus parade was in full swing during the run-up to Mardi Gras. Carnival goers packed the streets in droves, celebrating both the traditional festivities and the easing of tension within the city after weeks of violence and rioting.

Tré had been close-mouthed about where, precisely, they were going—only insisting that she wear the extravagant green and gold evening dress he'd bought her the previous day. It was by far the most amazing piece of clothing she'd ever owned, a satin confection obviously meant for Carnival, complete with a two-foot train that Duchess had needed to teach her how to deal with when wearing the high-heeled strap sandals that were part of the outfit.

She was dressed for a Ball to end all Balls. Her long, wavy hair was piled up in a riot of curls on top of her head, twisted through with ribbons of purple and green. A purple and gold half-mask covered the upper part of her face, the edges encrusted with rhinestones. Oksana had insisted on accentuating the little mole at the corner of Della's mouth—the one she had always hated—with a black eyeliner pencil.

"There," Oksana had said with satisfaction. "Just like Marilyn Monroe. Tré won't know what hit him, *ti cheri*."

The others had awoken early in the afternoon to dress in their own finery. Well... all of them except Snag, anyway. Della still had a hard time thinking of herself as fitting in with a group of such attractive beings, but even she had to admit, after seeing herself decked out in the antique full-length mirror in the bedroom, that she looked *good*.

Which, she reflected, was just as well, since she would be on the arm of a tall, dark, handsomely brooding vampire wearing a white tie and black tailcoat with a sash in the traditional colors of Mardi Gras, and a mask matching hers.

Now, she just had to keep the mental picture of how she was supposed to look firmly in mind when they arrived wherever they were going and she transformed back into human form. She'd been practicing for days, so she sincerely hoped to avoid a repeat of her first hideously embarrassing transformation, in which she had reappeared wearing only her bra, panties, and one sock... which had a hole in the toe.

Yeah. The less said about that particular performance, the better.

Below them, the crowds were growing thicker as they approached the French Quarter. The owl could hear the sounds of teeming life on the ground beneath them, and Della felt her newborn hunting instincts rise. Someday, she knew, she might feed from one of the countless thousands of humans celebrating the last days before Lent. But she was not yet ready to chance such a thing—content, for now, to seek nourishment from Tré when her hunger grew.

She was young yet — so very young, compared to the others — and she would not risk doing irreparable harm to some poor innocent, should her thirst for blood exceed her self-control. When she had explained all this to Tré and haltingly apologized to him for being a burden, he had made a sound deep in his chest that she couldn't readily identify, and drawn her into his arms, holding her tight and burying his face in her hair.

Now, Tré's owl was circling, honing in on a particular building below them. Owls looked at the world differently than either humans or vampires, but based on the crowds and their proximity to the river, Della was fairly sure this was St. Charles Avenue. They were close to Canal Street — only a few blocks away from it, she thought.

A curl of amusement rose, though she had no way to really express it while in bird form. It would have been a nightmare trying to reach this area from ground level. Impossible by car or public transit with the parade in full swing, and grueling on foot, through the dense crowds. Instead, they would both glide in on silent wings, with almost no one the wiser.

She followed Tré toward the huge balcony of the extravagant townhouse that was apparently to be their destination. People milled on the balustrade, talking, laughing, and sipping drinks. The soft strains of a piano emerged from within the house. As they approached, Della became aware of several familiar presences among the partygoers.

Eris. Duchess. Oksana. Xander. And another familiar aura that she couldn't quite place. But now, she needed to concentrate. Tré came in for a smooth landing on the balustrade, hidden from the people on the balcony by a row of lush, six-foot tall potted plants. The owl hopped down from the railing and Tré landed lightly on his feet in vampire form.

Della wasn't quite that skilled yet, so she aimed for the railing and steadied her balance with flapping wings for a moment before jumping down to the floor of the balcony while still in owl form. She thought very hard about all the clothing and small items she'd brought with her, and fixed a firm picture of her reflection in the mirror in her mind's eye.

Clothing. Hair. Makeup. Shoes. Jewelry. Mask.

She shifted into vampire form, accepting Tré's hand on her arm for support. She looked down — still dressed. She lifted a hand to her hair — still coiffed.

"Do I look all right?" she asked, just to be sure.

"Perfect as ever," Tré said, smiling down at her.

She smiled back. The soulful strains of Randy Newman's ballad, "Louisiana," filtered out from the piano inside. Xander appeared in front of them with a flute of champagne in each hand, which he tipped unceremoniously into the nearest plant pot. He handed them each one of the empty glasses and fished around for a flask inside his tailcoat.

"Took you long enough to get here," he said. "Here, have something to take the edge off."

He poured them both a generous draft from the flask and recapped it.

Tré glanced at the red liquid. "Do I want to know what this is, or where it came from?"

"Nope and nope," Xander said cheerfully. "Bottoms up."

Tré shook his head ruefully, but downed the glass all the same. With a shrug, Della did the same. The alcohol-spiked blood burned down her throat, warm and sharp.

"You're a hopeless degenerate, Xander," she accused fondly. The drink went straight to her head, leaving a pleasant buzz in its wake.

"At your service," Xander acknowledged with a smirk, and toasted them with the flask before making it disappear inside an interior pocket.

Della looked around, moving to the railing and craning to see up and down the street. "What is this place, anyway?" she asked, trying to orient herself. "And are we crashing this party, or are we invited?"

Eris joined them, with Oksana on his arm — both resplendent in their fine clothes and masks.

"We're invited," Eris said. "Xander *knows people*, apparently — as perplexing as that concept might be."

"Hey!" Xander protested. "People *like me*. I'm *charming*. You should try it some time."

Oksana swatted Eris on the arm with the fan she was carrying, no real ire behind the movement.

"Be nice to the person who got us private balcony access to Bacchus," she said, before turning to Della excitedly. "You'll never guess where we are, Della. You know the Cailey Townhouse, just downriver of Julia Street?"

Della's eyes went wide. "Nooo…" she said. "Seriously?"

"Yep!" Oksana said cheerfully. "Welcome to Mardi Gras Party Central, courtesy of a really rich guy who wanted a restored mansion where he could watch the parades go by with a hundred of his closest friends. And—apparently—with Xander."

Xander mock-glared at her. "See if I take you nice places again. Ungrateful sods, the lot of you."

Della was still in shock—she'd ridden past this place almost daily on the way to and from work. The tramline was just on the far side of the narrow street. The house was nicely restored on the outside, situated next to an apartment building called The Abbott, and across the street from a little bakery. But the place showed up frequently in human interest stories online or in the newspaper. The owner had picked it up for a song when it was a run-down tenement house, and spent a cool couple of million turning it into a residence fit for a king.

It was a hangout for rich people. Famous people. Not… *people like her*. Not receptionists from New Jersey. It was as though she'd gone to sleep and woken up inside a fairy tale.

Cinderella, you shall go to the ball.

She darted forward and kissed Xander on the cheek, startling him.

"Thank you for taking us nice places, Xander," she said, unable to stop the smile that was lighting up her face like a beacon.

Xander cleared his throat. "Well," he said, recovering, "at least *someone* appreciates my efforts."

"Your efforts are always appreciated, old friend," Tré said solemnly.

A smile quirked one corner of Xander's full lips, even as he struggled to regain his usual devil-may-care facade. "There, now. See how easy that was, Eris? *That's* more like it."

Eris huffed a breath of quiet amusement.

"You *have* to see the inside, Della," Oksana enthused. "Come on. This is the third story balcony. The second story one will be a better vantage point for the floats."

Della clasped Tré's hand and pulled him inside, following Oksana's lead. The house was amazing. Every available surface was finished with polished hardwood or solid marble, and decorated for Mardi Gras with streamers and beads. Even the statues were decked out with Carnival masks and jester hats. A grand staircase led down to the lower levels, where more party guests mingled and sipped drinks.

Looking down at the ground floor atrium, Della saw that it opened out into a ballroom, the floor a checkerboard of dark and white polished marble. Her breath caught.

"Do you dance, Tré?" she asked, looking up at him hopefully.

His mouth twitched beneath the mask. "Of course I dance, *draga*. One does not live five hundred years without learning a passable waltz. Come, then, if you are so eager for a turn around the floor. They're playing Tchaikovsky now, and it will be some time before the Krewe of Bacchus arrives."

The four of them made their way down to the dance floor, where Tré helped Della pin up the train of her dress so she wouldn't have to worry about stumbling over it.

"Where's Duchess, anyway?" Della asked.

"Sizing up the male contingent of guests, of course," Oksana said wryly. "We'll hook up with her outside on the balcony when the parade starts."

Della suspected that the male contingent had absolutely no clue what they were in for. Now, though, she let Tré take her in his arms and lost herself to the hypnotic *one*-two-three, *one*-two-three of the music, spinning slowly around the floor with her handsome lover gazing into her eyes.

Beside them, Xander danced with Oksana, despite their earlier teasing jabs at each other. With her floor-length gown, it was nearly impossible to tell that Oksana was wearing a prosthesis, unless one knew to listen for the telltale clack of spring-loaded metal against stone. Eris was quickly snapped up by a doe-eyed young human woman, whom he led gamely around the ballroom, genteel and reserved as ever.

Eventually, Della ended up dancing with all of the male vampires. She no longer felt the sense of intimidation she once had in Xander's or Eris' presence. Once, she thought, she would have been weak in the knees at the mere idea of dancing with two such strikingly handsome men. Now, while it was a pleasant enough diversion, it was Tré's eyes on her that warmed her core and made her heart beat faster.

He had, thankfully, gotten over his instinctive territorial protectiveness of her once she recovered from her turning and their mating bond settled — at least, to an extent, with the men he trusted like brothers.

But she still couldn't help it if the hint of a growl under his polite, "May I cut in?" made her heart swoop a bit as Eris handed her back to him.

This is where I want to be, she thought, settling into his arms. *Right here. Forever.*

They danced until the excited murmur of the other guests heralded the arrival of the first floats. Then, they hurried up to the second-story balcony, where they found Duchess waiting for them, wearing a cat-with-the-cream smile.

"Having fun?" she asked, taking them all in.

"This is *amazing*," Della enthused. "I still can't believe I'm actually here! What about you?"

"I always have fun," Duchess said, draping one arm over Oksana's shoulders, and the other over Xander's. "Xander, *mon chou*, please tell me your flask isn't empty? I'm *parched*."

"For you, Duchess, my flask is never empty," Xander said gallantly, and passed her the spiked blood.

Della basked in the happiness of being someplace so beautiful with the people who were quickly becoming family to her. She leaned back against Tré's broad chest and closed her eyes, drinking everything in. Again, she felt that strange brush of familiarity that did not belong to any of her fellow vampires, but before she could pursue it, a cheer from the street below announced the arrival of the first float.

The six of them pressed forward to get a spot by the railing, and she was aware of Xander shamelessly using his mental influence over the humans to clear a space for them. A sea of excited people milled a few feet below in the street, illuminated now by the strobing purple lights from the first float — Bacchus' chariot, adorned with gold trim and giant clusters of painted plaster grapes.

Della added her whoops and cheers to the crowd's as the masked and robed riders threw beads over the onlookers, then laughed in shocked glee when Duchess calmly unlaced her tight bodice and let her breasts spill out, the nipples artfully covered with a pair of tasseled purple pasties. A shower of beads and doubloons rained down on her. She grabbed several from the air and distributed them to Oksana and Della.

"Don't get any ideas, *draga*," Tré rumbled against the shell of Della's ear as he helped her arrange the cheap plastic necklaces, his fingers brushing her décolletage oh-so-casually as he did. "I'm not ready to share these perfect breasts with anyone else."

Della craned around to kiss him, her heart overflowing. "Don't worry," she said. "I have a theory that shamelessness is a side-effect of vampirism, but I don't think I've quite reached Duchess's levels of shamelessness yet."

Duchess smirked at her. "Ah, you're still young yet, *ma petite*. Give it a few hundred years."

They watched the gaudy floats go past one by one, their shoulders growing ever heavier with beads, thanks to Duchess' foolproof method of attracting the riders' attention. The head of the Bacchasaurus float had just passed by at eye level when Della's breath caught. That familiar presence was back, closer than ever, like cool spring water overflowing a stone basin.

"Ah. Francine," Xander said, turning to face the newcomer. "You're looking well. It's lovely to see you — our sincerest thanks for the invite."

Della's eyes flew to the wrinkled old woman with the coffee-colored skin, wearing African style clothing and a head wrap dyed in vibrant Mardi Gras green and purple. Her mouth fell open for a moment before she snapped it closed.

"*Laissez les bons temps rouler*, Xander, eh?" said the old woman. "Let the good times roll."

"Why, you've just encompassed my entire life philosophy in a nutshell, Madame," Xander replied, and kissed the knuckles of her extended hand in a courtly gesture.

"Wait," Della said, her brain trying to catch up with her mouth. "But... you're..."

"As I mentioned earlier," Eris murmured, "Xander *knows people*."

"Hello, Della," Francine said, looking at her with rheumy eyes. "Well, now. What have we here? I thought I sensed a change in the world, this past week."

"Hello again," Della said in a faint voice.

Madame Francine laughed gaily. "You needn't look quite so surprised, my dear. I like to know what's going on in my city, that's all."

Della swallowed, finally pulling herself together after her surprise. "Madame Francine. I need to thank you. If it weren't for what you said to me, I don't think I would have known what to do when the time came. You saved me, as much as Tré and the others did."

Francine's hazy eyes moved to Tré, who still had an arm around her shoulders. "Ha! Perhaps not *quite* as much as they did, child, but I'm pleased for you, nonetheless. So, you've thrown in your lot with theirs, then? Left your human life behind?"

Della nodded. "I have." A thought occurred. "Well… almost. I still have Jewel. My pet goldfish. Which probably isn't very vampire-ish of me."

She'd rescued the little fishbowl from her apartment once she'd recovered from her turning, and brought it to the plantation house. Perhaps it was her imagination, but the goldfish seemed a bit bewildered by events. Madame Francine made a soft sound of amusement, and Della had a sudden idea.

"I don't suppose your shop would benefit from a low-maintenance mascot to help greet visitors?" she asked. "We may be moving from place to place quite a bit, and it's not really practical to travel with a fish."

Francine smiled, the wrinkles on her face deepening. "I imagine that could be arranged, child. It's not every day that someone offers me a Jewel."

A small weight—one she hadn't even realized was there—lifted from Della's shoulders. "I'll come by on Ash Wednesday evening, in that case—as soon as it's dark enough. And… thank you again. I feel like what I did was the best choice, even though it means leaving my old life behind… fish and all."

Madame Francine lifted a wrinkled hand and brushed gnarled knuckles against Della's cheek. "Of course it was the best choice, Della. Look at you! You have become the very protection that you sought."

The idea circled through Della's thoughts for a moment before taking hold, sending tendrils of warmth through her heart. Tré's arm squeezed her tighter, holding her against him. She could feel his pride in her. His love.

"I can see that you still need to learn to listen to the unseen world around you, child," Francine continued gently. "Can't you hear it, now? The angel Israfael is weeping with joy."

And maybe… just maybe… Della *could* hear it, tickling at the edge of her mental awareness—a sound so pure and light that it made her heart swell.

She knew for certain, now. She had done the right thing.

EPILOGUE

Sevastopol, Crimean Peninsula. March 4th.

Bastian Kovac swore as he shook out his swollen and bloody knuckles. The Ukrainian agent who'd been sent to lure him into a fake money-laundering deal groaned up at him from his place lying on his back on the filthy floor of the dive bar. The man tried to lift his upper body into a sitting position, only to fall prone again, blood flowing freely from his broken nose.

"Come," Bastian told his current woman, who was still cowering in the corner, her eyes large and frightened. "We're leaving."

The bitch—*Sasha*—had been a recent acquisition of his, and one who was quickly outliving her novelty. She'd been a whore and a drug addict, and while her skill set did include having a tight ass and giving passable head, her drug habit was becoming increasingly expensive. Not to mention *irritating*.

Still, she was easy enough to keep in line with the occasional backhand to the face or threat of strangulation. And he could definitely use a good, hard fuck after this evening's epic shit-storm. A certain sniveling contact of his due for some serious payback after setting Bastian up with a *fucking narc*. A *Ukranian* narc, worse yet.

He gave Sasha a hard shove in the small of the back to get her moving toward the door, and she stumbled on the ridiculous stiletto heels she was wearing. She righted herself and seemed to hunch down, as though she were trying to appear smaller.

As if he was planning on expending any significant amount of his attention on her in the first place.

The bar was on the edge of the Kacha district of Sevastopol, home to an airbase and a lot of dingy gray tenement buildings housing railroad and dock workers. The central part of the city might have been a tourist destination, but out here, it was all brutalist Soviet architecture and the smell of quiet desperation.

Garbage lined the streets. This particular stretch of road smelled perpetually of piss and rat droppings. Bastian might have wished to deny it, but he felt strangely at home among the filth, human and otherwise. He'd grown up in just such a place, and while he had risen above it by doing things for money that weaker men weren't willing to do, business still seemed to drag him back down here to the gutters on a depressingly regular basis.

The room he was renting for the duration of his stay in Crimea was on the other side of the docks. The shipyards were deserted at this time of night, recent tensions between Russia and Ukraine having further eroded the already shaky economy of the area. Mud was creeping over the crumbling pavement of the road, as if trying to suck the man-made structures back into the earth.

Sasha slipped on a patch of the stuff, stumbling again and nearly falling.

"Keep moving," Bastian snapped, eager to get back to his flop, get himself off between those garishly painted red lips, and put this night behind him. "Watch where you're going, you stupid bitch."

She cringed again, hugging herself, eyes downcast.

Bastian shivered as a sudden blast of cold wind coming off the bay buffeted them. Even the fucking weather had it in for him tonight, it seemed. Sasha hugged herself tighter, her black miniskirt and halter-top doing nothing to protect her. Bastian shrugged his leather jacket a little higher around his shoulders and jammed his hands in the pockets.

The wind wailed past the abandoned cranes and through the broken windows of the warehouses, sounding almost like insane laughter. Bastian shook his head and frowned at the fanciful thought. A cold mist was rolling in as he watched, surrounding them like a muffling veil.

Sasha slowed. "I don't like this, baby," she said. "I c-can't see anything."

"Just follow the damned road," he growled, even as his own feet came to a halt, as if of their own accord.

The cold laughter came again, nearer this time. With no warning, Bastian was flat on his back, the wind knocked out of him, a suffocating weight crushing his chest as he was dragged off the pavement by an unseen presence and pressed into the cold muck. He flailed his fists, but there was nothing to hit — only the bone-deep chill and a feeling of tiny insect legs crawling over his skin.

He heard Sasha scream and caught a flash in his peripheral vision as she turned to run, hampered by her ridiculous shoes. Then, he was dragged over the edge of a pit in the ground and slammed into the sucking mud at the bottom. He fought to get free, but there was still nothing to fight against. The laughter tickled the shell of his ear this time; a sound of pure evil.

There is no escape from me, Bastian Kovac, said the unseen presence. *You will be mine, and together, we will bring this world to its knees.*

Bastian stopped fighting, his chest heaving like a bellows. "Who… are you?" he gasped.

I am your Master, said the voice. *And you will be my hunting dog. The teeth for my trap.*

"What do I get out of it?" Bastian asked, trembling as the cold filth he was lying in leached his body heat.

The laughter this time was maniacal. *You will get power, dog. More power than you could possibly imagine.*

Bastian licked his lips, contemplating the kind of power that an unearthly being like this might possess.

"… all right," he said eventually. "I accept."

A cold, slimy touch caressed his cheek, the gesture almost tender. *Oh, my arrogant dog… I was not asking your permission…*

Something reached inside of Bastian and *pulled*. His fingers scrabbled at the mud coating the sides of the pit, and he screamed in agony as his very essence was torn apart. It seemed to go on forever, an eternity of his own private hell.

Without realizing it, Bastian managed to claw his way out of the suffocating hole in the ground. He was *ravenous*. His insides had been torn out, and he needed to fill the empty space more than he had ever needed anything in his life.

A whiff of warmth and life pierced the veil of death surrounding him. He breathed it in, *thirsting* for that life. He had to have it. He had to have it *right now*.

The scent of sweat and cheap perfume called to him like a magnet called to steel. He plunged after it, abused muscles propelling him forward with inhuman speed. In what felt like no time at all, he was tackling the woman — the *whore* — to the ground, where she continued to scream and kick at him as he pinned her in place.

"Oh, my God! God have mercy on me!" she shrieked, the sound hurting his sensitive ears. "Get away from me, you son of a bitch! Don't hurt me, please, *don't hurt me!*"

The words meant nothing. Not when he could hear her pounding heart pumping blood beneath the fragile barrier of her skin. His Master's maniacal laughter split the night sky as Bastian surged forward and sank his teeth into the column of the woman's throat, ripping and tearing even as her body bucked and seized beneath his.

Blood and life force flooded his mouth like nectar, and he drank deep, pulling more and more into himself until her struggles subsided into twitches, and then, to nothing. He drained her dry, and let the empty husk fall back on the muddy pavement with a dull, lifeless *thump*.

Power coursed through him, until he felt that it would burst from his eyes like lightning. He reared up, his hoarse laughter joining his new Master's, until it seemed the darkness itself would burst open and unleash the denizens of hell upon the un-suspecting world above.

Bastian Kovac had spent his entire life seeking power. Now, power had finally sought him out in return.

The future was going to be *brilliant*.

finis

The *Circle of Blood* series continues in *Book Two: Lover's Awakening*.

To discover more books by this author, visit www.rasteffan.com

Printed in Poland
by Amazon Fulfillment
Poland Sp. z o.o., Wrocław